Go!

Hold On! Season 2

PETER DARLEY

GO!—HOLD ON! SEASON 2

Copyright©2015

PETER DARLEY

www.peterdarley.com

Cover Design by Peter Darley and Christy Caughie.

Other Titles in the Series:

Hold On! – Season 1

Run! – Hold On! Season 3

Hold On! - Tomorrow

"For my early readers,

whose eager desires to know

'what happened next'

enabled the completion of Go!"

Previously, on *Hold On!*

Brandon Drake was led in shackles along the corridor outside the Fort Bragg courtroom, his expression vacant. The complex sequence of events that had led him to this point flashed before his eyes.

He was a soldier: a sergeant with the Eighty-Second Airborne Division. After receiving a head injury in Helmand Province, he'd been relocated by corrupt Senator Garrison Treadwell to a weapons-testing facility in Washington DC. There, he unwittingly uncovered a plot within his own government to attack their own facilities. It had been an attempt to create excuses for profitable wars against innocent nations. One such target was Carringby Industries in Denver, Colorado.

Making use of advanced intervention equipment stolen from the facility he'd been assigned to, he rescued Belinda Reese, the secretary of Carringby Industries' CEO, from certain death at the hands of the senator's operatives.

Using the Turbo Swan, a small experimental test aircraft, he took Belinda to his safe haven, a cabin near Aspen, Colorado. Brandon believed the cabin had belonged to his late grandfather, and that nobody else knew of its existence.

After a race across America in an attempt to evade and expose Treadwell's corrupt faction, Brandon discovered his life was a lie. The cabin wasn't his grandfather's, and Brandon himself wasn't the person he thought he was.

He'd been the victim of a mind control experiment, which had altered his memories.

His true persona was that of a psychopath—a trait which now only surfaced during times of stress. The prime trigger for its characteristics was whenever the love of his life, Belinda, was placed in jeopardy.

He was finally arrested by the FBI and court-marshaled. During the trial, the remnants of his inherent personality came to the fore as Belinda was brought into the courtroom. The rampage concluded as he was subdued with a Taser.

Ultimately, he was found not guilty of desertion on the grounds of necessity. However, the verdict was contingent on him surrendering the location of the Turbo Swan, which was military property.

That decision gave Brandon an impossible problem. To reveal the location of the Turbo Swan would be to reveal the existence of the cabin—his only chance for total freedom. As such, he refused to comply, and chanced incarceration at the United States Disciplinary Barracks, confident he would escape.

Two somber-looking men, standing several feet away from the courtroom door, watched as Brandon passed them. One was a handsome young man, a little younger than Brandon. The other was much older with a snow-white beard.

"So, this is where it has led," the younger man said sadly.

"I don't know what to say."

"Isn't there something you can do, Dad? I mean, for Christ's sake he's—"

"Gone, Son. He made his choice. If you ask me, you're better off without him after that little scene in there."

The young man turned to his father, outraged. "Don't say that to me. I've been searching for him for most of my life, and now you're telling me to abandon him?"

"I just don't want to see you get hurt, that's all."

"I can take care of myself. And if you can't do anything, maybe I can."

"What difference does it make? You've got everything you'll ever need. Don't do anything to jeopardize that."

The young man exhaled as he watched Brandon disappear around the end of the corridor. "He's my brother."

One

Journey into Peril

Denver, Colorado, two years later

February 13th, 2016

Belinda Reese ran around her apartment frantically in search of basic essentials—toothbrush, toothpaste, shoes, clothes, and underwear.

She had begun to believe it was never going to happen. So much time had passed. But that evening, she'd heard an announcement that had been the sum total of all of her life's dreams fulfilled. Brandon Drake, her lover, was free.

It wasn't ideal. It wouldn't have been how she'd have wished for it, but knowing him as she had, she'd expected it. He'd even hinted at it with the last words he'd said to her at his trial. *'Wait for me.'* He was amazing. Who else but Brandon could have possibly escaped from Leavenworth?

Her last communication with him had been devastating. He'd given her specific instructions not to visit him at Leavenworth, despite the barracks' policy of allowing visitors. She'd assumed it was because of his masculine pride. Perhaps he didn't want her to see him caged like an animal. Now she realized he didn't want her anywhere near him because he didn't want her to be implicated in what he was planning.

His escape had been announced on the news by anchorwoman, Tara Willoughby. Belinda remembered with strained fondness the time Tara had interviewed her on live television. She recalled how nervous she'd been, only for her anxiety to become absolute terror as trained killers burst into the studio with guns waving.

Brandon had incapacitated them, and they'd managed to flee. They'd found themselves lost in the backstreets of Los Angeles evading the police, an assassin, and a street gang. It had been a nightmare beyond belief, and Brandon had to fight for their survival. She'd been forced to hide in the shadows. They'd had to find a place to disguise themselves and escape from the city.

As harrowing as that part of her life had been, it all came back to her with a certain ambivalence, the passage of time adding a touch of nostalgia to the horror. The fact that it had been Tara Willoughby's voice giving her the information Brandon had escaped warmed her heart. It seemed to bring everything full circle.

She dropped the last item into her case and sealed the clasps.

With a pounding heart, she looked around the room she'd lived in for two years. Her stomach turned over with guilt. Her employer at Stark, Rogers, and Blake Insurance, along with all of her colleagues, would never know what became of her. But as was her way, she hadn't been close to any of them. She'd discovered, at the time she'd been taken on as the boss's secretary, she could no longer relate to the banality of normalcy since Brandon. Everyday life seemed boring and uneventful.

However, her colleagues were people with feelings and she was walking out on all of them without a word. They deserved better. But Brandon was her heart, her love, and her life.

She picked up her case from the bed and made her way toward the door. After turning the handle, she paused and glanced behind her to see her living room one last time. "I'm coming, Brandon. Hold on."

Hold On!—The words he had said to her as he'd rescued her for the first time, gliding her off the roof of a burning skyscraper after it had been taken over by terrorists. Or at least, whom she'd believed at the time, were terrorists. Those two words had come to mean so much to her—a verbal exclamation mark with a very specific meaning: hope in a hopeless situation.

After taking a deep breath, she stepped out of her apartment, and closed the door behind her.

Anxiety filled Belinda's mind. She walked out onto the street, all the time fearing *they* would be looking for her in an attempt to locate Brandon. If they caught her before she reached him, they would interrogate her, even torture her to learn his location. Simply stepping outside immediately after his escape placed her in serious jeopardy.

She wondered if the young man in the business suit who'd just walked past her was one of *them*. He'd glanced at her momentarily. It might have been simply because he found her attractive.

She braved the pathway and made her way toward the Amtrak train station. There were several blocks to go and the thought of the distance chilled her. So much could

6

happen in the time it would take to get there. Persistently looking over her shoulder, paranoia consumed her.

A police car sped past her, its sirens blaring. She froze. Her heart raced with fear, but the car didn't stop. It wasn't about her. She exhaled with relief and continued on.

She realized there was no fun in her life. There hadn't been for a very long time. There'd been the briefest of laughs with Brandon—chuckles that had always been cut short by attacks from cruel officials, being kidnapped, tortured, and running. Always running. She asked herself, why, oh, why, did she want to go back to him?

It was because none of that was about *him*. He was incredible. *They* had been attacking him and he'd done nothing to deserve it. They had attacked her, and he'd saved her from them, just as he'd risked himself in his attempts to save so many innocents. All of his noble efforts had only earned him an indefinite term in a military detention facility. What did *he* have to laugh about?

Perhaps this was their new beginning. A time when they could both, finally, be happy together. She loved him and wanted the chance to be with him more than anything. If only she could reach the cabin.

She turned another corner. There were so many alleyways and streets to navigate before she reached her destination. She felt so vulnerable.

Another corner. Another alleyway. Any route to avoid being seen on the main thoroughfare. The hairs on the back of her neck stood on end as she moved onward. Gooseflesh formed all across her body. *They* were always there, at least in her mind, like phantom shadows coming out of the brickwork between the walkways. They wouldn't leave her alone.

Determined, she walked on with her case in a white-knuckled grip.

She came to the end of another alleyway and was beginning to feel confident. The railway station was in sight.

As she stepped onto a darkened back road, an unkempt young man appeared, as though his impatience had brought him out in the dusk rather than waiting for the night. His limp brown hair and sunken eyes indicated he was an addict.

"Gimme what you've got!" he said.

She shivered. "I-I don't have anything."

"You've got the case. Give it to me!"

"Go to hell!" she bellowed, defiant even through her fear.

"What're you gonna do, bitch? Stop me? I can take anything I want from you."

Belinda's heart raced in a way she hadn't known for two years: *Payne.*

But Payne was dead. Brandon killed him before her eyes. Payne had electrocuted her, placed sharpened wooden sticks under her fingernails, and waterboarded her. He'd been preparing to rape her when Brandon returned from the dead to save her. He'd come back after she'd seen him blown to smithereens.

The recollection comforted her for a moment. What if *she* couldn't die either? "Get away from me, you animal!" she shrieked.

The young punk pulled out a switchblade. She remembered the street gang in Los Angeles. There had been six of them, all armed with knives. Brandon had disarmed them all by kicking inwardly in a crescent movement, knocking the blades out of their hands in one strike.

She kicked inwardly, her foot connecting with the thug's wrist, knocking the knife out of his hand. Frantically, she seized the moment, lunged forward, and rapidly plunged her fists into his jaw.

Her assailant's face became bloodied. He held his right hand out in an attempt to quell the onslaught. "Stop!"

"Don't ever come near me, you son of a bitch!" She remembered the switchblade on the ground and suspected as soon as her back was turned, the thug would grab it and stab her. Kneeling, she picked it up, and held it tightly.

Stepping back, she collected her case before resuming her journey, her hands shaking. *What am I becoming?* was her immediate thought. And then, in a moment of exhilaration—*Hell, yeah!* Clenching her fists again, she savored the moment. She'd been attacked and she'd beaten her attacker. Why shouldn't she be proud of that? It was time, she realized, for her to start taking her own personal power back. She wasn't anybody's victim, and she'd had the best of teachers to show her how it was done.

Trembling but strengthened, she made her way forward, glancing back to check all was clear.

She ran through the maze of alleyways, desperate to avoid visibility on the highway. Her prior experience of interrogation procedures caused her anger to rise, and her lips curled with resentment.

She became uncomfortable holding onto the mugger's switchblade and decided to discard it in a garbage can just ahead of her. A pungent odor arose as she opened it. Holding her breath, she disposed of the knife.

As she exited the alleyway, she had no choice but to step onto a main thoroughfare again. The station wasn't far, but through the crowded street, the paranoia gripped her once again. More than ever, she was aware she was alone.

Her eyes darted around in every direction. Several more police cars passed her, and she froze each time. The fear wouldn't go away. It was a seemingly endless series of jumps, starts, and palpitations.

As the station came into view she became a little more relaxed. A slight smile formed at the corners of her mouth. She *was* going to make it. She'd be reunited with Brandon by tomorrow.

The toughest part was going to be the exhausting trek into the snow-covered mountains. Forty miles of brutal, freezing ice and snow. She quickly realized she'd have to spend the night in Aspen, and try to find a type of transportation that would take her as near to the cabin as possible. She'd need to rent a snowmobile at the very least.

She approached the station and there seemed to be no cause for alarm. She entered the ticket court, relieved she'd made it. It was crowded and easy for her to lose herself among the commuters. Excitedly, she joined a line to one of the ticket vendors. Immediately, another commuter stepped in behind her. She glanced around trying to spot anything alarming, but there was nothing. Everything was perfectly normal.

As she reached the halfway point in the line, she noticed a man in a suit talking on his cell phone, close to the station's entrance. There was nothing unusual about that. But it was the way in which he just glanced at her as he spoke into the phone. She looked away.

And then she slowly looked back. Their eyes locked. In an instant, she knew and could see he did too.

Her breathing became shallow, her palms were damp, and there was a heaviness in the pit of her stomach.

She gently eased her way out of the line and looked back again for a fleeting instant. The man was talking into his cell phone with a sudden urgency in his eyes, and he was persistently looking back at her.

She darted forward only to be halted by a hand on her shoulder. She looked around to see it was the man who'd been standing behind her.

"Belinda Reese?" he said.

That was enough. Without hesitation, she drove her fist into the man's nose and he recoiled with blood trickling onto his lip. He was stunned by her unhesitant assault, which gave her the moment necessary to run.

A number of men in suits emerged from the crowd like a swarm. Belinda barely missed being grasped by one of them as she dashed through the exit.

Out in the street, she ran as fast as her legs would carry her. The suitcase was slowing her down, her breathing was labored, and she didn't know how long she could keep up the pace.

Out of the corner of her eye she saw men she thought must be CIA or federal agents appearing on street corners all around her. "Oh God, no!"

The memory of what Payne had done to her filled her mind again. It would most likely result in a repeat of the ordeal if they caught her. That was unthinkable.

She saw a crowded street ahead and sprinted into it, trying to steal herself among the pedestrians in order to slip back into one of the alleyways.

She quickly saw her chance and darted back into the alley where she'd almost been mugged. Her emotions flitted between fear and rage. It was all so terribly unjust. She only wanted to be with her man and live her life in peace. Neither she, nor Brandon, had any desire to harm anyone, and yet both of them were suffering such overwhelming persecution. She questioned what right they had to do this to them? Why couldn't they just leave them alone?

Hopefully, Brandon would have the Turbo Swan sent back to the army, and that would be the end of it.

She continued running, but agents came up behind her within moments.

Seconds later, she lost her footing and found herself on the ground. A brawny agent twisted her arm behind her back and she swore loudly with the pain. She didn't know what was going to be worse. The sticks under the fingernails? Or the suffocation of waterboarding? She hadn't been able to decide on that before. They were both completely different types of horror. Consumed with panic, her tears flowed with unbearable dread.

"Take it easy lady and this'll all go smooth," the agent said. "We only want to talk to you."

She could hear the footsteps of several more agents hurrying toward them.

"Good job, Rogers," she heard one of them say.

And then, Rogers collapsed. The others followed, falling like dominoes beside her.

She rubbed her eyes and looked around her. It was such a familiar scene—being captured by the authorities and the authority figures just falling unconscious in front of her. It brought back a harrowing memory. Moore, Wyoming. She smiled with relief and excited exhilaration at the only thing it could mean. "Brandon."

Beaming, even through her exhaustion, she turned around to a sight she hadn't seen for two years. He stood before her in his black, bullet-resistant suit and the smooth black helmet with the visor. It was what he'd been wearing when he'd rescued her on that fateful first night. In his right hand was the sonic force emitter pistol. She realized the agents had been rendered unconscious by an intense concentration of ultrasound wave jolts.

Looking up she saw more agents turning down the alleyway behind him. The leader, a tall man in his mid-thirties, took out his cell phone, close enough for her to hear. "Sir, four men are down, but we have Reese in sight and an unidentified individual. I think it's Drake."

There was a pause on the line.

And then the reply came through. "Take him out."

Belinda heard and saw the official drawing his pistol. "Brandon, look out!"

The agent fired and the bullet struck him in the back, knocking him to the ground.

"No!" she screamed, and ran to him.

However, he rolled onto his back and fired at the agents with desperate speed, taking down four of them. But more were coming.

She knelt down beside him and held him tightly. "Are you all right, sweetheart?"

"I'm fine. It's Kevlar. Bullet proof."

"Of course."

Something wasn't right. His voice was different. He seemed to have some kind of a Southern hint to his accent. *Surely, he wouldn't have picked that up in Leavenworth.*

"Run to the end of the alley," he said. "Help's coming."

"Help? What help?"

"You'll see when you get there."

She frowned, confused. In addition to the new voice, his manner wasn't as it used to be.

He lifted his visor.

She looked up and saw it was Brandon's face—his eyes, his mouth, even his nose. But something was wrong. "B-Brandon?"

He didn't answer.

"Who are you?"

"Later. There's no time now. You've got to go." He pointed to the end of the alley.

Perplexed, she stood and picked up her suitcase.

Immediately, another three agents appeared at the opening of the alleyway, and they were closing in.

The man who looked like Brandon got to his feet and a bullet struck the armor of his left arm. Dropping the visor back into place, he fired at the agent who had shot him, but the sonic jolt missed its mark.

Belinda heard a familiar sound behind her. She turned to see a white van with blacked-out windows pull up at the far end of the alley. Her heart leaped. Was the real Brandon inside? It couldn't drive any nearer because the alley was too narrow. Seeing the problem, she ran toward the van.

The man in the Kevlar suit fired and took down another agent, but two were still coming. He got to his feet and started to run backward while firing at the remaining two pursuers. But nothing happened. His sonic force gun had depleted its charge. "Piece o' shit!" he spat.

Belinda glanced behind her. "Come on. Hurry."

He turned and ran toward her, but the agents were gaining on him. "Go!"

"Come on!"

"GO!"

Two

The Getaway

"You're in trouble, I'm coming out," a male voice said through the earpiece in the stranger's helmet.

"No!" he said. "If they see your face, you're screwed. Stay in the van."

He took a grenade from his tool belt and tossed it over his shoulder. A cloud of smoke engulfed the agents. Within seconds, they were stalled by tear gas.

"Come on!" Belinda urged him as she reached the van.

"I'm trying."

Belinda pulled the passenger's side door open, threw her case into the footwell, and jumped inside to avoid the cloud of tear gas.

Despite needing to get to safety, she felt concerned for the man running behind her—and the man in the driver's seat. She was taken aback by his gorgeous face, dark hair, and suntan. His chest protruded through his black t-shirt, visible through the open zip of a designer, black leather jacket. But it wasn't Brandon. "Who are you?" she said.

"I'm Alex." He handed her a blue blouse and a long blonde wig. "Put these on. Hurry."

She put the wig on without thinking. Questions spilled out of her uncontrollably. "Where's Brandon? What's going on? Who's that guy in the suit?"

Before he could answer, they heard the sliding side door being opened up at the back. It closed as quickly, followed by an urgent bellow of, "Go! Go! Go!"

Alex put the van in reverse. With tires screeching across the asphalt, they bolted forward.

"Put the blouse on. You've got to look different," Alex said.

Shielded by the blacked-out windows, Belinda unbuttoned her shirt, revealing her lithe, gym-honed physique. Alex was clearly too transfixed on getting them all to the next stop to notice.

A sense of déjà vu came over her again. They were racing away in a van through Denver after being rescued from the authorities. It prompted another memory—the Turbo Swan.

She buttoned up the blouse, turned, and pulled back the veil to the back of the van. What she saw was certainly not a test aircraft.

"Do you mind?" the young man said, naked and covering his groin with his hands.

"Oh, my God! I am so sorry." Nevertheless, she couldn't resist taking a longer look before pulling the curtain back. *Wow, he's pretty hot.*

But it was a thought that gave her cause for concern. She was in love with Brandon, and yet she'd just had a flutter of the heart over another man. Maybe it was because she was a perfectly normal, healthy woman of twenty-nine, who hadn't seen a naked man for two years. *Just hang in there. Hold on!*

Alex accelerated through the back roads of Denver. He reached behind to pull open the curtain a fraction of an inch. "Ty, hurry up. We're nearly there."

"Hey, Alex?" she said. "Who's 'Ty'?"

"It's a long story."

She rolled her eyes with frustrated impatience. "Isn't it always?"

The van turned onto the main highway and joined the traffic. Alex seemed extremely anxious, as was obvious from the dampness of his brow. Belinda empathized with him in a way very few others could. Being stranded in gridlock with the authorities in pursuit would have naturally given rise to profound stress.

"How did you find me?" she said. "And don't you dare say 'long story.'"

"When the news broke about Brandon's escape, he knew you'd be heading straight for him, but he knew how dangerous that was. We went to your apartment, but you weren't there."

"So how did you find me?"

"You didn't make it too difficult. We were heading back out when we saw agents chasing you through Denver. Ty suited up, jumped out of the van, and I went round to the other end of the alley to pick you up."

The thought of how lucky she'd been caused her to shudder.

Ty peered through the curtain. "OK, I'm done. Do we have far to go?"

"Half a block," Alex said.

Belinda looked at Ty properly for the first time. Somehow, he had Brandon's face, if slightly more feminine, and his hair was a little darker. It didn't make any sense. He was a man who looked like Brandon, who wasn't Brandon, but who wore Brandon's armor, and performed Brandon-style rescues. "Who are you?"

He smiled and held out his hand. "It's a pleasure to meet you, finally. I'm T—"

"We're coming up to it now," Alex cut him off.

Ty lurched forward as the van turned down another side road. "All right, get set. Grab your stuff and be ready to get out the minute I tell you."

Confused, she could only nod.

Alex pulled the van up alongside a gleaming red Porsche 911 Carrera, the only vehicle parked in a lane situated behind a towering, deserted textile factory.

"OK, Belinda. Get out now," Ty said.

She smiled a half-smile, threw open the door with her shirt across her arm, and jumped out. Reaching across to the footwell, she retrieved her suitcase.

Ty leaped out of the van attired in a t-shirt, jeans, a burgundy jacket, and gleaming black shoes. He threw the Kevlar jacket, pants, tool-belt, helmet, and boots into the trunk of the Porsche. He then turned to Belinda. "Gimme the suitcase."

She handed it to him and he threw it into the trunk. "The door's open. Get in."

He sounded so much like Brandon, save for the accent. There was the same resonance in his tone when he spoke with urgency. Brandon's words, on the night he'd rescued her two years before, rang out in her head: *Get. In. The. Back. Of. The. Van!* Ty had the same, stern, undeniable command when he said "*Get in.*"

"Where are we going?" she said.

"I'm taking you to the cabin."

She froze. "How do you know about the cabin?"

"I'll explain later. You have to trust me. I'll get you to Brandon, but we're wasting time."

Uncertain, she climbed into the Porsche, quickly noting it was far more comfortable than the space-restricted confines of the Turbo Swan.

She watched Ty through the rear-view mirror. Taking a step back, he returned to the van and grasped the open passenger's door. She heard him say to Alex, "Drive around town for thirty minutes. The jet's being refueled. After thirty, get to the airfield, and they'll take you back to Dallas. There'll be a cab waiting for you when you get home, OK?"

"You got it."

"OK, now go. Go!" Ty closed the door and slapped the van. He hurriedly returned to the Porsche and climbed in.

Belinda looked at him with more than a little exasperation. "That your favorite word?"

"What?"

"Go."

"Chill out, already. We're going for a cruise."

The Porsche shot forward. Belinda glanced in the rear-view mirror and saw the van back up. As the Porsche turned a corner she saw the police pull up behind Alex. "Oh, my God. I think your friend's just been busted."

"He's fine. It's just a white van and one of many. Nobody in it but him. They're not gonna be holding him for long on that. Trust me, Alex is fine. He's been very well briefed, and he's highly experienced."

"Well, that's good to know," she said sarcastically.

The Porsche turned onto the main freeway and headed toward Highway 70.

"How are we going to get up a snowy mountain in this?" she said.

"We're not. We're going to an airfield. I've got a chopper waiting."

"Listen, Ty, is it?"

"Yeah?"

"OK, Ty. It's not that I don't trust you." She paused for a second, and then said, "I *don't* trust you, Ty. Who are you?"

He grinned in a toying manner. "Wouldn't you just love to know?"

"Look, stop playing games with me!"

His expression changed, indicating he knew he'd crossed the line. "All right. My name is Tyler Drake-Faraday, OK?"

"Drake?"

"That's right. *Drake*."

She gazed at him as he joined the rush hour traffic. Something was connecting, but she still couldn't put it together. He looked like Brandon and he had Brandon's name, but what did it all add up to?

He glanced at her for the briefest moment before turning his attention back to the traffic. "I'm Brandon's brother."

"His brother? Brandon doesn't even know who he is. His memories were changed for delusions. He doesn't know where he came from. How can you be his brother?"

Tyler's irritated expression indicated that she'd just insulted his very identity. "So . . . what? You think I just had this face stuck on overnight?"

There was silence in the Porsche as it cleared the gridlock and soared onto Highway 70.

Belinda's mind became awash with emotions—shock, fear, anger, and love for the man she was going through hell to be with again. She glanced over at the man beside her with intrigue. It actually made sense. He looked so much like Brandon. "Brandon's brother. OK, I think I get that. Two of you. Oh, boy, am I gonna have my hands full."

He turned his head toward her and burst into laughter.

Belinda glanced at the road and saw he was about to collide with the median. "Look out!"

"Whoa!" He hurriedly twisted the wheel. "Thanks."

"Keep your eyes on the road and tell me why Brandon isn't here."

"He's not doing too well."

"What's wrong with him?"

"He's been shot. He's hanging in there, though. I think seeing you again will be the best medicine."

Speechless and deeply concerned, she looked ahead trying to guess what she would find when, at long last, she stepped back into the cabin.

Three

The Storm

"Look, everything's gonna be fine. Just keep your head down and get in." Tyler handed Belinda a headset and made his way over to the helicopter. A case containing Brandon's combat attire and sonic force gun were firmly in his grasp.

"Listen, are you sure you can fly this thing?" she said.

"Almost as well as I can drive."

"That's encouraging."

She looked around the small airfield. The Porsche was a fast car, and she couldn't be sure where they'd arrived. It was getting dark, but she estimated they were in a remote area, perhaps fifty miles from Denver.

Tyler's android phone rang and he answered it. "Alex? What happened? They let you go, right?"

Alex's vexed tone was audible even through the earpiece: "Yeah, they let me go, but only after making me feel like Charlie-goddamn-Manson."

"All right, buddy. I got everything worked out. Now get to this airfield. I've got a plane waiting for you."

"Yeah, but just remember you owe me one, Ty. This has got to be the craziest gig we've ever pulled off."

"Hey, don't worry, bud. I always come through, don't I?" Tyler winked at Belinda with an inappropriately unconcerned attitude. She didn't reciprocate.

"I guess so. I'll see you later," Alex said.

A tall pilot, approximately mid-forties with thinning brown hair, approached Tyler and Belinda.

"Hey, Dig," Tyler said. "Belinda, this is my pilot, Captain David Digswell."

Belinda forced a smile.

"Are the lap dancers on the jet?" Tyler asked.

"Yep," Digswell said.

"Great. Now, make sure they keep Mr. Dalton well entertained. That guy's just been through hell."

"You got it."

Belinda deduced Dalton was Alex's last name.

Tyler nudged her arm. "Come on. We've got to get to that north plateau."

She followed Tyler into the chopper. He climbed in, threw her case onto his own in the back, and fired up the rotors.

Belinda had never realized how frightening getting into a helicopter was. She remembered how flying them had been Brandon's vocation in the Eighty-Second Airborne Division. She climbed into the cockpit, startled by the harrowing force of the blades whipping over her head. Eagerly, she put her headset on to nullify the noise.

Tyler closed the door, muting the sound. He put on his headset and moved the mike to his mouth. "This is Faraday preparing for take-off."

She looked across at him suspiciously. "I thought you said your name was Drake."

"Drake-Faraday. I told you that." He pulled out a hip flask and handed it to her. "Johnny Walker Blue. The top of the line. Take it."

She took the bottle and drank deeply, the sharp burn of the spirit causing her to squint. "God, that's strong stuff."

"You need it," he said.

"You're right, but I still hate you."

"Sue me."

"I don't really."

"I know."

Tyler pulled on the collective lever and flew them into the night.

As the helicopter cut through the air, Belinda looked out of the window and saw they were already over the snowy mountains. "You said Brandon was shot?"

"He needs you."

The response came as a non-answer, and it was abrupt. "*He needs you.*"

He needs me. He needs me, repeated in her mind. Being needed—the same characteristic that drove Brandon. That drove them both.

The helicopter landed on the north plateau, two miles from the cabin, and the rotor blades slowed gradually.

"I picked up your snow boots from the cabin." Tyler took the boots off the back seat and handed them to her.

Belinda's eyes widened with excitement. She remembered the day Brandon bought them in Aspen for her. The fact that she was about to wear them again, at the cabin itself, thrilled her heart.

Tyler handed her a shawl, gloves, and a Russian-style, fur-lined hat with an insulated facial guard. "Put these on too. It's minus ten out there."

"All right, take it easy." She couldn't understand why he'd suddenly become so stern.

As if in response to her thoughts he took a deep breath. "It's been a long day."

She looked at him and smiled empathically. "I know. I'm sorry, Tyler. I do understand. I know what this can do to you."

"You got that right. The cabin is just beyond the ridge."

Belinda grasped his wrist, and tears came to her eyes. *I've waited for two years for this moment.*

Tyler placed his arm around her shoulders. "Hey, hey. It's all right. Everything's gonna be OK. I'll get you to him and everything will be fine. Let's just get down there."

Belinda grasped the snow boots and gazed at them for a moment. As she put them on, she focused on her feet falling into them, persistently questioning if it was really happening. Was she actually returning to utopia?

"Are you ready?" he said.

"As ready as I'm ever gonna be."

"Good. This is it. Let's get going."

Tyler grabbed the backpack, opened the side door, and stepped out. Belinda took her suitcase and followed.

They walked with difficulty through the thick snow, and further heavy snow was beginning to fall.

"How far is it to the cabin, Tyler?" she shouted over the cutting wind.

"About two miles."

"Two miles?"

"That's right."

"I thought you said it was just over the ridge. Why couldn't you have landed a little closer?"

"Because there is nowhere closer. You can't land a helicopter on a snow slope. This is a two-mile-high snow slope. That's the ridge."

"Well, why didn't you land by the cabin?"

"Because the only flat spots around there are where the cabin is, and the space where those trees are behind it. You need flat, clear space for a helicopter. Those rotor blades aren't gonna forgive any obstacles. The cabin is in the worst possible place for landing a chopper."

"You still haven't told me how you know about the cabin," she said. "It's a secret place Brandon got himself sent to Leavenworth for."

"I'm not happy about it, believe me. We had no choice but to come here. I've just seen what happens to those who might know too much. Being chased through the streets by agents isn't my idea of a party."

The snowfall descended ferociously.

"Did you say two miles?" she said.

"Yeah."

And then it became a blizzard. The snow beat against Belinda's face, cutting into her to the extent that she couldn't go any farther. "Tyler, I can't move."

"Neither can I. Jesus H. Christ!"

The snow whipped at them mercilessly. Belinda held her hands out as the onslaught continued. "Tyler!" The force of the storm forced her back, causing her to twist and turn blindly. "Tyler!" she cried again, but she couldn't hear anything over the deafening sound of the wind.

She staggered back and felt herself sinking. In an instant, she knew she'd stepped into a snowdrift. Her lips quivered as she became submerged. The snow continued to fall in on her, smothering and suffocating her, and virtually burying her alive.

Four

The Lucky One

"Belinda, where are you?" Tyler braced the palms of his hands in the snow, pushed himself up, and grasped the suitcase.

"Tyler," he faintly heard her cry.

Realizing she'd hit a snowdrift, he scurried around in the deluge with desperate speed. "Hang in there. I'll get you out."

The snowfall thickened as his fists pummeled desperately into the snow. "Oh, hell. Where are you?" He punched again in an attempt to prevent ice from forming, all the time knowing he might accidentally injure her. Using his hands as shovels, he burrowed snow away from the area. The snowfall grew heavier, whipping at his face painfully. As fast as he cleared the snow away, it was filled in again.

Panic gripped him the longer time went by without finding her. Not only would it be a tragic and horrific way for Belinda to die—freezing and suffocating, buried alive—but what would it do to his brother? Brandon was severely injured and desperately needed medical attention. How would he survive learning Belinda had died when they were to be imminently reunited?

He widened the area of his search, moving six feet to his right, but there was nothing under the snow. It made no sense. She'd been standing right next to him.

Two yards to his left, a shower of snowflakes burst up out of the ground. Tyler barely heard it, but placed his forearm across his brow and looked across. He could scarcely make out two gloved hands protruding through the snow. "Oh, thank God. Just try to stay calm. I'm coming."

He burrowed through the fresh, relatively-soft snow, shoveled it away as fast as he could, and cleared her face. Together, they managed to pull both arms free. Tyler reached under Belinda's armpits as she strained to pull herself free. With them working together, she gradually came out of the drift.

Belinda coughed violently, spitting out a mouthful of snow. The storm continued to beat against her with merciless persistence.

Tyler angled his face down toward her to avoid the snow. "Belinda, you've got to turn over. Keep your face away from the blizzard."

Once her face was out of the direct line of the onslaught, he placed his arm across her shoulders and held her tightly. "Now, hang on to me."

"W-what is h-happening?" she said through chattering teeth.

"Some kinda freak snowstorm. Never seen anything like it."

She held him with her free arm, and they moved through the storm.

Tyler struggled to see through the snow but worked out the direction of the blizzard was west-to-east. With his arm around Belinda, he led away from the flow of the storm.

Within five minutes, he thought he could make out something approximately twenty-five feet away. *Maybe it's a tree?* "Keep your head down and move straight ahead."

"Where are we going?"

He pointed ahead. "Over there. Come on."

"With e-everything t-that's happened t-trying to get here," she said, "it's like the gods are t-trying to keep B-Brandon and me apart."

"Seems that way, but I don't buy it."

They plowed farther through the forces of the elements. When they had reached approximately one hundred yards from where they'd started, he could see it wasn't a tree they were heading toward. It was a cluster of them.

"This is it," Tyler said joyously. "Our asses are saved."

They quickly arrived at the trees. The wind-driven snow continued to soak them, forcing them to keep their eyes forward.

Tyler led Belinda into the aspen trees and settled in front of one that was the farthest into the cluster. The trees behind it acted as an additional break against the storm. Finally, they sat and huddled close to one another with their backs braced against the tree.

"W-we made it," Belinda said in a thankful tone. Her teeth continued to chatter incessantly.

"Yeah, we sure did. You gave me one hell of a scare back there."

"I gave myself one hell of a scare b-back there, too. Felt f-for sure I was dead."

"Well, you're not, but we're not out of it yet. We've got to sit it out 'til it slows down."

"S-so, what's your story, Tyler? Help m-me take m-my mind off it."

"A long one," he said. "I almost met you once before, you know."

"How so?"

"I was at the trial."

She looked at him surprised. "You were at the t-trial? I n-never saw you."

"Well, I was at the back with my dad behind all the off-duty soldiers in the courtroom. He has connections to Fort Bragg, which is how we could get to the trial. You were really upset."

"Why didn't you s-say something?"

"Wrong time. Wrong place. I wanted Brandon to be free so badly. I'd searched for him since I was twelve years old."

"Since you were twelve?"

"Yeah. I was the lucky one. Found out at twelve I was adopted. I had it all. My dad's one of the wealthiest guys in Texas. He's the founder and CEO of the Faraday Corporation. Best schools. Best friends. But there was always something missing. Finding my birth family became an obsession. Dad was real supportive. I finally found Brandon just as he was being taken to freaking Leavenworth."

"So what happened? How did you get involved with his escape?"

"Visited him regularly while he was there. We hit it off real quick. After about a year, he hinted to me what he was up to, and when he was gonna do it, so I got myself prepared. It took a long time, but he broke out of that place all by himself."

She looked at him questioningly. "B-but you said he was shot."

"He took a bullet on the run, not far from the grounds. I picked him up, got him to one of the airfields my dad commissions in Kansas, and we flew here."

"And after that you came for me?"

"Yeah. Alex was already on the way to Denver. We'd planned all of this."

"So, who is Alex?"

"One of my closest friends. He works in my dad's marketing department. We recruited him out of Los Angeles. He's a really great guy. Me and him are pretty tight." Tyler chuckled mischievously. "My dad would freak out if he knew what the two of us were up to."

"That's s-so amazing, Tyler. I had no idea. Brandon d-didn't want me anywhere near Leavenworth."

Tyler laughed. "Proud jerk. With Brandon, you don't give the guy a chance to say no. I just showed up there unannounced."

Belinda gave a strained smile. "Guess I should've been m-more assertive with him."

After another powerful gust of snow-filled wind, the blizzard began to abate.

"Hey, you feel that?" Tyler said. "It's stopping."

"Yeah."

"Let's give it a few more minutes, and then we'll get the hell out of here. This has gotta be the c-coldest I've ever been in my whole damn life. You must be even colder after being under the snow for so long."

"I'm f-frozen solid," she said.

Gradually, the snowfall slowed to a scattering of random snowflakes blowing in the wind. They finally stood with snow falling off them, and walked back in the direction they'd come from. Taking a right turn, they exited the trees.

"The ridge is just a few yards ahead," Tyler said.

"OK."

They quickly reached the edge at the top of a steep snow slope. The gradient was fierce, but manageable.

"Now, take it steady getting down there," Tyler said. "It can be a real son of a bitch," "Getting Brandon down here while he was injured was no walk in the park, I can tell you."

Cautiously, she began her descent, her suitcase in one hand, and her other tightly gripping Tyler.

"Two years ago," she said, "Brandon and I came back from Los Angeles to find Treadwell sitting in the living room in the cabin."

"Yeah, he told me about that."

"It was the c-creepiest moment of my life. After Treadwell shot himself, Brandon placed the body in a sack and p-pulled it all the way up this ridge. I realize now how harrowing it must have b-been for him."

"Yeah, Brandon's a tough guy, no doubt about it."

Very carefully, she placed one foot before the other, careful not to slip.

"You're doing fine," Tyler said.

"Thanks. What kind of b-business is your father in, Tyler?"

"He manufactures helicopters. He has clients all over the world. The US Army, Air Force, numerous police forces around the US and Europe, global corporations, rich playboys, you name it."

"Wow. That explains your helicopter and sports car."

"Like I said, I got lucky."

Belinda slipped and her suitcase fell from her grip.

Tyler braced his feet into the snow at a sideways angle and held her hand to prevent her from rolling down to the bottom. "Easy, easy. I've got you. Just hold—"

"Don't say it!" she barked.

"Say what?"

"It."

He shook his head, confused, but held onto her hand so she could pull herself back up.

Once she was on her feet, they looked down and saw her suitcase as a speck a few hundred yards down the slope.

"You OK?" Tyler said.

"Yeah, I guess," she replied, a little shaken.

"All right, concentrate, and let's get to the cabin in one piece. We'll pick up the suitcase when we get to it."

Very carefully, they continued their descent.

Five

Behind the Door

Arriving at the bottom of the ridge, Tyler and Belinda came to a small snow hill, no higher than six feet. Belinda braced herself for what she would see on the other side. It wasn't a steep climb, just enough to obscure her view. Suitcase in hand, she climbed the few footsteps up and over the hill.

Finally, after two years, there it was. Her mind flooded with memories as she gazed at the cabin just a few yards ahead of her. To her left was the short path that led to the clearing with the snow-coated forest behind them. Her dream had come true at long last.

The Turbo Swan was still parked outside in the spot they'd left it before they'd headed out to North Carolina, two years earlier—the journey that had led to Brandon's arrest. Their separation, and Brandon's incarceration in Leavenworth, had all happened due to that damn machine being parked outside the cabin.

"Well, here we are," Tyler said cheerfully.

She looked up and noticed there was no smoke coming from the chimney.

"Now, why in the hell hasn't he got the log fire going," Tyler said. "The guy must be freezing his nuts off in there."

Belinda silently concurred. Brandon used to have the fire burning almost every waking hour. "I do hope he's all right."

"Let's get inside."

They walked up to the front porch. Tyler took out the key and opened the door.

Belinda remained a step back for a moment, apprehensive about what she was going to find behind the door.

Tyler stepped inside first. "Brandon? I've got a surprise for you, bro."

No reply came.

He turned to Belinda. "Come on. He's got to be in here somewhere. Let me find the light."

Slowly, she moved closer and then stepped inside. Tyler found the light switch and flicked it on.

Before them was a man huddled in the corner of the room, wrapped in a blanket. His hair was damp and his eyes were sunken. His skin appeared ashen and coated with perspiration. A makeshift bandage around his shoulder showed blood soaking through it. Shivering violently, he loosely held a three-quarters-consumed bottle of gin.

Horrified, Belinda looked upon the face of a virtual stranger. "Brandon?"

He looked up with a glazed expression. "Mom?"

***

Agent Andrew Wilmot stepped into Deborah Beaumont's office at Langley with the hint of a swagger. "You're working late. How is he?"

"Very annoyed."

He nodded, somewhat complacently. "What are your plans for dinner?"

With her spectacles resting on the end of her nose, her piercing, contemptuous hazel eyes would have cut through the resolve of most men. But not Wilmot. Deborah was an attractive woman of thirty-seven, and the loyal secretary of Strategic Detection of Terrorism Director Elias Wolfe. Her manner had always been cold, overly-proper, hopelessly humorless, and apparently, asexual. Just the type Wilmot loved to conquer.

"That's a shame," he said. "I was thinking of taking you to KFC."

Shaking her head, she sneered.

He moved on to the adjacent office and knocked.

"Come in, Agent Wilmot."

He finally cringed, knowing what this was about. There was the possibility of inconveniences on the horizon. Such concern was not something he'd ever show to Deborah.

Wolfe turned with a stern, clearly-displeased expression as Wilmot entered. "I just received the report of all communications during the incident with Belinda Reese earlier."

"Yes sir?"

Wolfe moved closer to him. "I trusted you, Andrew. You're an exceptional operative, which is why you were promoted to my second-in-command. But what the hell were you thinking?"

"I don't follow you, sir."

"You gave a direct order to take out Brandon Drake. We're not a law-enforcement agency. It was a breach of protocol."

"Sir, he'd put down four men. I made a decision I'd make again in a heartbeat."

"We need him!" Wolfe said with undeniable assertion. "And why the hell did you permit all of that goddamn commotion through the streets of Denver? They were just supposed to track her. We're covering our asses here. Everything about this has to be off the record, and those idiots made a public spectacle of it."

Wilmot was silent, having no words to justify his actions.

Wolfe took a deep breath, exhaling loudly. "He used a sonic force emitter and tear gas. Hardly lethal."

"I had no way of knowing that, sir. I wasn't there."

The director's expression relaxed. "Neither was he, as it happens."

Wilmot frowned. "What do you mean? They saw him."

Wolfe walked back to his desk and rummaged inside a drawer. "Reports from Leavenworth show that in two years he had only one visitor, and according to sworn statements, he took a bullet in the shoulder. He wouldn't have been in any condition to rescue his girlfriend, I can assure you." He took out an eight-by-ten black and white photograph, and placed it on the desk.

Wilmot studied the image of the young man in the shot. "That's Drake. Isn't it?"

"*A* Drake. Not *the* Drake."

Wilmot shook his head, bemused.

"That's a photograph of Tyler Faraday, Brandon Drake's brother. He's also the adoptive son of Charlton Faraday, founder of the Faraday Corporation. I'm sending you out to Dallas immediately. Find out whatever you can. You can sleep on the jet."

"Yes, sir."

"Steven McKay, the brother of your late colleague, Martyn McKay, managed to have an inquest into his brother's death opened. Now we need Drake more than ever. He just broke out before we could get to him. I couldn't give a rat's ass about his escape from Leavenworth, or the Mach Turbo Swan. McKay isn't the only one who believes his brother was murdered, and if there's a shred of truth to it, we have to know. Any last trace of Treadwell in the CIA and SDT has to be rooted out. Brandon Drake might be the only one left who knows anything."

"Martyn McKay was unstable and on the edge, sir. There's no doubt in my mind that he killed himself."

"I sure hope you're right. Let's be certain. We need Drake. I'll even try to push for a presidential pardon for him. See if that sweetens him up."

Wilmot made his way out of the office, deep in thought.

Stepping out the building, he walked across the parking lot to his Camaro. After climbing in, he took a cell phone out of the glove compartment and selected a contact. It was answered almost immediately. "Garrett? We need to get prepared," he said darkly. "Wolfe has now become a liability."

Six

Cabin Fever

Belinda knelt beside the bed in the cabin cradling the back of Brandon's head with her palm. Her clothing was still damp from the snow, but she was barely conscious of how cold she was. Her only thoughts were for her man.

Brandon shivered uncontrollably, despite being huddled under a thick, goose down comforter. Whenever his eyes opened they rolled, unable to focus.

Tyler entered the room. "The fire's blazing and it's warming up a bit. How is he?"

"He's delirious and burning up." Her voice quivered with the anguished pangs of emotion. "We've got to do something, Tyler. He needs medical attention urgently."

"I know, but what can I do?"

"Why did you come for me?" she snapped. "Why didn't you go get help for him?"

"He was nowhere near as bad as this when I left him, but my coming for you was what he wanted. You had to come first. He made me promise. If you ask me, it's a damn good thing he did, otherwise they'd have caught you. God only knows what they'd have done to you, or what information they might have gotten out of you. Absolutely everything could've gone right down the crapper."

She was momentarily silent, but finally conceded. "I know you're right. But what are we gonna do? I mean, just look at him."

41

Tyler moved closer to the bed and peeled back a corner of the comforter to just below Brandon's shoulder. Carefully, he unbound the blood-caked linen tied around the gunshot wound.

As the binding came away, Belinda slapped a hand across her mouth in horror. Raw flesh coated with coagulating blood was visible below Brandon's collar bone. It appeared to be a neat exit wound, but the surrounding tissue was severely inflamed.

"How well do you know this place?" Tyler said.

She tried to gather her thoughts. "I suppose as well as anyone could. There's not much to it. Living room, basement, kitchen, bedroom, and bathroom. That's about it."

"OK, he obviously drank the gin to ease the pain, so he's gonna need water. Do you know if there's anything in here like . . . ? I don't know. Disinfectant?"

"I'll see what I can find." With that, she made her way out to the kitchen.

Searching through the drawers and cupboards, her mind came alive with memories, and dreams she'd had of those memories. Her most powerful recollection was of her first view outside the kitchen window, the morning after Brandon had rescued her from Treadwell's pseudo-terrorists. The peace, the serenity, and the magnificent sight of those snow-coated trees were a treasured memory that had helped her through the last two years.

The bear cub came to her mind in a moment of desire that this living nightmare had never happened. *Snooky. Whatever became of you?*

Abruptly returning to her task, she opened the cupboard under the sink and found a meager offering of dishwashing and surface-cleaning products. But nothing was suitable for application to human flesh. There wasn't anything that would help with an infection.

However, she noticed four two-liter bottles of filtered water. Taking one, she returned to the upper cupboards for one of Brandon's magnum-sized coffee mugs.

With the bottled water and the mug in hand, she hurried through the bedroom, into the bathroom, and looked through the mirrored door cupboard above the wash basin. There was nothing helpful there either.

"Bro, can you hear me?" Tyler said, holding onto Brandon's hand.

He'd never gotten over how closely he resembled his brother since he first laid eyes on him in the courtroom. On the day he'd met him face to face at Leavenworth, his first words had been hesitant as he'd tried to process the unique moment of gazing directly upon a virtual mirror. He'd been right since he was twelve years old. There had been a part of himself out there in the world he needed to be reunited with.

But there his other self now lay, injured, shivering, delirious, and kissing the veil of death. "You can't die. I won't let you." Enraged, Tyler hurried out of the bedroom and into the living room. His gaze darted aimlessly all around him trying to find something—anything that might help his brother through the night.

He noticed the remainder of the gin in the bottle over in the corner of the living room. *Alcohol.* He took the bottle and ran back to the bedroom.

Belinda had already returned to Brandon's side. She unscrewed one of the water bottles, poured it out into the coffee mug, and drew Brandon's head up. "Try to drink, baby."

His lips tasted the rim of the mug, but he was notably senseless.

"We need washcloths, towels, anything like that," Tyler said.

She placed the water mug next to the bed and ran back into the bathroom.

Tyler took Brandon's hand and knelt down beside him again. "Take it easy, bro. This might just work."

Within a minute, Belinda returned with a handful of towels.

Tyler turned to her. "All right, I need you to help me roll him over onto his side."

She placed her hand underneath Brandon between his shoulder blades, and eased him over. The towel came away from where it had adhered to his dried blood, exposing the horrifying entry wound.

Tyler took one of the washcloths and poured a splash of gin into his brother's open flesh. Brandon's weak groans indicated his delirium, much to Tyler's relief. Were Brandon fully conscious, the pain would've been unimaginable.

He immediately pressed the cloth against the wound and cascd Brandon onto his back again. He then set about emptying the remainder of the gin onto the exit wound.

Tyler secured another towel onto the injury and bound it all up again with the linen. "That's all we can do for now. Hopefully the alcohol will act as an astringent until the morning. I'm gonna fly back out to Dallas first thing, but I need to think of a plan."

"Go back to Dallas and do what?" she said.

"Get some antibiotics, morphine, and some medical advice, at the very least."

Tyler knew there was no chance of him being able to sleep, despite his exhaustion. *Two hours there, two hours to sort something out, two hours back again.* Such was the reality that tortured his mind, with his brother possibly dying beside him. There had to be something he could do to help him.

And there was.

Seven

Desperate Measures

Tyler took out his android phone and noticed the time on the digital clock: 23:57. *He's gonna kill me*. Regardless, he searched through his contacts until he found the number.

His call was answered quickly, and he exhaled with relief as a familiar male voice came through the receiver. "Brett. It's Tyler Faraday."

"Tyler? What can I do for you at this hour?" It was one o'clock in the morning in Dallas, and Brett Fleetwood was notably lethargic.

"This is the biggest thing I've ever asked of you, but I'm absolutely desperate."

"All right, now just take it easy Tyler, and tell me what's going on?"

Tyler could clearly hear the man's wife groggily saying, "What's going on, Brett?" It was such an uncomfortable moment. He knew he was waking up a man and his wife in the middle of the night, but he had no choice.

"Somebody—" Tyler paused to collect himself. "Somebody close to me has been seriously injured, and it's a very delicate situation. I have nowhere else to turn."

"Where are you?"

"I. . . I can't tell you."

There was a momentary silence on the line. Brett was obviously confused by Tyler's words.

"Doc, the reason I can't tell you is for your own protection. I need you to trust me."

46

"Of course I trust you, Tyler. Hell, I've been your physician since you were two years old."

"If I can get you flown out here, can you be ready by the morning to come and help us?"

"I . . . I'm not sure Tyler. I've got—"

"Look, I'm begging you! My brother may be dying," Tyler said, unable to hold back his tears.

"Brother?"

"It's a long story."

"Well, what kind of injury is this?"

"He's been shot in the shoulder. It looks like a clear entry and exit wound, but he's burning up with fever."

"When was he shot?"

"About twenty hours ago."

"Oh, my God. Have you been keeping pressure on the wound?"

"Yes, but it's drying up now. All I had to clean up the infection was gin."

"Gin? You put gin on it?"

Fear came over Tyler that he might have unintentionally harmed Brandon. "Well, yeah."

"Well, it's better than nothing, at least temporarily."

Tyler gave a sigh of relief. "So what do I do now?"

"Keep him warm. He could go into shock, so keep him wrapped up. Now, I need you to do something for me."

"What's that?"

"I need you to get photographs of both injuries, entry and exit, and email them over to me right away. I need to see them enlarged so that I'll know what I'm dealing with."

"I'm on it. I'll call you right back."

"Wait a second," Fleetwood said. "Do you have my email address?"

"It's in my phone."

"Good. Now get those shots to me yesterday."

Belinda looked up at him sharply. "What's going on?"

"I'm making arrangements to have medical help brought here."

"You're what?"

"It's a man I'd trust with my life, and if we don't do this, Brandon could lose his. I need photographs of his wounds."

Eagerly, Belinda unbound the linen from Brandon's shoulder.

Tyler took the photograph with his phone camera. "And the back."

They eased Brandon onto his side again and removed the towel. Tyler took the second photograph. "All right. Wrap him up again. I've got to get these sent off, pronto."

As Belinda redressed the wounds, Tyler located Fleetwood's email address, forwarded the photographs to him, and then called Fleetwood back. "All right, I've just sent the shots to you."

"Give me a moment to check my mail," Fleetwood said.

Tyler waited for two minutes, the tension getting the better of him. "Doc, you still there?"

"I'm here. I'm just opening up the file now . . . Wow. Did you take these in HD?"

"Yeah."

"Well, I've got to tell you, they're perfect. With the zoom imager I've got on here, it's almost like I'm on top of him."

"Well, what do you think?"

"Do you have any idea how far away he was from the shooter when he was shot?"

Tyler closed his eyes and tried to think. He didn't see Brandon get hit, but he'd been waiting around a corner close by when it happened. "Two hundred yards, maybe a little more."

"Two hundred yards?" Fleetwood said, clearly amazed.

"Yeah."

"In that that case, whoever shot him wasn't only a hawk-eye marksman, but he most certainly didn't want to kill your brother. It's a clean shot from a distance that's missed the collar bone, every organ, and caused minimal tissue damage."

"Really?"

"Do you have any idea what kind of precision that would take?"

"No, I don't. Look, Doc, is he gonna make it?"

"He's going to be just fine, barring the need for a few stitches, pain killers, and a few antibiotic shots. Trouble is, I need to get to him to administer them."

"I can arrange that."

"How soon?"

Tyler's mind raced. Alex and Digswell would be arriving in Dallas by around 2:00 a.m. Fleetwood would have to meet them at the airfield, and Dig would have to fly him all the way back again. That would be another two hours, plus the time to get him, via helicopter, to the ridge, and then the trek to the cabin. "Shouldn't take more than six to eight hours max, even allowing for bad weather."

"Tyler, just take it easy," Fleetwood said. "I know you're upset, but you need to listen. Make sure your brother is as warm as possible, and that he has water. The fever is going to dehydrate him, and the shock is going to make him feel cold even though he might not be. If you take good care of him, he'll make it until I get there, all right?"

"I'll make this up to you, Brett."

"Don't worry about that. Now, where do you need me to go?"

"I'm gonna make the arrangements now. Can you give me a few minutes?"

"Sure."

Tyler noticed Brandon's eyes opening. He opened his mouth but no sound emerged, and his eyes darted about the room deliriously.

Tyler searched for Alex's cell phone number. He knew Alex had an advanced-range satellite phone, but would he be able to pick up a signal in the jet? Nevertheless, it rang out.

"Hey, Ty." Alex's tone seemed to have warmed slightly since their last communication, softened perhaps, by the sight of two beautiful pole dancers gyrating in the middle of the jet.

"Alex, I need to talk to Dig."

"Sure. Why? What's going on?"

"I'm about to piss him off, big time."

Brandon seemed to become more agitated by the moment, and a barely-audible word fell from his lips. "Em-il-y."

Belinda rapidly spun around. "Oh, my God. He's waking up. He's talking."

"Em-ily."

Captain David Digswell came on the line. "Yes, sir. Is everything all right?"

"Dig. Look, man, I know this is a lot to ask, but I'm gonna cut to the chase. When you drop Alex off, I need you to pick up another man, a Doctor Brett Fleetwood, and fly him back out to Denver immediately afterwards."

"Mr. Faraday, that's not safe. You're asking me to fly through the night without any sleep."

Tyler knew Dig was right and screwed up his lips in frustration. And then he remembered he had $7,000 in cash in his suitcase. He knew it would be a bribe, but in a desperate situation he had no choice but to try. "I know what I'm asking you to do here is run a goddamn gauntlet, Dig. That's why I insist on paying for a day and a night in one of Denver's top hotels for you, along with two thousand dollars in cash."

"I'll be as quick as I can, sir."

Tyler grinned, ended the call, and turned to Belinda. "We can relax. Brandon's as good as new. I've got the doctor, the pilot, and the money." And then a thought occurred. "Oh, shit. How much is Fleetwood gonna cost me?"

"Who's Fleetwood?" Belinda said.

"My doctor. I'm having him flown up here. If I don't have enough money on me—"

"What?"

"Dammit!" he exclaimed in humiliation. "I'm gonna have to call my dad."

Brandon became frantic in an almost-convulsing manner.

"Oh, baby," Belinda said. "You're gonna be fine. Tyler's got help coming."

He shook his head maniacally from side to side. "N-no. T-Tyler . . ."

Tyler knelt down and gripped his brother's hand. "I'm here, bro. Everything's cool. Try to relax."

"N-no. It's not OK. P-please, Ty. Don't . . ."

"What? Don't what?"

"Don't call your dad."

Eight

House Call

Tyler stepped out of the helicopter at the top of the ridge, made his way around to the other side, and opened the door for his guest.

Dr. Brett Fleetwood cautiously followed him out into the snow attired in thick layers of arctic clothing and headwear. With his medical bag in his grip, his eyes were bound by a large handkerchief,

"I'll take that off now, Doc." Tyler briskly removed the blindfold.

Fleetwood opened his eyes. Dawn was breaking, and the moonlight illuminated the snow beneath him. He'd been flown from Dallas to Faraday's airfield outside Denver, then blindfolded, led into the helicopter, and brought up to the ridge. For over two hours, he'd seen only the interior of the jet, then darkness, and now snow. "Where the hell have you brought me to? The North Pole? On second thought, don't answer that."

"All right, Doc, I can't even begin to tell you how much I appreciate this. I'm gonna have to put the blindfold on you again when we get to the bottom of the ridge."

"I understand." Fleetwood couldn't help but notice the trees to his right in the distance. It was dark, and they were so heavily coated with snow he couldn't be certain what species they were. *Aspen* was a calculated guess, but he decided he really didn't want to know.

Tyler led the harrowing trek down the ridge.

"I still can't get over it," Fleetwood said. "Brandon Drake is your brother, and you helped him escape from Leavenworth? Do you have any idea how serious a mess you guys are in?"

"Only too well."

"It's been all over the news, and he has more than his fair share of fans. This thing has virtually divided the entire country."

"Really?"

"Ty, you've got no idea. Police have been placed on alert all across the nation, and people have been having parties in the streets over this."

"No way."

"Seriously. I guess the whole thing has tapped into the innate human resentment for authority."

Tyler shot him a shrewd grin. "Did you party too?"

Fleetwood smiled coyly. "Had a few drinks at home. I remembered Brandon's trial and the scandal about Treadwell. There was something admirable and compelling about the story, and about Brandon, no matter which side of politics you're on."

"I had no idea."

"Well, the sooner we get to him, the sooner we can get him back to good health."

They finally arrived at the base of the ridge. Fleetwood gazed at the snow hill before him.

"This is where I'm gonna have to blindfold you again, all right?" Tyler said.

"The less I know, the safer I'm going to be."

Tyler wrapped the handkerchief around Fleetwood's head again and gently held his shoulders from behind. "All right, I'll guide you. I need you to put one foot in front of the other and walk up that incline you just saw. I'll be right behind you."

Steadily, the two men scaled the snow hill. Tyler carefully eased Fleetwood down the other side until they were on flat, snow-covered ground.

"Just a few more steps, Doc." Tyler guided Fleetwood across, and up onto the cabin's porch.

Belinda stepped out of the kitchen as the front door opened. Her heart missed a beat. First, a blindfolded stranger entered. Then Tyler followed with his hands on the man's shoulders, steering him. Her mouth fell open with elation and relief. *Oh, my God. He actually did it.*

Tyler acknowledged her with a nod, but she held herself still to avoid alerting Fleetwood to her presence.

Tyler opened the bedroom door, maneuvered Fleetwood inside, and closed the door behind them.

Belinda paced the living room restlessly, her anxiety at all-time high. She'd endured almost twenty hours of relentless tension and stress. It kept playing over in her mind. She'd been spared no trauma—paranoia, a near mugging, running for her life, and coming close to being buried alive and freezing to death. Now, the love of her life was at death's door, with no certainty he was going to be saved.

Tyler seemed like such an extraordinary man, but in a different way from Brandon. He was clearly obscenely wealthy, but with such a strong streak of selflessness. It was abundantly clear that, despite his fortunate background, nothing meant more to him than his family.

Fleetwood's vision adjusted as Tyler removed the blindfold, finding himself in a bedroom with no idea where. He removed his headwear to reveal a messy covering of graying hair.

Tyler knelt down beside Brandon who was still ghostly-pallid and damp with perspiration. However, his eyes opened and he seemed to be becoming coherent.

"Hey, bro," Tyler said. "I've got help for you. Now, just relax and everything's gonna be fine."

Brandon turned his head toward Fleetwood. He attempted to extend his hand from under the sheets, but the pain in his shoulder was clearly too severe. "How're you doing, Doc?" he said weakly.

Fleetwood smiled. "I'm fine, thank you, Brandon. But I need to take a look at you. How are you feeling?"

"Sore. Hung over."

"Did the alcohol ease the pain?"

"Can't remember."

Fleetwood placed his medical bag on the carpet and prepared an anesthetic syringe. "I don't want to waste any more time, Brandon. You were shot almost thirty hours ago. I'm going to have to stitch you up immediately, and then give you a strong shot of antibiotics."

"I understand. Thank you."

Fleetwood released the air bubbles from the syringe. "You'll feel two tiny scratches, and then your shoulder will be frozen. You won't feel a thing."

Brandon managed a smile. "Music to my ears, Doc."

"Are you allergic to any antibiotics?"

"Not that I know of."

Fleetwood turned to Tyler. "Come closer, Tyler. I need you to watch what I'm doing because I'm going to leave you with some tetracycline shots. I'll teach you how to administer them, and afterwards, I'll give you a crash course on removing the stitches."

Tyler nodded nervously.

"All right. Let's get started."

Two hours passed before the bedroom door opened again. The blindfolded doctor, with his medical bag in hand, stepped into the living room guided by Tyler. "I've got you checked into the Four Seasons Hotel for the night with Dig," Tyler said. "He's gonna fly you back to Dallas tomorrow."

"Thank you, Tyler."

"No, Doc. Thank *you*. I still can't figure out why you won't let me pay you for all this."

"With the amount of money your father has put into my cancer research project, this is the least I could do."

Fleetwood knew Charlton Faraday's generosity had a personal element attached. Twenty-eight years earlier, Charlton's wife of five years had passed away from breast cancer at the age of twenty-nine. His loss had crushed him beyond endurance, and he felt an obligation to do whatever was in his power to reduce such future suffering.

As they reached the door, Fleetwood paused and turned slightly. "I can't see you, but it would've been a pleasure to have met you, Ms. Reese. You have a rather phenomenal tale to tell."

Belinda looked at Tyler, astounded that Fleetwood knew she was there, but she didn't say a word.

And then, the two men were gone.

***

Andrew Wilmot walked briskly across the Faraday-Dallas airfield toward the helicopter landing pad. It was a particularly warm day for February, and he couldn't help noticing the difference in climate compared to Washington D.C.

He waited while the rotor-blades of a newly-landed chopper slowed to a crawl.

A tall, bearded man in a pristine blue suit and Stetson, stepped out of the helicopter. Had he not been so lean, Wilmot thought he would've been a dead ringer for Santa Claus. "Mr. Faraday? Charlton Faraday?"

"Howdy," Faraday said in a deep, Texas accent. "What can I do for you, young fella?"

Wilmot took out his ID badge and showed it to Faraday. "I'm Agent Wilmot with SDT. Homeland Security. I'm here on official business, sir. Your secretary told me where I could find you."

"Just been testing the new *Air Shark*," Faraday said excitedly. "One of the best we ever made. Flies like an eagle, but it'll bite your ass off if you get in front of it. So, what's goin' on? I thought you intelligence boys kept your identifications secret."

"SDT is a unique sub-division of Homeland Security. One of the reasons it was set up was to enable conventional investigations with civilians."

"I see."

"I need to talk to you about your son, sir."

"Tyler?"

"Yes, sir. Do you have any idea where I can find him?"

Faraday looked as though he'd just been punched in the stomach. "No, I haven't seen him since Monday. What's this all about?"

"You haven't seen the news?"

"Not since yesterday afternoon. I've been kinda busy."

"Brandon Drake, your son's natural brother, escaped from Fort Leavenworth in the early hours of yesterday morning. We need to talk to Tyler so that we can eliminate him from our inquiries."

Faraday's face turned almost as white as his beard. Seeing his distress, Wilmot made the decision to disclose a hint of the real reason SDT wanted Brandon. "We're not interested in your son, sir, and we're not interested in arresting Brandon Drake. SDT isn't a law enforcement agency. We need Brandon's help on a matter of national security, and we were hoping your son might be able to help us find him."

"I have no idea where he is, Agent . . . ?"

"Wilmot."

"Of course. I apologize. Tyler's his own man, but I don't know anything about this."

Wilmot casually studied the look in the older man's eyes. After a few moments, he was confident he was telling the truth. He took out his card and handed it to Faraday. "If you hear anything at all from Tyler, sir, I'd really appreciate it if you'd have him call me."

"I'll do that."

"Thank you for your time. You have a nice day now, sir." Wilmot turned and made his way back across the airfield.

As he approached his cab, he pondered the suspicious look he'd seen in Faraday's eyes: the look that told him Faraday wouldn't be willing to disclose his son's whereabouts, even if he knew.

He took out his cell phone and waited for two rings. A familiar female voice answered. "Heidi, this is Agent Wilmot at Director Wolfe's office. I'm going to email you an authorization for an NSA satellite trace on all cell phones registered to one Charlton Faraday, and his son, Tyler. I want conversation details and pinpoint locations on every one of them."

Nine

The Agenda

Brandon had been slipping in and out of consciousness all day and hadn't been coherent or conversational. Belinda still hadn't spoken to him. Anxiously, she made her way to the bedroom.

As she opened the door, his head turned to her.

"Hi. You're awake." she said with a beaming smile.

"Barely. My shoulder's still numb, so I'm not complaining. You look so beautiful."

Her hand came across her mouth as she suppressed her tears.

"Hey, hey, what's wrong?" he said.

"I have missed you so much, for so long." She sobbed as the sum total of two years' hoping was finally released.

Weakly, he said, "Oh, baby. Come over here."

She wanted to hold him so badly while he was conscious of her. Wary of aggravating his wounds, she approached him with caution. She considered how cruel it all was. All she had wanted was to hold him. Now they were reunited, even that was denied them.

Brandon could only embrace her with one arm, but she knelt down beside him and rested her head on his chest. "I love you so much," she said.

"I never stopped loving you, all the time I was away," he said, his voice hoarse with a hint of gravel. Nevertheless, his emotion was unmistakable. "There wasn't a day I didn't long for you."

"Me too."

"They loved your cooking, though."

"*My* cooking?"

"Yeah, you remember. You taught me how to do it right."

She chuckled recalling their mishaps in the kitchen during the early days.

"Are you gonna be OK living here with me for awhile?" he said coyly.

"Are you kidding? It'd take an army to drag me out of here."

He managed a smile.

"I slept with you last night. Did you know that?" she said.

"You did? How could I have not known?"

"You were out of it big time."

"Yeah, well, must've been the sedative. It's not over yet. It's gonna be weeks before I'm fit enough to do what we've got to do. But recovery's gonna be the fun part." He shot her a devilish grin.

She looked up from his chest, confused. "What do you mean? 'What we've got to do'?"

He exhaled and his eyes became weary again. "Tyler found me. I couldn't believe it. Thought I was seein' things. All I ever wanted was my family, babe. Then I found out I never had one. My mom, my dad, my grandfather. . . None of them were ever real people. They were just delusions."

"I know, sweetheart. I remember how painful it was for you."

"I couldn't get over it. Just couldn't process it. It tortured me day and night. But Tyler changed everything. He spent so long searching for us. Now, he has a lead."

She frowned, puzzled. "*Us*? A lead on what?"

"Not on what. On *whom*." He looked her in the eye with a glow of hope in his own; a radiance that seemed to strengthen him against his debilitation. "We have a family. There is another Drake."

"Another Drake?"

"Tyler and I have a little sister. He found some information about her from the Hall of Records. Her name is Emily, and she's in Nevada. Can you believe that?"

"You have a sister?"

"Yeah. That's what this is all about. Tyler helped me to get out of Leavenworth. Together, we're gonna find Emily. We're gonna put our family back together. Then he's gonna help us to get out of America and disappear forever somewhere, where we can just live our lives in peace."

Belinda shook her head frantically. "No, Brandon. It's too dangerous. If Tyler can get us out, let's just go."

"Not without seeing Emily. I need to find her, baby. She's my sister. I need this. I need a true identity. Without it, what is freedom worth?"

Her face flushed with desperate anger. "The police, the FBI, and the army are out to get you. You're all over the news. Practically everyone in the country knows what you look like. You can't do this!"

"It's worth the risk to me. It's worth everything . . ." His eyes rolled, and his head sank into the pillow as he lost consciousness again.

Exasperated, Belinda let go of his hand and stood. The walls of the bedroom seemed to close in on her. She'd been through it all before and didn't believe she could face such an ordeal again—the fear, the stress, the panic, and the relentless danger.

But Brandon was her life, her heart, and her soul. He was determined to find Emily, and she knew what he was capable of when he had his heart set on something. Trying to talk him out of it would be like trying to stop a runaway train. There was no room for compromise. It was a no-win situation, and the pangs of resentment began to build within her. "Damn it, Brandon!"

***

"What the hell did you think you were doing?"

Tyler was taken aback by the first experience in his life of his father's rage. Charlton Faraday was one of America's pioneers, and an essentially astute, hardened business tycoon. But Tyler had always been the apple of his eye, the one who was spared the wrath.

The office, positioned on the thirtieth floor of a gleaming high-rise in downtown Dallas, was a testament to Faraday's wealth. From the plush cream carpet, to the brown leather recliner chairs, to the top-of-the-line personal computer on Charlton's oak desk, everything was spotless. The windows spread across the length of the room providing a birds-eye view of the sprawling metropolis.

"Dad, I-I—"

"I told you at Fort Bragg, two years ago, to let this go. Brandon is trouble. I knew it then. I know it now."

"He's my brother," Tyler said with an assertion he'd never had to summon before.

Charlton stepped from around his desk and came toward him. "A government agent came to the airfield yesterday looking for you." He reached into the lapel pocket of his suit jacket, took out the card, and gave it to Tyler. "Agent Wilmot from some special Homeland Security division. He said they needed Brandon to help them with an investigation, but I didn't buy a word of it. You're in deep, Son, and I'm worried sick about you."

Tyler swallowed hard. "That's why I didn't call you. Brandon told me all phones registered to us would be under NSA surveillance."

"Oh, that's just great. They're gonna know all my business, all my dealings, *and* my private conversations."

"I-I'm sorry, Dad. I really am, but I had no choice."

"Did Alex help you?"

Tyler stared at the floor, deeply reluctant to sell out his best friend. "Of course not. Why would you say that?"

"Because I know the kind of crazy shit you two get up to, that's why."

"Yeah, well—"

"Why, Tyler? Why?"

Tyler stepped closer to his father with conviction in his eyes. "I am a blessed man, Dad. All thanks to you. You put the silver spoon in my mouth that I was born without."

"So why risk what you have? This is what I just don't understand."

"I was born in hell. I know that now. The more I researched my history and where I came from, the more I knew I had to find the others." He lowered his head in recollection. "I . . . I remember him, Dad. I remember Brandon. I couldn't have been even two years old. But I remember the bigger boy. *Bannon,* I remember calling him. I had to find him again. Please try to understand."

"But Brandon was a military prisoner, and you helped him escape. You broke serious laws. Federal laws."

"That's right, Dad. How could I have done anything else? I was given the brass ring, and Brandon was tossed in the trash can. He fought to survive, and because he fought he was punished with a choice of prison or the army. The bastards then stripped him of his life by brainwashing him."

Charlton tilted his head as though he was trying to assimilate Tyler's reasoning. "You're doing this out of a sense of guilt over what you have?"

"Not guilt, Dad. Duty. And love. I was spared for a reason. That's what I believe."

Charlton took a step back, coming down from his anger. "You're going after the girl now, right?"

"It was only by chance that I learned about her when I was researching my adoption. I hired a private detective to find out where she is, but I still don't even know what she looks like. I have no memory of her. All I know is nobody wanted her, and because of that, she's spent her entire life in a goddamn—"

"It's not your fault, Tyler."

"But it's my responsibility to put it right."

"Why?"

"Because I was spared."

Charlton was silent, but after a few moments, he spoke again. "You know, when I lost my Sarah to cancer, I was robbed of the chance to have a child with the only woman I'd ever loved. You were brought to my attention at that orphanage, and my heart just melted." He wept as he recalled the moment. "I loved you from the moment I saw you."

Tyler was more uncomfortable than ever seeing his father, a titan, so emotionally vulnerable. Tears and Charlton Faraday didn't mix. "Dad, look, I didn't wanna upset you, I just—"

"I am so damn proud of you, Son."

"E-excuse me?"

"You said it yourself. You have it all. And yet you're willing to risk it for the sake of others. You're a man of integrity. Far beyond wealth or vocational success, there is nothing more precious than that. I have no moral right to stand in your way."

Stunned by his father's words, Tyler looked at him vacantly. "Dad? What are you saying?"

Charlton dried his eyes and pulled himself together. "I'm saying I was wrong, Son. You need to do what you need to do with this . . . agenda. No matter how much I'm gonna be worried sick about you."

Tyler threw his arms around him, and they held one another for a moment. "Thank you, Dad."

"I'll do whatever I can to help you."

Tyler reached into his pocket and handed his father a cell phone. "Take this and keep it on you. It's not registered to anyone. I've got the number, and I'll call you on it, all right?"

Charlton took the phone and nodded, his expression an amalgam of deep concern and enormous pride.

Tyler turned and made his way toward the elevator.

Charlton watched anxiously as the elevator doors closed.

Ten

Contact

Brandon gnashed his teeth pulling his body weight up on an overhead support beam in the cabin's living room. Four weeks had passed since his escape from Leavenworth. Despite his eagerness to get back in shape, the pain in his shoulder was still debilitating.

"Eight—n-nine—oh, God—t-t-ten." Dropping to the carpet, he fell to his knees grasping his shoulder.

During the last week, he'd begun the process of restoring his fitness by briskly scaling the ridge every morning before breakfast. However, his upper body muscularity was already going into atrophy. He was paranoid about becoming unfit, especially with the potential risks he faced when he finally left the cabin. Regardless, this time he realized he'd been a little over-zealous.

Tyler had stayed with him and Belinda to help with his care, and Tyler had successfully removed his stitches as Fleetwood instructed. Scar tissue formed across the entry and exit wounds, but Brandon knew he still required at least another two weeks rest before attempting anything strenuous. Impatience had got the better of his reason.

Belinda stepped out of the bathroom with a bucket of cleaning materials. She'd comfortably taken to a life of domestic co-habitation. It was the happiest and most secure she'd ever felt.

69

Concern overcame her when she saw Brandon wincing in pain, and hurried over to him. "What happened?"

"Pull-ups," he said.

Kneeling down, she looked into his pained eyes. "Pull-ups? Are you out of your freaking mind?"

He looked up at her with a sheepish grin.

"It's too soon, Brandon. You're not well enough to put yourself through that kind of exertion."

"I didn't hear you say that last night." He winked at her painfully. "Or the night before."

After taking a deep breath, she quickly succumbed to laughter. Her fingers combed through his thick, ever-growing hair. "I love you. I just don't want you to hurt yourself."

"I'll be fine. I know I'm not ready to work on my lats, yet. Or my biceps. Or my chest. Oh, shit, I'm a goddamn invalid. If anything happens to an arm or shoulder, you can't really do anything." He looked away from her almost shamefully.

"I don't care what your body looks like. All I care about is you. Now, take it easy."

"Yes, sir."

"Stop kidding around, Brandon. This is serious."

"How's the bathroom," he said, changing the subject.

"Sparkling."

"You didn't have to do that, you know. I can clean up."

She laughed. "No, you can't. When I first came here, it was a mess. You hadn't even done the goddamn dishes."

Before he could respond, the sat-scrambler phone buzzed on the liquor cabinet. Brandon stood and answered it. "Hey, Ty. How's it going, bro? What are you calling me on?"

"It's a burner phone, so quit worrying. I'm at the top of a ski-slope in Switzerland with a beautiful woman," Tyler quipped. "You are so gonna love the hell outta me, buddy. I got your money invested in a top interest account in Bern yesterday. They didn't ask any questions after they checked my history through the Faraday Corporation."

"Great," Brandon said with a victoriously-clenched fist.

"I went in with the one million, one-hundred-forty thousand, like you wanted."

"Yeah?"

"So, let's go back to the beginning. You started out with one million, two hundred gees, right?"

"Right."

"Well, with this account I've put it in, you're gonna have the forty-eight you blew on vans and shit, *and* the twelve grand you've held for living expenses, back within about twelve weeks."

Brandon was silent for a moment.

"Hey, Brandon? Hello? You still there?"

Brandon cried a deafening, jubilant cheer and noticed Belinda's inquisitive, intrigued look. "How the hell did you do that?" he said gleefully.

Tyler chuckled. "Hey, when it comes to investing money, I know what I'm doing. It was my favorite hobby when I was in preschool."

"You are *the man*, you know that?"

"I have my moments. Anyway, how are you doing?"

Brandon cringed. "Not as well as I'd hoped, unfortunately. I just had a little setback working out."

"Just take it easy. You're rushing it, bro."

Brandon glanced at Belinda. "So my commanding officer keeps telling me."

"How's Belinda doing?"

"Great. We're happy. Everything's peaceful. It's everything we ever wanted. But if I were you, Ty, I'd stay in Switzerland just a little while longer. I'm still not sure what your situation is with the authorities."

"Hey, don't worry about me. I'm having myself a fine old time."

"I'm still worried about Emily," Brandon said.

"Well, I've got to admit, it's not a life I would've chosen, but to each, their own."

Brandon's lips pursed with moderate anger. "They took her in when she was a baby. I doubt she's ever known the meaning of choice."

"At least she's safe for now. That's all that counts."

Brandon looked over at Belinda again, this time with concern. "Don't be so sure of that."

"What do you mean?"

"Never mind. Just have yourself some fun, Ty. I'll call you soon."

"All right. Take care, bro. I'm going for a ski."

Brandon put the phone down and sat in cold contemplation.

Belinda walked over to him and placed her arm around his shoulder. "What was all that about? You were up and down like a roller coaster."

"Tyler invested Payne's money. He says the sixty thousand dollars I took out will come back in interest within three months."

"Three months?"

"You got it."

"So, why are you so glum?"

He picked up a calling card Tyler had left behind on the cabinet and stared at it. "This has to end."

"You're not actually thinking of making contact, are you?" she said.

Without a word, he picked up the sat-scrambler again.

***

"What was your general impression of Sergeant Drake during the time he was here?"

Mike Johnson, an MOS 31E-grade army corrections specialist at Fort Leavenworth, pondered how he should respond to Agent Wilmot's question. Sitting across him in one of the guardrooms, he didn't want to seem biased. "Well, sir, I suppose I'd have to say he was a model prisoner. He did what he was told, he was popular with the other detainees, and a particularly good cook."

"A good cook?"

"Yes, sir. That's how he got assigned to kitchen duty."

"It's also how he managed to break out, isn't it?"

"With all due respect, sir, I really don't think that's fair. We've analyzed his escape, and it's become apparent he'd been working on this breakout since he arrived."

Wilmot leaned forward, his expression bearing all the signs of condescending sarcasm. "So, he gave you two damn years to figure out what he was up to, and you still blew it."

Johnson swallowed hard. "He was handling an early morning food delivery. Once the stock was in, the security locks would've secured him in the kitchen. After we thought the door was locked, he was left unattended for just a few minutes. It seems he'd found some way of messing with the electronics of the internal security system. He knocked out the security cameras and disabled the door lock."

"And?"

"He apparently fixed a pre-prepared steel sheet to his back somehow, snuck out, and braced himself underneath the delivery truck with metallic straps. By the time we knew he was missing, the truck was already off the grounds. He then released the straps and fell onto the road."

"And you saw this happen?"

"Yes, sir. I was on lookout duty that morning."

"And what did you do?"

"Five of us went after him. I fired a warning shot, but he kept running. I had no choice but to shoot him." The pangs of regret struck Johnson in a way he couldn't disguise.

Wilmot tilted his head derisively. "You're kinda sympathetic toward this guy, aren't you?"

Johnson exhaled. In the two years he'd known Brandon Drake, he'd developed as close to a friendship with him as was possible with any inmate. It was clear that Agent Wilmot was a jerk, whose own sense of self-importance superseded his professionalism. Adherent to duty and honesty, Johnson had always strived to be an exemplary corrections specialist with a commitment to fairness. Occasionally, duty conflicted with his heart. "Sir, my own feelings had no bearing on the performance of my duties. I shot Sergeant Drake. Isn't that enough?"

"What happened after that?"

"I shot him at a range of approximately two hundred yards. He'd made considerable headway before he dropped from the delivery truck. From there, he made it on foot into the residential area. By the time we got there, he'd disappeared."

"Mmmm. . . Those damn Ferraris sure can move, can't they?"

"I don't know anything about that, sir."

Wilmot leaned closer to Johnson. "You're absolutely sure Tyler Faraday hadn't been anywhere near here for two weeks prior to Drake's escape?"

"Absolutely, sir. All records were thoroughly examined and submitted to Director Wolfe's office on request."

"And all the time Drake was here, he never mentioned anything about a hideout? Where he planned to run to?"

"Not that I know of."

"Nothing was overheard during conversations between Drake and Faraday?"

"No, sir."

Wilmot sat back again, his eyes boring into Johnson's. "OK, I think we're done here for now. But I can assure you, Mr. MOS thirty-one-E, all personnel here are gonna be grilled repeatedly until we find out what the hell happened. A large section of this country is still celebrating the fact this place is an unforgivable failure, not to mention its history."

"History, sir?"

"Grigware, Banghart, Jones, and now Drake. Not a good track record."

Johnson looked away in exasperation.

As Wilmot stepped outside the guardroom, his cell phone rang. He answered it. "Yes."

"This is Brandon Drake, and I wanna propose a deal to you."

Wilmot shivered with surprise and the effects of an extremely unpleasant flashback, having suffered a severe beating at Drake's hands, two years earlier. That aside, they hadn't been formally introduced. He knew there was no possibility of Drake knowing the agent he was talking to was the one he'd beaten up in Morgan, Wyoming. "I'm listening."

"I was to be released from Leavenworth if I surrendered the Turbo Swan back to the military. I'm willing to give it back to you . . . in return for my freedom."

Surprised by the call, Wilmot considered the particulars. Wolfe wanted Drake to help him with his investigation into the remnants of Treadwell's operation, unaware that the inquest could lead to Wilmot himself. If Drake turned himself in and actually knew something, Wilmot could lose everything. He knew he had to dispose of Drake at all costs. "Done. You name the time and place."

"I'll let you know."

The line went dead.

Wilmot took the cell phone away from his ear, concerned he hadn't responded in the most effective way. It was vital to his plans that he get to Drake before Wolfe did.

***

Brandon put the sat-scrambler down. Belinda watched as he gazed aimlessly at the floor. "What did he say?" she said.

He shook his head. "Something's wrong. It was too easy. He assured my freedom, but he has no authorization to do that. They're up to something. I just don't know what."

"What are you going to do?"

"There's nothing else I can do." He looked up at her with conviction. "We go on as planned. We wait for Tyler. By that time, I should be back to full strength. But I really think you should stay here."

"No way."

"Coming to Nevada with us could not only be dangerous, it could be upsetting for you."

During the last four weeks, she'd decided she would stand by Brandon, regardless of her initial objections to what he was planning. He wasn't the same person he'd been when they first met. His warm levity was notably diluted, but subconsciously she'd already expected that after everything he'd been through. She loved him more than she'd ever loved anyone, and where he went, she was determined to follow. "I can handle it."

He turned away and his hand brushed a bottle of vodka on the cabinet. Belinda noticed the desiring look in his eyes.

Eleven

An Unknown Past

After six weeks indulging himself in the Alps, Tyler braced himself for a return to prospects that were not so appealing. All of his travels had been accomplished with the use of Faraday Corps' private jets, thereby enabling a more discreet and less-visible itinerary. However, there was no doubt the authorities would've been able to intercept him had they wanted to. His question remained—why hadn't they?

He closed the helicopter door, suitcase in hand. His apprehensive gaze settled on the tip of the ridge. *Oh, shit. Here it comes again.*

Making his way forward, he prepared himself for the arduous descent.

He was alerted to a strange humming sound coming from below. As it came higher, it changed pitch to the mild screech of a jet-engine. Or a turbo.

For the first time, he bore witness to the electric-blue spectacle that had become a media legend. It rose up and hovered before his stunned eyes.

The left side door rose upwards and Brandon leaned out slightly. "Hey bro. You want a lift?"

Smiling with relief, Tyler hurried over to the right side of the Turbo Swan. Not only would it spare him a harrowing trek, he was finally going to discover a unique and inimitable flying experience.

Belinda opened the cabin door to a warm and elated reception from Tyler. Brandon followed.

"Hey, Belinda. How're you doing? I've got to say, you're looking great." Tyler hugged her and kissed her cheek. Dropping his suitcase, he removed his insulated hat, jacket, and snow-boots. "Well, I've heard about it, seen it, but I'd never experienced it The Turbo Swan is the most amazing aircraft I've ever imagined."

Belinda smiled. "I know. How far did you go in it?"

"We just took it for a spin around the mountains. I can't get over how small it is inside. It's just a pod, but it's so damn formidable. How the hell can it withstand grenades and all?"

"It's the alloy shell," Brandon said. "The team who developed it had been working on the formula for years before I was assigned to Mach Industries. It took them a long time to make the metal so tough but lightweight."

"My dad would go wild if he ever saw it. I mean, he'd be like a little kid."

Changing the tone of the conversation, Brandon said, "I don't care what anyone says, we're taking it with us tomorrow. It's not up for debate."

"Whatever you say," Tyler said. "In that case, I'll have to pick up a van first thing tomorrow."

"Just make sure it's a really big Sprinter. The 'Swan might be small, but it's still got to fit in the back."

Tyler opened up his suitcase, took out a folder, and handed it to Brandon. "This is it, bro."

"What?"

"Everything you ever wanted to know about . . . *you*."

Brandon's fingers trembling as he gripped the folder. "This is the file?"

"I wanted to give it to you after you got out of the slammer, but you weren't very coherent. Then I had to get out of the country. It's been in my room at the ranch all this time."

Belinda noticed Brandon's shaking hands. "Are you OK, sweetheart?"

"I'll take you through it," Tyler said.

They sat on the leather couch, and Tyler took the file from Brandon. He fished out a photograph of an impoverished-looking couple in their twenties, who appeared to be standing outside a trailer. Wearing a cheap, pink and white dress, the woman seemed weathered beyond her years. Her dark-blonde hair hung limp and looked like it hadn't been washed in a month.

The man standing beside the woman looked hardened and unkempt. There was coldness and anger in his eyes. *Savagery*. He looked as though he would tear a man's throat out simply for looking at him cross-eyed.

"That's them, Brandon," Tyler said. "That's our parents. Chuck and Linda Drake, Keldian Trailer Park, Charlotte, North Carolina, twenty-eight years ago. Both were unemployed and on welfare. This is where we came from." He took out a newspaper clipping and handed it to Brandon. It bore the same image and the story of how Chuck Drake, in a drunken rage, had stabbed his wife to death before hanging himself. "Your friend David told you the rest, right?"

"Yeah. On the day everything went to hell."

"The day the FBI picked you up?"

Brandon nodded as he studied the image of his parents. Linda Drake was so very different from his memory of 'Annabelle Drake', the woman who'd been constructed in his mind as his illusionary mother.

The man, Chuck Drake, offered the very antithesis of how he recalled his imaginary father, 'Major Howard Drake'—a polished, proud, and respectable-looking delusion.

Brandon couldn't put it together in his mind. Having not been given the chance to process what had happened to him, it was so confusing. Soon after learning the truth about his past, he'd found himself adjusting to life at Leavenworth. Since before his escape, he'd lived with a sense that his very soul had been brutally torn from him.

"Maybe we could do this later," Tyler said.

"No," Brandon said, choked. "Keep it coming."

Tyler tilted his head slightly, showing his reluctance. He handed Brandon a photograph of a child of preschool age. "This was you at four years old."

Brandon gasped at his first view of himself from a time in his life of which he had no recollection. Belinda edged closer and placed a comforting arm around his shoulders.

Tyler handed him a photograph of another child. "This was me. Still think I was the better looking one," he said with a chuckle, clearly attempting to lighten the mood. "Did I ever tell you I remember you?"

"You remember me?"

"Yep. Just vaguely. I remember the bigger boy called 'Bannon.'"

Brandon placed his arm around his brother's shoulder with tears rolling down his cheeks.

Tyler tapped his hand affectionately and continued. "It all makes sense, though. We were taken in by the authorities and placed in different orphanages. At that time, my dad was supplying a new helicopter engine to—guess where?"

"Where?"

"Fort Bragg."

"No way."

"Yeah. He adopted me and took me back to Dallas. You weren't adopted. You wound up in foster care with these guys." He handed Brandon a photograph of a middle-aged couple who looked to be slightly more affluent than the Drakes. "Joe and Gretchen Cassidy. Do you remember these people?"

Brandon studied the photograph but felt he was looking at total strangers. "No, nothing."

"The last time you saw them was nine years ago. You're sure nothing's there?"

Brandon looked at the picture intently, almost trying to convince himself there was a glimmer of recognition, but he knew he was fooling himself. "Nothing. Are they still alive?"

"Yeah, but I don't think you're gonna want to see them. This guy Cassidy was apparently abusive, according to your court transcripts. It's believed he's largely responsible for your violent temperament. It's why you were given the army as an option after getting busted by the police so many times."

Brandon put the photographs aside. "I . . . I have no memory of any of these things, Ty. Honestly. All I remember are people, incidents, and places that were never real. My true memories don't begin until four years ago when I woke up in the hospital."

"I understand, bro. I'm really am sorry." Tyler took out another photograph. "Here's the last one."

Brandon looked at a photograph of a baby in a crib. "This is Emily?"

"That's all we have of her. I have no idea what she looks like now. I guess we'll find that out when we get to Nevada."

Brandon stood, his gaze not moving from the picture in his hand. His feet automatically shuffled across to the liquor cabinet. Barely conscious of Tyler and Belinda watching, he unscrewed a bottle of vodka, put the rim to his mouth, and drank deeply.

Twelve

Sister

Sister Veronica walked apprehensively along the corridors of her convent. At twenty-four, she'd retained an almost child-like youth, an innocence that showed a profound distance from the world outside the Carmelite Sisters of Obedience.

Conflicting emotions, mostly negative, soared through her heart: hope, guilt, shame, desire, uncertainty, sadness, but above all—fear.

The convent was the only life she'd ever known. Her vocation had led her to some deeply rewarding experiences, working in Africa with her sisters, bringing water and food to those who starved. She'd received a commendation from her bishop for her aid in the Hurricane Sandy tragedy. Closer to home, she was still active with her church, assisting with the homeless and the elderly.

However, her highly-restricted view of the world had left her with just enough insight to conflict with her beliefs. Was it truly necessary for her to be a member of such an order to do good in the world? She'd questioned the validity of the doctrines of obedience, poverty, and chastity, and prayed for forgiveness for her questioning. She'd received no answers, other than the gnawing feeling that those questions were justified.

She'd been dissuaded from reading the Bible by the church's hierarchy, with no explanation as to why. Regardless, she had, during moments of curiosity, studied its pages. Reading its tales of violence and war, she'd experienced a sense of horror rather than reassurance, and began to question the nature of that with which she was affiliated. However, she dared not petition the abbess for clarification. Fear had become her overriding state of mind.

Her faith shaken, this was her day of reckoning.

The airless corridor seemed to stretch beyond its usual distance. The convent had retained its humble, archaic appearance since its foundation during the 1840s.

Her heart fluttered, and her palms grew damp as the door came into view. Gingerly, she came to it and knocked.

"Come in."

Nervously, she stepped inside the windowless office. The crucifix on the wall, the rosary on the mantelpiece, and the statue of the Virgin Mary taking center stage on the desk, seemed to be collaborating to instill her with gut-wrenching guilt.

Reverend Mother Bernadette, the abbess of the order, sat before her with cold, harsh eyes. Sister Veronica couldn't detect a hint of sympathy as she looked at her. The debilitating feeling she'd felt all of her life struck her heart with terrifying resonance—the threat of feeling judged.

The reverend mother pushed a sheet of paper bearing the Papal seal toward her. "Your petition to be released from your vows has been denied."

Sister Veronica's lower lip quivered.

"It is considered your mind is not sound, and that you require more time to contemplate and pray in order that you might acquire greater clarity."

Speechless, the pangs of conscience tore at her.

The abbess stood, her visage gradually assuming a hint of compassion. "Why do you feel the need to do this, my child? Life among the sisters is all you have ever known. Our order took you in, cared for you, nurtured and loved you since you were an infant. The Lord led us to you. We delivered you from a life of potential wickedness. The wickedness from whence you came."

"I-I know, Abbess. And for that you have my eternal gratitude. But I truly believe my vows were made in error."

"You were made aware of the seriousness of such a commitment. In your heart, you will always be a nun. Being released from your vows will never change that. There is no walking away. You are not prepared for life on the outside. It would be extremely hazardous for you."

The abbess' aggressive, dominant tone struck something in Sister Veronica. She had worked in the outside world. She'd met people who were happy and free—women who had husbands and children of their own. It made them no less than she was. They were kind and loving, charitable and compassionate. Why could she not have such freedom? What were the virtues of poverty, chastity, and obedience? How might her poverty help the poor? In what way did her chastity show love? What did it provide other than divisiveness? And what authority could the order demonstrate that demanded her obedience?

Such questions pounded inside her head repeatedly, cutting through her fear of the abbess. Anger began to replace it, drowning out the bane of trepidation, and it clearly showed in her eyes.

"Go to your cell this instant, Sister Veronica," The abbess said sharply.

"That's not my name!"

The lines on the abbess' aged face deepened. Her cheeks flushed, creating a rare contrast to her usually-permanent, chalk-white complexion. "How dare you speak thus to me?"

Sister Veronica's moment of rage passed in deference to the more familiar temperament of submission. "F-forgive me, Reverend Mother."

"Go to your room and pray for forgiveness. You will not eat for twenty-four hours. Water will be sent to your room within the hour while we dine. Perhaps a penitent fast will help you toward clarity."

"Yes, Reverend Mother." Sister Veronica turned and made her way out of the office.

The abbess sat down and listened as the sound of the young sister's footsteps receded along the corridor.

She opened a drawer, took out a folded newspaper, and studied the story and photograph of the striking young man on the front page:

```
America Divided Following Remarkable
Prison Break of Sergeant Brandon Drake
```

She looked up at the office door, deeply saddened. "Why, Emily? Why now? If only you knew the terrible life we have spared you."

***

Sister Veronica paced her basic cell situated on the upper floor, thirty feet above ground. It was one of only five in the convent that had a window. She gazed across a sprawling view of the Nevada desert. Even the word 'cell' conveyed a message she had come to abhor. She was a prisoner tormented by the sight of the free landscape.

She knew her sisters were dining in silence below her. She glanced at the jug of water on her bedside table, the only sustenance with which they had provided her. In her heart, she knew what had happened to her was unjust and wrong.

She thought of Father Henry, a wonderful, caring man with whom she'd worked, providing aid and comfort to the needy. Did she truly need to wear a habit to continue helping people? Would the church turn her help away simply for being a lay person? And if so, was it really an organization worthy of her affiliation? *Why, oh, why didn't I think of these things before I committed myself to my vows?*

Finally certain of her convictions, she grasped her habit and removed it. Her flowing auburn hair fell onto her shoulders.

She walked across to her oak wardrobe, opened it up, and took out an unassuming white blouse and a pair of khaki trousers. She'd worn them last when she'd been working in New York and Wisconsin after the Hurricane Sandy disaster. They, along with a light denim jacket, were the only civilian clothes she owned.

Looking up at the crucifix on her wall, she lowered her head, the sting of guilt plaguing her, yet again.

Following a muttered prayer for forgiveness, she withdrew from her repentance. Her robes came away, and she re-attired herself in preparation for joining the human race.

Placing what few essential possessions she had into a small shoulder satchel, she was startled by the click of a key in the door lock. Her heart pounded as she hurried across to discover she was locked in. Horror, and an overpowering feeling of being entombed, gripped her. She knew that now, more than ever, she had to escape.

She took a key from her bedside drawer, opened up the window, and looked out over the ledge. Even in the dim light of the dusk, the ground seemed so far below. A chill gripped her at the thought of the drop, knowing it was her only means of escape.

She tore every sheet away from her bed, emptied her linen drawers, and tightly bound one sheet to another. She then twisted them into a series of crude ropes, estimating each sheet measured approximately six feet in length.

Finally, she bound the seventh length of bedding. Never in her life had she felt such a sense of threat. But never before had she requested to leave.

The distance from the window to the door was perhaps seven feet. She wrapped the first sheet-rope around the doorknob and tied it as tightly as she could.

She took her satchel from the bed, looped it across her shoulder, and climbed up onto the window ledge.

Trembling with vertigo, she pulled the linen rope under her buttocks, and gripped the slack with her left hand.

As she eased her way out of the window she realized how unsteady she was.

With great care, she held the sheet and relaxed her left hand slightly, dropping down just a few inches. The jolt took her breath away, but she persisted, bracing her soft-soled shoes against the stone wall.

As she dropped another few inches, out of reach of the ledge, she became fearful of the sheet breaking away from the door handle. "Oh, my dear Lord, please help me."

Steadily, she descended two feet, then four, then six.

Within three caution-ridden minutes, she was halfway down. Terror consumed her as she detected the tension in the sheets.

After two more minutes she chanced looking down. If she dropped her feet, she would be no more than three feet from the ground. That gave her the confidence to lower herself just a few more inches.

The sheet unraveled and broke away from the door. She fell the last two feet onto her back, the impact forcing the air out of her lungs. The sheets shot out through the open window to land on top of her.

Taking the time necessary to collect herself, she brushed the dirt off her clothes. She muttered a prayer of thanks that she'd fallen from such a shallow height.

She looked out across a dust-laden road, barely distinguishable from the desert. Uncertainty gripped her. She had so few belongings and only thirty-three dollars to her name.

The nearest town was Woodville, four miles away—the place where the main diocese was located. Everybody in the town knew her. Maybe she would find someone who would be sympathetic to her plight.

In that moment, she knew 'Sister Veronica' was no longer, and Emily Drake had just been reborn.

Ridden with anxiety and a pounding heart, she began to walk. Her pace soon quickened, propelling her headlong into the desert night.

Thirteen

The Runaway

Father Henry Gerard opened the door to the vestry of St. Mark's Diocese in Woodville, Nevada, at 6:00 a.m.

At thirty-two, he'd never married or known the touch of a woman, having accepted his calling to the priesthood at the age of sixteen. Father Henry, as opposed to Father Gerard, was the name he had affectionately adopted from the townsfolk.

He changed into his long black robe and white collar, constantly mindful of his need to prepare for Sunday's sermon.

He made his way down into the cellar to check the mousetraps. The church's long-standing problem of rodents eating into the wine racks, records, and storage boxes created his first daily task.

Entering the archaic, dank room, he switched on the light and approached the far corner to check the first of four traps.

As he knelt down, he instinctively knew he wasn't alone. Slowly, he turned. There was nothing but terror in the eyes of the young woman huddled in the corner behind him. "Sister Veronica?"

"I'm so sorry, Father," Emily said. "I became disoriented and fell asleep. Please, I beg you. Just let me be." She stood and made a move to leave.

"But whatever is the matter, Sister."

"I had nowhere else to go to. I will find somewhere, but I needed a safe place to sleep. Please, forgive me."

"Forgive you?"

"Rome refused my petition to release me from my vows, but I cannot return to the convent."

Smiling compassionately, he knew what she needed more than anything was a friend. "You must be hungry. Would you care to join me for breakfast?"

Stopping in mid-stride, she nodded.

Sitting opposite Father Henry, Emily hungrily devoured a plate of bacon and eggs. "I really appreciate this," she said.

"You have to go back," he said. "You can't just run away like this."

"They locked me in my room. I don't belong in the order any longer. I no longer believe in the church. I—" She paused as she prepared to say something so unthinkable she'd never dared even contemplate it before. "I don't think I even believe in God any more. I have been so unhappy."

"So, why did you take your vows?" he said with an objectionable tone.

She looked up from her plate fearfully. "It was all I had ever known. I didn't know what else to do. I acted in error. Does the church not teach forgiveness and understanding?"

He exhaled and replied, "You're right. It's not my place to judge. But what are you going to do?"

"I don't know. Find work, maybe. Try to survive."

The sound of a car pulling up outside halted their conversation. Emily looked up sharply, having eaten the last of her breakfast.

Father Henry looked at her, and they held one another's gaze with ominous knowingness. Finally, he stood. "I have to tell them the truth. You know that, don't you?"

Emily got out of the chair and picked up her satchel.

Henry quickly opened up the cupboard above the sink and reached for a coffee tin. He took out five $10 bills and placed them on the table next to her. "This is all I have."

She stared at the money in silence.

Henry exited the kitchen and walked into the church to see the bishop and Reverend Mother Bernadette coming toward him. The bishop's deep-set, piercing gray eyes seemed almost accusatory. "Your Grace. Reverend Mother."

"Sister Veronica has fled," the bishop said, wasting no time getting to the point.

"I know, Your Grace."

The abbess' eyes widened eagerly. "You've seen her?"

"She is here. She spent the night in the vestry's cellar."

"Oh, dear Lord. That poor, lost, precious soul."

"Where is she?" The bishop said.

"She's very fearful, Your Grace. I would advise the most delicate approach."

"Where. Is. She?"

Father Henry turned reluctantly. "Follow me."

Along the short journey across the aisle to the kitchen, Henry was seized with ambivalence. If Emily was still in the kitchen, he hoped she might be persuaded to return and find peace in the convent again. She had been such a wonderful and caring person throughout her life. The order and the community would suffer greatly at the loss of her.

However, the look of desperation in her eyes made him think that to force her to stay would be the worst of all cruelties.

He opened the kitchen door and noticed the money was gone. The room was empty and the door was open. He turned back to the bishop and the reverend mother. "She's gone."

***

"I can't believe you bought this. You must be crazy," Brandon said as he drove a shiny, jet-black Mercedes-Benz Sprinter toward the Utah border.

"It was a steal," Tyler said. "Brand new, these babies go for forty-five gees. That dealer you told me to try in Aspen only wanted twenty-one. I'm telling you bro, I know a guy in Fort Worth who'd be willing to pay me thirty for it."

"Let's hope you're right."

"I am right, so quit worrying. We're going to Nevada, so let's do it in style. Anyway, how's the shoulder feeling?"

"It twinges occasionally, but it's almost as good as new. Just needed some time, is all."

Belinda sat comfortably on one the seats behind Brandon and Tyler, a linen veil blocking her view of the Turbo Swan in the rear. She smiled at the way in which Brandon and Tyler were so familiar with one another. It seemed so strange. In less than two years, Tyler had entered the game and developed this close, fraternal relationship with her man. A hidden drama had occurred, and she'd known nothing of it. "How do you think Emily's gonna react to you guys when she sees you?" she said.

"I have no idea," Tyler replied. "But we've got to meet her, let her know we're alive, and that we care about her. After that, who knows?"

"Yeah, but if she's a nun, she might be averse to having anything to do with anybody from the outside world. She might shun the two of you."

"Nah. Why would you think that? They do missionary work."

Belinda looked away with profound disquiet. "You're right. I guess I just don't have a very good opinion of religion."

Brandon glanced behind at her. "It's great to have you with us, baby, but I really don't want you to get upset by this place."

Tyler frowned. "When are you guys gonna tell me what this is all about?"

"That's up to Belinda, Ty."

"All right, time out, you guys," she said. "I'm fine. I'm more concerned about someone recognizing Brandon."

"I've done the research," Tyler said. "There are no 'Wanted' posters out for him, and the shot of him on the TV when he escaped was his mug shot from two years ago—shaved head and terrible lighting. Even I had a time recognizing him. Look at him now. Shoulder-length hair and a few days growth on his puss. Totally different guy."

A sense of uncertainty came over Belinda. "There was no mistaking what he looked like on our TV interview two years ago."

"You said it. Two years ago. Folks have memories like sieves." Tyler nudged Brandon playfully. "I remember it, though. You are one photogenic dude, you know that?"

Brandon brushed off his brother's smartass remark and looked at the clock on the dashboard. "It's coming up to five in the afternoon. We're not gonna reach there by tonight, you know."

"If we don't, we don't. We'll just find somewhere to crash. I have a few possibilities in mind."

"Wherever we stay, we've got to make sure it's somewhere secure," Brandon said. "No cheap shitholes. Not with the Turbo Swan in the back."

"Are you kidding me?" Tyler said.

"Two years ago, Belinda and I stopped off at a rundown motel in Wyoming. We woke up the following morning to find our van had been stolen in the night, along with the Turbo Swan, and all of our money in the back. It led to all hell being let loose."

Tyler chuckled. "You honestly think I'd shack us up in a shithole?"

Brandon laughed finally. "You've got a point, there."

They'd been on the road for over eight hours, with only two stops for food and restrooms. At nine o'clock in the evening, they pulled up at the Peppermill Wendover Hotel on the Utah/Nevada border. Brandon approached the hotel parking area, completely exhausted.

But Tyler was relentless. "It's a casino hotel, bro. I'll get us checked in, dress up like a high roller, and get down there. I thrash the hell out of them every time."

"How about we get some goddamn sleep, Ty?" Brandon said with a hint of annoyance.

"OK, chill. You guys go to bed, have yourselves a party or whatever. Just keep your head down. We don't want anyone making you. I'll go play Blackjack for awhile. I'm too restless to sleep."

"Just remember, we've got to be up early tomorrow."

Tyler laughed. "I'm always up early. To take a leak."

"All right. You do what you've gotta do. We're turning in."

"Yeah, you go for it, bro."

Brandon gave his brother a slightly judgmental stare. "Hey, Ty, do you ever think about anything other than money?"

"Sure I do. I think about family. Money is power, and power is safety and security for that family. You with me?"

Brandon was quiet, feeling like a hypocrite. He knew, without Tyler, he would most likely be back in Leavenworth for life, and with no possibility of the future stability he hoped to create. For the first time in his life, he was within reach of a true family. Who was he to argue with the one who had enabled it all?

Regardless, Tyler did have a juvenile, devil-may-care attitude, and it presented the question of how seriously he was taking all of this.

Brandon drove up to a space in the indoor parking area. He and Belinda got out of the van with their travel bags in hand.

Tyler exited the van last and approached a patrolling, twenty-something parking attendant. "Hey there."

"Hi, sir. Welcome to the Peppermill," the young man said.

Tyler pointed to the Sprinter. "Listen, I wanna make sure that van over there gets touched by nobody, know what I mean?"

"Sir, we operate the highest security here in order to ensure the safety of our guests and their property."

"Of course you do." Tyler reached into his inside pocket and took out a $100 bill. "But I don't want it to go unappreciated. What's your name?"

"Zak, sir. Zak Potter."

"Well, Zak. I just bought that monster over there, and she's my pride and joy. You make sure she's still there in the morning, and there's another five of these babies in it for you."

Zak smiled at him appreciatively and took the money. "Thank you, sir."

"Don't mention it. I'll see you at around eight tomorrow morning, all right?"

The elated attendant nodded his eager affirmation.

Tyler smiled and made his way back to the van.

"OK. We all set?" Brandon said, pulling a baseball cap low across his forehead.

"Sure are."

As they walked across the parking lot toward the hotel foyer, Brandon kept himself behind Belinda and Tyler. Neither of them seemed to notice as he secretly withdrew a small bottle of gin from his jacket pocket.

Fourteen

The Middle of Nowhere

By 8:30 the following morning, Brandon, Belinda, and Tyler were on the road again. Tyler was a little disappointed his hour of indulgence in the casino had only netted him $700.

He noticed Brandon wasn't himself, which was apparent from the unfocused look in his eyes as he drove onto the desert road. Even his skin had taken on an unusual pallor. "Hey, bro. You feeling all right? You don't look so sharp?"

"Yeah, I guess." Brandon's voice was notably weak and lethargic. Something was clearly wrong.

"You sure?"

"Just haven't woken up yet." Changing the subject, he said, "So, what'd you win last night?"

"Not good. Seven hundred."

"That's bad?"

"Yeah, well, I guess it paid off Zak."

"Who?"

"Zak. You know? The parking attendant guy."

"You seriously gave the parking attendant seven hundred dollars?"

"Six actually, and it was worth every penny for him to pay extra-special attention to the van. How much is the Turbo Swan worth?"

Brandon was quiet for a moment as he calculated the monetary value of a machine that couldn't really be quantified. "It's completely unique. There's nothing on it you'll find anywhere else. The experimental, bonded titanium shell, the engines I put together, the internal electronics, a shit load of man hours . . . Maybe a few million dollars."

Tyler raised his hands in vindication. "So, I rest my case. Six hundred bucks to a needy kid to keep an eye on it has got to be the bargain of the century."

Belinda took in the desert scenery around her. The sun was bright, and it was becoming warmer the farther they drove into Nevada. Having never seen this part of America before, she was amazed by how different it looked from Colorado, or Massachusetts where she'd grown up. To her eyes, it seemed more like another planet, much less the same country.

The van suddenly jolted to the right and the tires screeched. All three passengers were startled witless by the shock. Brandon struggled to hold the vehicle steady, but the steering wheel was torn out of his hand. The two left side wheels left the surface. The van slid forward, half on the right side wheels, and half on the chassis perched on a ditch, producing a shower of sparks.

"We've got a blowout," Brandon said.

"What's happening?" Belinda yelled.

"I can't hold it!"

He pressed his foot to the brakes, slowing the right-side wheel. Gradually, the van decelerated to a standstill.

They sat for a moment, considerably shaken. Brandon appeared suddenly awake, opened his door, and looked down the dusty edge.

"I'll go take a look," Tyler said.

Belinda jumped down onto the road and walked around to the other side with Tyler.

After a moment, they peered inside the van. "We're screwed," Tyler said. "The left front tire's blown, and half the van is hanging off the edge. There's no way we're gonna get it back onto the road."

Brandon rubbed his face, nodding despondently. "Figured as much."

"I'll call the auto club." Tyler took out his android phone and selected the auto club contact, but it didn't ring out. He looked at the screen and exhaled. "Damn. No signal. We're in a dead zone. How about the Turbo Swan?"

"Life and death only," Brandon said. "We fly that out of here, it's gonna be seen. It's got an ascension height of a hundred-fifty feet, max. It'd be like writing our names in the air."

"So, what are we gonna do?"

Brandon pushed the door open and jumped down, spending a few moments looking around him. Belinda followed his gaze. There was nothing in sight. No stores, houses, gas stations, or establishments of any kind. It was just miles of desert for as far as the eye could see.

"So, I guess that's it," Brandon said hopelessly. "We're stranded in the middle of nowhere." He leaned against the vehicle and rested his head against his elbow.

Belinda said, "Look, why don't we wave a few cars down, see if anyone'll give us a ride to a garage?"

Tyler concurred. "That's as good an idea as any."

Without a word, Brandon walked around the van again, aimlessly. Trance-like, he jumped down the ditch and walked back to the driver's side. He knew what would help him endure his plight. Deep inside, he was aware there was a serious problem in him even contemplating what he was going to do, but he couldn't help himself. The urge was so very strong.

After climbing back up onto the seat, he reached underneath and pulled out a hidden shoulder bag. He felt around inside, quickly found a bottle of vodka, and pushed the bag back. Obsessively, he unscrewed the bottle top, and put the rim to his mouth.

Only four cars had driven past Tyler and Belinda during the first hour. Nobody had stopped and the heat was becoming oppressive.

"Looks like the milk o' human kindness just dried up at the tit," Tyler said, frustrated.

Belinda giggled. "You have a terrific way with words, Ty."

"It's a gift. You think Brandon's all right?"

"He's . . . I don't think he's doing too well."

"Yeah, well, I'd have thought he'd at least help us out here."

"I think he's developed a real problem dealing with stress. I think we should just let him be for now."

They watched eagerly as a beat up station wagon came closer toward them from the horizon. They waited for a few minutes until the car was virtually on top of them. A scruffy young man in a checked shirt looked out the window as he slowed to a crawl. And then he sped up again.

"Hey!" Tyler cried out, but it was futile.

Belinda glanced at him with the same feeling of outrage. "What an asshole."

Another thirty minutes passed, along with three more cars, shattering their hopes even further.

And then the perfect chance appeared in the distance.

"Is that what I think it is?" Tyler said.

"You know what? I think it is."

As the vehicle came closer, they could see it was a worn tow truck with a crane and hook.

"Oh, my God. This is it." Tyler stepped out into the middle of the road and waved his hands for the truck to stop. Belinda immediately joined him with the same eagerness.

The truck slowed to a stop. A gruff, bearded man, who appeared to be at least fifty, stepped out. "Hi, there. Need some help?"

Tyler approached him. "Sir, please, you've got to help us. Our front tire blew out, and we got launched off the damn road. Can you help us lift the van off the edge of the verge? I'll pay you."

"I'm Earl," the man said with a deep, gravel-like voice, and extended his hand to Tyler. "Now, don't you worry about a damn thing. I'll have that van of yours outta the ditch in no time."

Tyler beamed. "Seriously?"

"Sure. C'mon. Let's get the sumbitch hooked up."

Tyler and Belinda gave one another a jubilant high-five.

"You ain't seen much traffic out this way, I guess," Earl said.

"Not much. And what we have seen has been about as much use as tits on a boar," Tyler said.

Belinda turned away laughing at his deadpan way of making Texan, humorous statements.

They looked behind them as Brandon appeared. It was abundantly clear something was very wrong with him. His eyes seemed glazed and unfocused, and his demeanor looked particularly *happy*. "Hi, guys. Need some help?"

Earl replaced the shattered tire with the Sprinter's spare. Belinda kept Earl entertained with her charms and a deliberately-revealed cleavage at the front of the van. It was imperative that the old guy didn't get a glimpse of the military hardware in the back.

Finally, Earl slipped his crane-hook under the front tow bar of the Sprinter. Tyler sat behind the wheel of the van. The crane lifted the front of the van off the verge while he turned the steering wheel and Earl lowered the crane.

Brandon and Belinda watched, but Belinda couldn't help noticing how unsteady Brandon was on his feet.

Once the van was down, three of the four wheels were back on the road with the left rear tire half perched on the verge. With one depression of the accelerator, Tyler brought it back up onto the road.

Earl turned off the truck's engine and unhooked the crane.

Tyler stepped out of the van. "Hey, man. How much do I owe you?"

Earl smiled. "I'll get the invoice."

"Ty, can I talk to you for a second?" Belinda said.

"Sure."

She led him around to the side of the van and saw the driver's side door was still open. "Ty, I think Brandon is seriously sick. I don't think we can go on."

"Are you sure?"

"He's staggering all over the place, and he's as white as a sheet."

Tyler rubbed his forehead. "What do you think it might be?"

"I have no idea."

Tyler pointed to the strap under the seat. "I didn't put that there. What is it?"

Belinda climbed up, pulled the strap, and drew out the backpack. The moment she opened it up, she felt her blood turn to ice at the sight of vodka bottles. Several of them were empty.

"What's in it?"

"Oh, my God, Ty," she said tearfully.

"What?"

"He isn't *sick*."

Brandon smiled at Earl with drunken abandon. "Y'know what, bud? You're a f'ckin' life-saver."

Earl stepped out of the truck's cab as another individual arose inside, seeming to emerge from the footwell—a young man wearing a checked shirt. He exited the truck with something in his hands, but Brandon couldn't make out what it was. He couldn't even be sure if it was one man or two. Whoever it was, the young man threw whatever he, or *they* held, to Earl.

"Hey, were those guys havin' a nap in that ol' truck?" Brandon said with intoxicated laughter.

"Oh, there was only one guy in there, you drunken jerk."

"So, how much do I owe ya, bud?"

Earl replied in a gruff voice, "Just the van should settle it."

Brandon finally noticed the double-barreled shotgun aimed at him, but it didn't seem to matter.

Fifteen

.45

Brandon staggered toward the two men before him, laughing insensibly. "The van? You want the van? Sure. Jus' help yourself."

The younger of the two men smiled. "Hey, Pa. This is gonna be easier than we thought."

Earl chuckled. "You got that right, Bobby."

Bobby became aware of a clicking sound in his right ear, followed by a crippling sensation in his left arm.

Earl turned around sharply to see Bobby writhing in pain with his arm twisted up his back. Tyler held him with a .45 aimed point-blank at his temple.

"Drop the gun!" Tyler bellowed. "You hear me? Drop it!"

Earl slowly lowered the shotgun onto the ground.

Belinda appeared from behind the van.

"Kick it toward me!" Tyler said.

Earl complied. Belinda ran forward, picked up the shotgun, and trained it on Earl.

Earl raised his hands in surrender. "D-don't do anything. Just let us go, and that'll be the last you see of us."

"It had damn well better be."

Earl walked backward to his truck, his gaze on the rifle at all times.

Tyler released Bobby and pushed him forward.

A glint of recognition appeared in Tyler's eyes. "I know you, you son of a bitch. You're the one who slowed down in the station wagon earlier and then drove on again. What were you doing? Weighing us up for a heist?"

Bobby turned, ran past Brandon, and climbed into the truck. Earl pressed his foot on the gas.

Belinda handed the shotgun to Tyler and ran to Brandon. He no longer had the ability to stand still, and his eyes were rolling. It was clear he was on the verge of losing consciousness.

She gripped him under his armpits and held him steady. "Sweetheart, let's get you back in the van. You're not well."

Tyler joined her. Together they guided Brandon up the step and onto the passenger's seating area.

"Strap him in," Tyler said. "I'll drive."

Belinda pulled the seatbelt around Brandon and caressed his cheek sadly. "Why, Brandon? Why?"

Tyler stowed the shotgun under the seat along with the .45.

"Where'd you get the pistol, Tyler?" she said.

"Back home. It's a Super Carry HD. One of the best. I wasn't gonna take another chance with that crappy sonic thing Brandon sent me to Denver with."

Brandon slurred a response. "Ol' Archie the whiz made it. Funny ol' guy. Had hair a' th' sides of his head. None on top. He never finished the power cell thingy before I took it."

Belinda gently pushed up his eyelids, but all she could see were the whites of his eyes. "He's passed out."

"We've got to get out of here," Tyler said. "There's every chance those two bozos will be back with reinforcements."

"You've got a point. Let's go."

They hurriedly closed the side doors. Tyler pressed his foot onto the accelerator and glanced at his unconscious brother. "What do you think's wrong with him? Why would he do something like that at a time like this?"

Belinda shook her head in despair. "I should've seen it coming. I can't believe I missed the signs."

"What do you mean?"

"When I first met your brother, his life was nothing but stress. He was consumed with guilt over being unable to save everyone else on the night he rescued me. It was like he truly believed it was his responsibility to save the world."

"Yeah, I always got that impression about him too. When I first met him at Leavenworth, he was real emotional and just wanted to throw his arms around me. He sobbed like a baby."

Belinda succumbed to tears. The thought of Brandon so alone in such a vulnerable place was unbearable.

"He talked about you all the time," Tyler said reassuringly. "He loves you, you know."

She nodded but was unable to speak.

"Hey, everybody gets hammered once in awhile. I've done it plenty of times. Maybe that's all it is. I bet you have too."

"Sure I have. But think about it. What state was he in when I saw him for the first time after he escaped?"

Tyler glanced at her with a look that suggested he knew where she was going with this. "Drunk."

"Exactly. And have you noticed how he's been sipping on gin and vodka since he's been back?"

"Not really."

"Well I have. He made it look so casual and harmless. After you showed him the pictures of his real family, what did he do first?"

"You're right. He headed straight for the liquor cabinet."

"Right. And why always gin and vodka?"

"I don't know."

"They're the least likely to leave a smell on you, Ty. He's been doing whatever he could to hide the fact that he's got a problem."

Tyler checked the satellite navigation unit on the dashboard. "Well, we're about two hours away from Woodville. I just hope he's sobered up by then. I'd hate for this to be Emily's first impression of him."

"Two hours? Don't hold your breath. How did you find Emily, anyway?"

"It wasn't easy. I had to hire a private detective in the end. Brandon was easy enough for me to trace on my own. He'd left quite a trail behind him with police records, court transcripts, and military records. But Emily had just vanished. She was eventually traced to this Carmelite convent. She works with St. Mark's church in Woodville. She goes by the name Sister Veronica."

Upon hearing terms like 'Carmelite convent,' 'St. Mark's church,' and 'sister,' Belinda shivered.

At four o'clock in the afternoon, Tyler pulled up on a dusty roadside beside the church. Brandon was still in a deep sleep.

Tyler became apprehensive the moment he turned off the engine, and looked down at his hands. "Damn it, I'm trembling."

"Are you OK?" Belinda said.

"No."

"Want me to come in with you?"

"You don't have to do that. Stay here and watch over Brandon."

"I hardly think he needs watching over. He's seriously away in dreamland."

After a moment, Tyler concurred. "To tell you the truth, I could use the support. Thank you."

"OK. Let's do it. You're gonna meet your sister for the first time, and I'll be with you every step of the way."

Tyler took the keys out of the ignition, climbed out, and closed the door behind him.

Belinda linked her arm with Tyler's in a gesture of support as they walked across the path to the front entrance of the church. The closer they came to it, the chill running through Belinda's heart grew ever colder.

Disturbed by the vibration of the doors closing, Brandon stirred, and his eyes fluttered open.

Sixteen

Ghosts of the Past

With Belinda by his side, Tyler pushed the church door open to an unexpected sight. Seven nuns, five priests, and a bishop seemed to be in conference, with no congregation members in sight.

A young priest broke away from the gathering to greet them.

Tyler noticed Belinda's sudden movement and couldn't miss the fear in her eyes. There had been an underlying abhorrence of anything religious in her since he'd first met her. Yet neither she, nor Brandon, would tell him what it was all about. This time, he knew he had to force the issue. "Belinda, what's wrong? You look terrified."

"You deal with the son of a bitch."

"May I help you," the young priest said.

Tyler turned to him and forced a smile. *Shit. What do I call this guy? Father? Brother? Padre?* After a moment, he gave a contrived, convivial, "How're you doing, sir? We're looking for someone. Maybe you can help."

"Certainly. Who might that be?"

"Well, it's a kinda complicated story." Tyler reached inside his jacket pocket, took out his business card, and handed it to the priest. "My name is Tyler Drake-Faraday, Executive Investment Specialist for the Faraday Corporation. My father owns it."

The priest smiled warmly. "Well, that sounds fascinating, but—"

"I'm sorry, sir. Maybe I should explain." He paused to brace himself against the fluttering in his stomach. "I was adopted, and I'm trying to find my sister. We traced her to here."

The priest frowned. "Here? I'm afraid I don't understand."

"We were all separated when we were very small. She was just a baby. Her name is Emily Drake. Do you know her?"

"I'm sorry. I've never heard of her. Perhaps if I pass you over to—"

"Sister Veronica." Tyler said.

The priest's expression dropped, and Tyler noticed. "What's wrong?"

"You're Sister Veronica's brother?"

"Yes, sir. Do you know her?"

"I think you need to talk to the bishop. Would you mind bearing with me for a moment?"

"Sure."

As the priest walked away, Tyler turned back to Belinda. "Something's wrong. I can feel it."

"Something's always wrong when it comes to these twisted places."

Tyler cringed. Between the look on the priest's face when he'd said Sister Veronica was his sister, and Belinda's hostility, none of this looked like it was going to pan out favorably. To add insult to injury, Brandon was passed out drunk in the van.

He watched as the priest conferred with the bishop. Then the bishop said something to the gathering. Most of them turned away and exited the church. Tyler noticed

Belinda backing away as the parade of robes crossed her path.

The bishop approached Tyler. "Mr. Faraday, is it?"

"Y-yes, sir. How do I . . . ? I mean, what do I . . . ?"

The bishop smiled. "Do not allow my appearance to distress you. We are all God's children. Not one above another. I am Bishop Neville Jessop. Please, take a seat."

"Thank you." Tyler relaxed and sat in the nearest pew while Belinda stood behind him.

"You say that Sister Veronica is your sister?" Jessop said.

"Yes. We were separated as children. There were three of us. Me, my brother Brandon, and Emily." Tyler took the photograph of his baby sister out of his pocket and handed it to the bishop. "This is the only photograph I have of her." He watched the clergyman's knowing expression as he took the photograph.

"There is no need to convince me, Mr. Faraday," Jessop said. "Your resemblance to Sister Veronica is astonishing. I could see it the moment I laid eyes on you. Would you give me a moment? I have something for you."

"Sure."

They waited as Jessop disappeared into the back of the church.

Moments later, the bishop returned with a photograph. Fascinated, Tyler took it, and cast his eyes upon the answer to a question he'd had for many years—what did his sister look like? He gazed, mesmerized, at a color photograph of a nun standing against a backdrop of storm wreckage. The close, quarter-length shot left her face clear and identifiable. Despite the habit, to Tyler's eyes it was the

115

face of a female version of himself. "Oh, my God," he said with quavering emotion. "Is she here?"

"I'm afraid not," the bishop said.

Tyler looked up sharply. "Where is she?"

"If only you had arrived yesterday. You might have been able to persuade her to stay."

"Stay?"

"She fled. She was here only this morning."

"W-well, where is she? Where did she go?"

"We don't know, but we are all very worried about her. This is what we were all discussing when you arrived."

"B-but—"

"What did you do to her?" Belinda said in an accusatory tone.

"My child, nobody did anything to Sister Veronica," the bishop said.

"Yeah, I'll bet."

The reverend mother strode over to join them with a stern, domineering expression. "You just watch your tongue, young lady. We are all deeply worried about Sister Veronica. She is lost in the world now, with no knowledge of life outside the convent. She is terribly vulnerable, and an outburst like that is not likely to help matters."

"Why did she run away?" Belinda demanded.

"She had a crisis of faith."

Tyler turned back to the bishop. "Do you have any idea where she may have gone?"

The bishop shrugged his shoulders. "The nearest town is Wolverheath, five miles south of here. After that, there's Crispin Rock, another four miles along. They're small towns, but they have stores and motels. There's nowhere

116

else she could have gotten to on foot, but she might have hitchhiked and picked up transportation away from the area. We are very worried about her."

"Well, why don't you call the police? Send out a search party? Anything?"

"She's legally an adult. This is out of the jurisdiction of the law. She has the democratic right to go wherever she pleases. Our concern is for Sister Veronica, personally. We feel she is ill-equipped to navigate life on the outside."

"How much money does she have?" Belinda said.

"I'm sorry?"

"How much money does she have? Is there a chance she could get picked up for vagrancy?" She tilted her head and gave the clergyman a sardonic stare. "That wouldn't look very good for your pious image, now would it?"

Tyler turned to Belinda angrily. "What is it with you? This isn't helping, Belinda. I've got enough to deal with right now, so you just go outside and cool off. I'll handle this, OK?"

"As you wish."

Tyler waited for her to leave and then resumed his conversation. "I'm sorry, sir. She's been through a lot. Please forgive her rudeness."

Jessop placed his hand on Tyler's. "Think nothing of it. May I ask who the lady is?"

"I guess she's kinda like my . . . sister-in-law."

The bishop squinted inquisitively. "I see."

"Kinda."

Belinda stepped out into the blistering heat and took a deep breath.

A thirty-something woman of apparent Hispanic origin approached the church with a young girl of approximately twelve at her side. They appeared to be impoverished judging from their shabby clothing. The mother's weathered face showed an age beyond her natural years. She glanced at Belinda, but the brief exchange offered no desire for communication on either side.

However, Belinda's heart was overcome with empathy and concern for the girl.

The door opened, and Tyler and the bishop stepped out. The abbess followed.

"We pray that you find her, Mr. Faraday," Jessop said. "I believe God has sent you at this, the most desperate time of her life."

Tyler looked at him skeptically. "You really believe that?"

"I do. You have not come here by chance at this very moment of all times. That's far too much of a coincidence. Yours is a divine mission."

"I doubt that. If the big guy in the sky had anything to do with us being here, he'd have got us here yesterday."

Through the open door, Belinda watched as Father Henry entered one of the confessionals. Her heart pounded as the Hispanic woman led her daughter into the adjoining cubicle. Belinda's own protective, maternal instinct took control of her. Her feet shuffled unnoticeably past Tyler, the abbess, and the bishop.

Stepping onto the aisle in a trance, she made her way toward the confessional. In her mind, voices—ghosts of the past—echoed, driving her forward.

Have you something to confess, my child?

118

Yes, Father.
Can you tell me about it?
I-it's difficult, father.

He knew.

Belinda continued forward, slowly.

Have you touched yourself in a way you know you shouldn't have?
Y-yes, father.

Her fists clenched. The confessional was within reach.

It's all right, Belinda. Join me in here and show me how you do it.

She paused in the grip of shame, disgust, and absolute rage.

No, no. You're not doing it right, Belinda.

Her breathing deepened, paralyzing her.

Let me do it for you.

She had been a child of only thirteen, lonely, and without emotional support. He'd taken advantage of that.

Her following life experiences flooded her mind. She'd suffered an inability to trust any man, leading to fleeting sexual encounters, never destined for anything more. Loneliness was always the result. She couldn't get close to any of them.

And then there was Brandon, who had rescued her, and whom she adored. Yet he'd led her to a life of running,

119

life-threatening danger, torture, relentless heartbreak, and constant fear.

But it had all started with Father Turney. He'd been the first in her life of dominos that pushed the next one, and the next, until the solid structure of her possible future had collapsed before it had even begun. She would not permit it to happen to another.

She heard the mumbled sound of the young girl opening her heart to Father Henry, and violently opened the confessional door. Her heart pounded with a combination of compassion and determination. "Go!"

Frightened, the young girl stood and hurried past her.

"Excuse me," the priest said. "This was a private, spiritual moment for my parishioner. Please leave."

An all-consuming fury infused Belinda, completely destroying her reason. She exited the confessional and tore open Father Henry's door. "This is *my* 'private spiritual moment,' you sick bastard!" With that, she plunged her fist into his nose. The nasal bone split upon impact, causing him to recoil with blood spurting from his nostrils.

The ferocious assault continued, but Father Henry didn't raise a hand in defense. It was as though he knew what Belinda was, and what she'd been through. "Please, forgive us," he muttered.

Belinda's knuckles collided with his jaw for the last time before she felt herself being lifted bodily away from the confessional.

"Easy, easy," Tyler said as she struggled in his arms.

The bishop and the abbess hurried up behind him. The reverend mother rushed to Father Henry's aid. The young girl shielded herself behind her mother.

Tyler gripped Belinda by the shoulders. "What's wrong with you?"

She looked at him and gradually became aware of what she'd done, struggling to process it.

Father Henry wiped the blood from his nose and approached Tyler. "Please, let her be. It isn't her fault."

The girl's mother called across to Belinda, "You are a monster. May God have mercy on you!" Turning with her daughter, they briskly made their way out of the church.

Tyler turned to the bishop and Father Henry. "Look guys, I'm really sorry. I have no idea what's the matter with her. But if there's anything I can do—"

"Watch over her, and keep her from harm," Father Henry said.

They followed the woman and her daughter to the church entrance.

Before they reached the door, they saw the woman freeze at the sight of a tall, masculine presence in the doorway. She looked up into his dreary-eyed face and a glint of recognition came across her eyes.

"Hi," Brandon said sleepily. "I'm looking for my brother and my girlfriend. Do you know if they're in here?"

The woman looked behind her.

Brandon followed her gaze and waved at them obliviously. "Hey, guys. What's happenin'?"

The woman looked downward, clearly trying to recall where she knew Brandon from—and then looked up at him again.

Tyler became concerned as he watched the woman staring at his brother. Brandon returned her stare with an inebriated, confused look. But Tyler knew instantly that, regardless of her economic circumstances, she clearly owned a television set. He recalled Dr. Fleetwood telling him that Brandon's escape from Leavenworth had divided the American people. The look on this woman's face indicated she wasn't one of those who wanted his autograph. Paranoia came over him. In addition to everything else, he instinctively knew that all hell was about to be unleashed upon them.

He grasped Brandon by the arm and turned him around. "Come on. We've got to go."

"Is Emily here?"

"No."

The woman waited until the three strangers had disappeared. With one hand tightly holding her daughter's, she took out her cell phone.

Seventeen

Vipers

Emily approached the town of Crispin Rock, overcome by fatigue. Having walked for miles across desert land, she was in desperate need of rest.

It was four in the afternoon, and the sight of Rocker's Tavern on the opposite side of the main high street looked extremely appealing. She'd never stepped inside a bar before. The convent had taught her that such were places of iniquity and drunkenness, notwithstanding she'd heard rumors of priests who frequented them. She'd never experienced alcohol beyond the thimble's quantity provided for communion.

But the bar was a place where there were other human beings and a sorely-needed place to sit down.

Racked with apprehension, she gingerly pushed open the door and stepped inside. She noticed the bar area ahead of her, and then her attention transferred to the rest of the room. There were posters and advertisements for bands that were due to appear at various dates, an overhanging fan, and a spattering of men sitting and drinking beer around the tables.

The creaking wooden floor was the only audible sound as she stepped forward. The patrons ceased their conversations in mid-sentence, creating an ominous atmosphere. The eerie silence exacerbated her apprehension.

The owner of the bar, a tall, overweight male with long hair hanging in his eyes, acknowledged her. "Afternoon, ma'am. What can I get for you?"

Nervously, she replied, "W-well, I was just wondering if I may have . . ."

"Ma'am?"

"A glass of water."

"You sure can. And please, take the weight off." He gestured to one of the tall chairs at the bar. "By the way, I'm Bill."

"Thank you. I'm Emily." As she sat, the feeling of her feet leaving the floor was indescribably ecstatic.

Bill placed a pitcher of water and a glass on the bar. Emily poured it out eagerly, never having known a thirst like it.

"Where are you from, Emily?" Bill said. "You staying around here?"

The question made her feel uncomfortable, but she was adamant she wasn't going to lie. She wasn't eager to reveal she was an escaped nun either. "I'm from . . . Nevada. I'm just traveling right now. Looking for work."

Bill briefly glanced over her shoulder. She turned in the direction he was looking to see a young, Latino male in the corner of the bar. He seemed to be watching her with particular interest. She turned back to Bill and noticed him shuddering.

The man in the corner stood and came toward them. She noticed the patrons recoiling in discomfort. The atmosphere was permeated with tension, but Emily didn't know what to make of it.

Bill leaned forward, about to say something, but backed away as the Latino male arrived beside her.

Emily looked up at the young man and couldn't help noticing how handsome he was. She became captivated by his thick, perfectly-groomed black hair, flawless olive complexion, and the most striking brown eyes. Dressed in crisp jeans, a white vest, and a denim jacket, he caused her heart to flutter in a way she'd been taught could lead her to hell.

"I'm Fabian," he said.

She returned his smile awkwardly. "Emily."

"I heard. So, Emily, you're looking for work. What kind of work?"

She shrugged. "Well, I-I can cook, clean, sweep up. I can learn pretty much anything, I suppose."

"Have you been traveling long?"

"Just a couple of days."

"Well, I can find work for you if you're interested."

Emily smiled warmly. "What would I be doing?"

"Something I've got a feeling you were born to do."

"What's that?"

"Helping people. Bringing happiness to them."

Her heart leaped. "Whereabouts? Are you from around here?"

"No. Los Angeles."

"Los Angeles? I've never been there."

"Oh, you'll love it."

She poured herself another glass of water and drank deeply.

"When was the last time you ate?" he said.

She looked away from him, a little embarrassed. "Breakfast."

"Breakfast? You must be starving."

"I . . . I suppose I am quite hungry. But please, you don't have to buy me food. I'll be fine, really."

"It's not that I *have* to. But I'd like to. What say we quit this joint and go get something to eat?"

Despite her apprehension, her hunger prompted her response. "I'd like that, but . . ."

Fabian frowned. "But what?"

"I'm rather embarrassed. I only have eighty-three dollars, so it will be difficult for me to return the favor."

He smiled broadly. "Are you kidding me? Where I come from, the gentleman always pays."

"Well, if you insist. That's very kind of you. Thank you."

"No need to thank me. Shall we go?"

"Sure, I guess so," she said with some uncertainty. As she stood, she was immediately reminded of how sore her feet were the moment they touched the ground.

She turned back to Bill behind the bar. "Thank you so much for your kindness."

He didn't respond.

The patrons watched as Emily exited the bar with her hand in the crook of her new escort's arm. The door closed.

A hard-looking, shaven-headed man sitting at the far side of the bar stood up aggressively. He was about to intervene when Bill grasped his arm. The two men looked into one another's eyes for a moment. Sadness and regret consumed Bill as he shook his head at his customer. "We'll have a massacre on our hands."

The patron backed away. Bill knew the anger in the other man had suddenly been replaced by the same grief he, himself, was feeling. He shook his head, unable to accept what had just happened.

"We've got to do something. We can't just let that bastard take her."

"We have no choice, Galen," Bill said. "If we interfere, they'll kill every last damn one of us and burn the place down." He gripped Galen by the shoulders and looked pleadingly at him. "We have families. We can't fight vipers like that. They're way out of our league, you know that."

Galen broke away from Bill and began to pace the room.

Bill looked over at the closed door. "May God help her."

Eighteen

The Wire

"Air traffic reports show Tyler Faraday flew to Switzerland for six weeks in one of his father's private jets. He invested just over one-point-one million dollars with La Roche and Co. in Bern, returned to Dallas five days ago, and disappeared just as quickly." Agent Wilmot dropped the report onto Director Wolfe's desk. "I think trying to track this guy down is a waste of time and manpower, sir."

"Why do you say that?"

Wilmot was highly protective of the fact that he'd heard from Brandon Drake during the time Tyler Faraday was in Switzerland. In an attempt to throw Wolfe off the scent, he proceeded to put forth his alternate case. "From the personnel we interviewed at Leavenworth, there's no tangible reason for us to believe Faraday was complicit in his brother's escape. And Faraday's trip to Switzerland is in keeping with his *vocational* activities."

"Oh?"

Wilmot produced one paper after another from his file and placed them on Wolfe's desk in turn. "Four months ago, he spent two weeks in London conducting an investment deal with the daughter of Rudolph Hemingford, a financier in Westminster . . . from the honeymoon suite of The Dorchester Hotel."

Wolfe picked up the paper and glanced over it.

"Three weeks prior to that, he returned from a four week vacation in the Cayman Islands with one of the models from Ford Models, Inc. Two months before that, he was in Tokyo discussing the purchase of some tech for one of his father's helicopter designs with the Takagu-Mitsushi Corporation." He placed the paper on the desk. "Shall I go on?"

"I get the picture."

"This guy's a professional vacationer who happens to be an expert in investment and finance. The day Faraday adopted him was the greatest lottery win in world history. He has it made."

"So it seems."

"I really think going after Tyler Faraday to find Brandon Drake is a waste of time."

The conversation was cut short by Wolfe's portable phone beeping, and he took it out of its cradle. "Wolfe here."

Wilmot watched, intrigued, as the director's eyes widened.

"OK. . . . She's sure it was him?" Wolfe hurriedly scribbled down the details on a notepad. "Thank you. I'll dispatch a unit out there right away." The call ended.

"Sir?" Wilmot said.

Wolfe handed him the note. "Brandon Drake has been seen in Nevada *with* Faraday and Belinda Reese. Apparently Reese assaulted a priest."

Wilmot cringed knowing he'd just made an ass out of himself by saying the hunt for Tyler Faraday was futile. Now, his entire agenda was on the line. If Drake knew anything about Treadwell's surviving cell, it could lead to Wilmot himself facing considerable time in a federal penitentiary. He knew, no matter what, that he had to act immediately.

"There are no fine details as such," Wolfe said. "It seems they were looking for someone at St. Mark's Catholic Church in a place called Woodville, Nevada." He gestured to the paper in Wilmot's hand. "Whoever it is, chances are they're searching for them in nearby towns."

"Drake's an escaped fugitive, and he's showing his face in public? It doesn't make sense."

"The information came from the Nevada Highway Patrol. I want them kept out of it. Don't take an entire unit. I want this kept low-key, and I don't want Drake to feel threatened. At all costs, you let him know you're not with law enforcement, and that we need his help on a matter of national security. You understand?"

"Yes, sir. I'll get right on it." Wilmot headed for the door.

Wolfe stood sharply. "Take Jed Crane. You're a damn fine agent, but he's got a knack for diplomacy that you don't. And tell Deborah I need to see her."

"She's gone home, sir."

"What?"

"She left a couple of hours ago. It's nine o'clock, sir."

Wolfe looked at his watch. "Damn. Looks like this is gonna be a long night. I have a lot of calls to make." He picked up his phone.

Wilmot departed the office with haste. Looking around to ensure the corridor was deserted, he took out his encrypted cell phone. After selecting a number he had on speed dial, the call was answered almost immediately. "Garrett. Now's the time . . . That's right. Tonight."

As he ended the call he became aware of a presence behind him. He turned abruptly to see Agent Crane approaching. *Dammit.*

Jed Crane, a tall, strapping operative in his early thirties, with male model looks and perfect blond hair, was the last person Wilmot wished to see at that moment.

"I've just had a call from Director Wolfe," Crane said.

Wilmot managed a faux-smile. "Don't worry about it. I've got everything under control."

"That's not what Director Wolfe said. He insisted I accompany you to bring Drake back, with specific conduct instructions."

Wilmot took a deep breath in an attempt to contain his annoyance. "All right, I'm taking Kerwin and Rhodes. We're keeping it low key, but we don't take any unnecessary chances around Drake. He's lethal, you understand?"

"You got it. Is Garrett coming with us?"

"No." With that, Wilmot hastily made his way along the corridor.

After a moment, Wilmot came to his senses and recalled his previous experience with Drake in Wyoming. Knowing Drake's physical capabilities, there was the possibility of a serious problem bringing him in should he become volatile. He realized Crane's diplomatic skills and temperament might be useful after all.

It was past midnight when Wolfe exited the elevator and walked into the indoor parking lot toward his new BMW. Ten consecutive nights of overtime and early rises were taking their toll upon him.

For the past two years, his life had been a series of daily ordeals. First, there had been Treadwell, his long-standing friend and ally, who was revealed to be a murderous politician who sought to elevate America to celestial heights by creating arbitrary wars. The situation had become a living nightmare when it became apparent that Treadwell might have operatives within the intelligence community. Wolfe's own cell, SDT, was most likely infected, given that it was established under Treadwell's recommendation. It was now under examination by Congress as part of an investigation into the possible murder of one of its own operatives.

Treadwell's two captured recruits, Ogilsby and Woodford, who had been incapacitated by Drake two years earlier, had been unofficially disposed of only weeks before the investigation began. The details had not been made public, but they were considered, at the highest levels, to be serious internal security risks. Both had gone to their deaths defiantly protesting that they had given everything they knew to Wilmot, who, in turn, denied he'd received anything at all. Wilmot's word was taken over those of two disgruntled turncoats. The only remaining man alive who might know anything helpful was an escaped, highly-elusive fugitive.

Wolfe opened up his BMW, sat in the driver's seat, and put his seat belt on. He turned the key in the ignition, and the radio came on. His MP3 recording of Tchaikovsky's Piano Concerto No.1 began.

He exhaled deeply and relaxed into the leather seat, unwinding to the soothing, classic melody. After giving himself a moment, he turned the key.

A wire shot out from behind the seat and cut into his Adam's apple. Gasping for breath, he tried to pull the wire away from him, but to no avail.

As the veil of darkness overcame him, he caught a glimpse of his assailant in the rear view mirror and immediately realized who had organized his murder.

Elias Wolfe's final thought was the knowledge that one of the most significant cells in American intelligence was about to fall under the control of a traitor.

Nineteen

A Cruel and Unjust Road

The motel door slammed shut behind Tyler. The outrage in his eyes was unmistakable. "What the hell do you guys think you're playing at?"

Brandon and Belinda looked at him from the edge of the bed. Brandon was still intoxicated, but had returned to a state of moderate, conscious awareness. Tyler's rebuking tone wasn't helping his pounding head.

"Well?"

Belinda stood and approached Tyler. "I'm sorry for what happened. I truly am. I don't know what came over me."

"Yes, you damn well do. You've both been keeping this from me for weeks. You were given every chance to keep out of it, but you were having none of it. We're on the run, lady. Brandon's wanted! Now, I don't care how personal the problem is, I want some answers outta you. Why'd you attack that priest?"

She looked away. "You mean you haven't figured it out yet?"

Tyler took a deep breath and lowered his volume. "I know it was none of my business before. But that's changed now. This problem you have has jeopardized us all."

"I know."

"We parked the van behind the church, so I don't think anybody saw what we were driving. But I'd be amazed if the police haven't been contacted."

She turned back to him. "What do you suggest we do?"

"You two stay put. We might be hidden away in a desert motel, but we're still in the next town only five miles along. I'll try doing some investigating on my own tonight. They're only a handful of stores and businesses in Wolverheath. I'll see if anybody knows anything about Emily. Tomorrow morning we'll head on to Crispin Rock."

Belinda nodded sorrowfully. Brandon's head remained shamefully bowed.

Tyler walked over and knelt in front of him. "What's going on, bro? I mean, look at you. You were a hero. A legend. Why are you wasting yourself like this?"

Brandon's weary eyes rose slowly. "I . . . don't know. I just don't know, Ty."

They remained staring at one another for a painful moment.

Finally, Tyler stood and made his way to the door. "You two had better get your shit together, and I mean pronto. I can't do this on my own." Stepping outside, he banged the door shut behind him.

***

Bishop Neville Jessop responded to a knock at the church door at 7:00 a.m. Four men in pin-sharp, dark suits stood in the doorway.

"Good morning, gentlemen," Jessop said. "What can I do for you?"

"I'm Agent Wilmot. These are Agents Crane, Kerwin, and Rhodes. We're with SDT. Homeland Security. May we come in?" Without waiting for permission, he walked past the bishop.

His three associates followed. Crane visibly cringed. Kerwin, a particularly obtuse character, used his shaved head, broad frame, and nightclub-bouncer looks to maximum, intimidating effect.

Rhodes was more conservative in appearance, with a generous amount of dark hair, although his arrogance was apparent, nonetheless.

Wilmot noticed Crane's uncomfortable body language, indicating a lack of solidarity with his companions. He knew Crane viewed them as embarrassments.

Wilmot turned to Jessop. "We've just spoken to one of your parishioners, Rosetta Mendez."

"Oh, yes?"

"She tells us she saw Brandon Drake in here yesterday afternoon, and that his girlfriend beat the crap out of one of your . . . what do you call your kinda guys?" Wilmot rejoiced in doing his utmost to intimidate the bishop by displaying absolute disrespect. Having always harbored contempt for the religious, he considered them deluded dreamers who had no concept of reality.

"There was an incident with Father Henry," Jessop said, apparently unfazed.

"Is he here? Because we'd sure as hell like to talk to the guy."

Father Henry appeared through the kitchen door at the far end of the aisle. Even from a distance, his misshapen nose and twin black eyes left no requirement for an introduction.

Wilmot smiled sarcastically. "Whoa. Looks like the little minx really can pack a punch, doesn't it?"

The bishop finally retaliated. "Agent Wilmot, I would very much appreciate it if you would state your business."

Wilmot circled around him in a manner befitting the high school bully. "Yeah, I bet you would."

"Is there anything I can help you with?" Father Henry said.

"Definitely," Wilmot said. "Would you mind telling me why Belinda Reese used your face as a stress reliever?"

"I don't know."

"You press charges?"

"No."

"Why's that?"

"She was clearly troubled. She needs care and love, not punishment."

Wilmot turned back to the bishop. "Where did they go afterwards?"

"We have no idea. Nobody even saw what they were driving."

Wilmot's brow furrowed in suspicion. "Why the hell not?"

"We were all rather shaken at the time, and we were concerned about Father Henry."

"And that's all? What were they doing here?"

Jessop didn't answer immediately. It was clear from the look in his eyes that he harbored a degree of sympathy with the Drake brothers.

Wilmot rolled his eyes and exhaled. "I'm waiting."

"They were here looking for their sister, Emily Drake. She was a nun with our Carmelite order, but she decided to leave."

"Sister? Where did she go?"

"I have no idea, and neither does anybody else. We are extremely concerned about her."

"I'm sure. Where could she have gone?"

Hesitantly, Jessop replied, "There's our town, Woodville, and then Wolverheath and Crispin Rock farther along. But I find it unlikely you'll find her in either. All it would've taken is for someone to have given her a ride somewhere."

"Their sister might not be in either of those towns," Wilmot said. "But I'm willing to bet my bottom dollar our three stooges are." He tapped Jessop on the shoulder with contemptuous disregard. "Thanks, Padre."

Wilmot made his way out the church, stopped in his tracks, and turned to his three associates. "Drake's in one of these towns. I can feel it. When we find him, I want him taken alive. Are we clear? And you never know, if Faraday and Reese were to attack us, or try to stop us from taking Drake in . . . *anything* could happen."

Kerwin and Rhodes grinned with pack-animal sadism.

"But take it from me, Crane, Drake's not someone you want to get physical with. If you can persuade him peacefully, you'll be making our job one hell of a lot easier. The other two are expendable."

"I can handle Drake. Nobody has to be harmed," Crane said.

"OK, just don't underestimate the son of a bitch."

Bishop Neville Jessop sat in a pew, deep in thought. His reluctance to guide Wilmot to Brandon Drake's possible location had been excruciating—the dilemma of obeying a legal responsibility with the Judas kiss. He wasn't under the seal of the confessional this time, but he had no desire to lead an arrogant, despicable miscreant like Agent Wilmot to his quarry.

Despite the havoc the presence of Belinda Reese and the Drake boys had caused, he suspected they were traveling along a cruel and unjust road.

Twenty

Highway to Hell

Emily awoke in a room at the Days Inn South Lenwood Hotel in Barstow, California, feeling particularly refreshed. Fabian had insisted on buying her dinner at the hotel the night before, and paid for her room. She couldn't deny her pangs of guilt at having accepted his generosity with no means by which she might reciprocate.

Having showered and dressed, she made her way downstairs to the restaurant for breakfast.

According to Fabian, it wasn't a prestige hotel, but to Emily, it was a paradise compared to the stifling environment from which she'd escaped. Her sense of enjoyment exacerbated her guilty conscience. Her life had been one of self-denial, with the indoctrination of the message that suffering was a virtue. Any form of pleasure or enjoyment for 'the self', she'd been taught, was, indeed, a step on the road to damnation. Despite her waning faith, the thought briefly crossed her mind that her feelings of humble self-abasement and guilt would remain with her for life.

The elevator doors opened, and she stepped out into the crowded foyer, across to the restaurant. She immediately noticed Fabian sitting at a table in the far corner reading a newspaper, and quickened her pace toward him.

He looked up and smiled. "Good morning. How did you sleep?"

"Oh, just fine, thank you. You are very kind," she said with gentle graciousness. "This hotel is just wonderful. I've never stayed in a place like this before."

"Oh, this is nothing. Please, take a seat and have some breakfast."

"Thank you."

He placed the newspaper on the table. "You were very quiet over dinner last night. I'm not trying to pry, but are you sure there's not something you want to talk about?"

She looked away, desperately wanting to avoid the subject of her past, if for no other reason than to not make him feel uncomfortable. Finally, she realized there was no way around it. "All right, I'll tell you, but I really don't want to."

"What?"

She took a deep breath. "I'm a nun."

Fabian grinned. "A nun? Come on. You're putting me on."

"Well, at least I was until a couple of days ago. I escaped from the convent. I just . . . never mind."

"You escaped?"

"I couldn't take it anymore. They wouldn't release me from my vows, so technically, I'm still a nun. I just don't feel like one."

"Well, after breakfast, we'll hit the road, and then we'll stop off and get you a new set of clothes."

She looked away, somewhat saddened. "You don't have to do that. Please—"

"I want to spoil you." He stroked her cheek, but she recoiled. "What's wrong? You are so beautiful."

"P-please don't."

He took his hand away. "I'm sorry, I just thought—"

"What do you do, Fabian?" she said, intentionally changing the subject. "What's this job you have for me?"

"Well, you said you liked helping people. I know of people who need help. I think a kind, thoughtful person like you could really help them get to where they want to be."

She tilted her head pensively, unable to deny her curiosity about what the job entailed. "Are they poor?"

Fabian paused in a contemplating manner for a moment. "In a way."

"I'll do whatever I can," she said. "It will be so good to be able to serve people, and have my freedom too."

Fabian stood and stepped around to the side of the table. "I need to use the restroom. Get yourself some breakfast. I'll be back in a minute."

Emily watched him walk across the restaurant, wondering where her life was taking her. Fabian seemed so wonderful. She couldn't help but trust him.

She noticed the newspaper on the table and picked it up, excited that she could sit at a hotel breakfast table and freely read the paper.

Her eyes shot to the left as her own name caught her attention. It was a page three article on the case of the escaped military prisoner, Brandon Drake. She became intrigued as she read the story and studied the face of the man in the photograph. There was something about his features that seemed so familiar, especially his eyes.

Or was it just her imagination? Could her mind have been playing tricks on her simply because this particular fugitive had the same name as her?

142

Fascinated, she continued to read.

Fabian turned a corner in the reception area and took out his cell phone. He shook his head in astonishment at his stroke of good fortune. On reflection, he realized how being a nun fit Emily so well. She had such a shy, extremely polite, and modest manner. The way in which she wore no makeup, and bore a face of such profound innocence, made her claim highly convincing.

Regardless, he could see her bone structure was strong. Her green eyes left no doubt in his mind that with minimum cosmetics, she would be one of the most beautiful women he'd ever seen.

He searched through his list of contacts, found the number, and made the call. "Hey, it's me. What would you say if I told you I've got your most profitable squeeze, ever . . . ? Yeah, we'll be hitting the highway soon, so I'll be back with her by the afternoon. She doesn't suspect anything. She's a runaway nun, ridiculously naïve, and as dumb as they come . . . OK, but don't forget, I want a serious cut for this." He ended the call and returned to the restaurant.

After breakfast, Fabian settled up the tab at the reception desk. With Emily by his side, he departed the hotel and walked across the parking lot to his silver Chevrolet Corvette. "You ready?"

"I-I guess so," she said.

"OK, jump in and let's hit the road."

Once Emily had closed her door, he started up the engine. The car shot forward, screeching the tires slightly.

With unnecessary acceleration, he sped onto the road in the direction of the highway.

Twenty-One

Nowhere to Run

Belinda awoke beside Brandon to find him shivering and perspiring heavily. "Brandon? What's wrong?"

"I don't know. I feel hot. Feverish."

Abruptly, she sat up and noticed his skin was white and damp. "Oh, my God. You've got withdrawal."

"G-guess so. I'll be all right."

"Not for another few days. Why, Brandon? Why didn't you tell me you'd got a problem?"

"Didn't t-think I had."

"How long have you been drinking?"

"How long?"

She grasped his shoulders tightly. "I need you to listen to me. When was the last time you can remember going a day without touching any alcohol?"

"I don't know. Three, maybe four weeks."

"Three, maybe four weeks? And you didn't think there might be a problem?"

He clasped his clammy, quivering hands over his ears. "Please, don't shout."

She exhaled, exasperated, and climbed out of bed. "Get up and take a shower. What you really need is medical attention."

With a look of profound loathing, he lifted his head off the pillow.

***

The night before, Tyler had found that most of the people in Wolverheath knew Sister Veronica. However, nobody had seen her during the time since she'd fled the convent.

He parked the van in a lot outside a small shopping mall in Crispin Rock. From there, Tyler, Brandon, and Belinda proceeded to inquire at every store they came to with their only photograph of Emily.

With each passing moment their anxiety escalated, and Brandon's condition was worsening. He tried valiantly to hide his shaking hands and perspiring brow by looking downward, his long hair and baseball cap acting as a makeshift mask. The perspiration made it impossible for him to use his usual prosthetic disguise methods. They all knew what they were doing was hazardous, but they had no choice. Emily was missing, and they had to find her, no matter the risk. It was an impossible situation. They'd found themselves putting their own liberty, perhaps even their very lives in danger, but were compelled to act in the absence of an alternative.

They spent almost four hours asking if anybody had seen the woman in the photograph, but it proved fruitless.

After stepping out of a small bookstore they noticed Rockers Tavern directly opposite. Tyler and Belinda had been avoiding it since they arrived in town, fearful of how the sight of alcohol might affect Brandon. Standing on the opposite side of the street, they stared at the place with unease.

"I'll be OK," Brandon said weakly.

Tyler took out the keys to the van and handed them to him. "Brandon, go sit in the van. You don't need to go in there."

A pleading look crossed Brandon's face. "Please, Ty. I know I'm a wreck. I know I've screwed up. But I can handle it. I'm not gonna be able to live with knowing I couldn't even help trying to find her."

Tyler glanced at Belinda, their fears in sync. What would be the worst? Risking Brandon looking at bottles of alcohol for a few minutes? Or risk the problem getting worse by having him live the rest of his life with an enhanced feeling of failure and shame?

"All right," Tyler said. "But we're gonna be watching you like goddamn hawks. The first sign of needing a drink, you get the hell outta there."

"You have my word."

Tyler held his gaze for a moment. "Jesus, man. You look terrible."

"Thanks."

"Come on. Let's get this over with."

They crossed the road and entered Rockers. Brandon immediately averted his eyes from the bottles behind the bar. It had been an arduous morning for him. After a shower and an attempt at breakfast, he was still perspiring and shaking. His performance capacity was practically zero. Against Belinda and Tyler's advice, he fought through his incapacity to aid in the search for his sister, the ravenous urge for a drink ever present.

It was surprisingly busy inside. They waited a few minutes for the manager to finish serving before seizing a moment to catch his attention.

"What can I get for you guys?" the manager said.

Belinda took Brandon's hand and squeezed it. "Take a deep breath," she whispered.

He gripped her hand tightly. Being in the bar was every bit as tough as he thought it was going to be.

Tyler took out Emily's photograph and showed it to the manager. "Sorry to bother you, but we're looking for someone. Have you seen this lady?"

The man's eyes showed recognition as he gazed at the photograph.

"You've seen her, haven't you?"

Brandon's face shot up as a fleeting surge of adrenaline coursed through him, temporarily anesthetizing his tremors and splitting headache.

"Jesus forgive us. She was a nun," the man murmured. "Who are you guys?"

"We're her family," Tyler said. "Is there anything you can tell us? I mean, we're real worried about her."

The manager looked up at them with an agonized expression. "I'm Bill," he said finally. "She was here yesterday afternoon."

Tyler lurched forward. "Seriously? Do you have any idea where she went?"

"Unfortunately, I do."

"Where?"

Bill was silent.

"Come on, man. Tell me."

"She left with a guy named Fabian Rodríguez. Puerto Rican clown."

"Who's that?"

"He's from Los Angeles. He's a scout for a seriously dangerous outfit."

"What kind of dangerous outfit?"

"Organized crime. Drugs, prostitution, kiddie porn, human trafficking, you name it."

Brandon swallowed hard and came closer to the conversation. "Who are they?"

"They're the most powerful underground organization in L.A. It's controlled by a guy they call Sapphire, but nobody's ever seen him. All I can tell you is you don't mess with these guys. Anybody who does anything that gets in their way gets blown to hell."

"You let him take her?" Tyler exclaimed.

All conversations in the bar ceased at the sound of his outburst.

"Don't think for a minute any of us are happy about this," Bill said. "There wasn't a man in here who didn't want to help her."

"So why didn't they?"

"You don't get it, do you? If any one of us had done anything to stop him—anything at all—they would have killed every last damn one of us. We have families. Please try to understand."

Brandon tried to process what he was hearing through his palpitations, incessant fever, and constant shaking. He'd never felt so helpless in his life, and he knew it was his own fault. He couldn't forgive himself for letting Emily down with his indulgent stupidity in her most desperate hour.

"Can you give us any information on where this Sapphire operates from?" Tyler said.

Bill shook his head. "A lot of activity with them goes on around the Avenue Nineteen area. That's all I know. But please don't go there." He put his hand on Tyler's. "I'm so sorry I couldn't do anything to stop this. But you've got to believe me. The lady's gone, and she's not coming back."

Tyler took his hand away and stood back defiantly. "Oh, yes she is, goddamn it!"

"They'll be in L.A. by now, and if she's a nun he ain't gonna put her out on a street crawl."

"What are you talking about?"

"He'll sell her to the highest bidder, and she'll be gone forever. I'm sorry. I truly am."

Tyler shook his head and backed away toward the entrance. "No. We'll get her back, no matter what."

"Don't be crazy," Bill said.

"Oh, we're gonna be the craziest these bastards have ever seen." Tyler tapped Brandon's shoulder. "You'd better shape up fast. Come on."

Belinda followed them out.

Brandon glanced at Bill who looked back at him as though he was convinced they were walking toward their deaths.

Tyler threw open the doors at the moment three cars sped to a halt on the opposite side of the road.

Immediately, two car doors flew open. Two suited officials exited from one, and an attractive blond man from the other, their pistols trained on Brandon.

"Please, put your hands behind your heads and stand where you are," the blond man said.

"Oh, my God, not now." Brandon's heart pounded fiercely, his panic increased one-hundredfold by his inability to help Emily. He stood as still as possible, shivering, regardless of the Nevada heat.

The third car door opened and a fourth man stepped out with a gloating smile. Brandon vaguely recognized him, but he couldn't quite recall from where.

"Hi, Drake," Wilmot said with victorious sarcasm. "It's been a long time."

Brandon didn't answer, but continued to look at the man questioningly. *Where do I know him from?*

"I've waited two damn years to get your ass where I have it. And you want to know something else, soldier?"

"What?"

"You're not looking too good."

Twenty-Two

The Inside Man

Crane raised his palm toward Brandon in a gesture of peace, and lowered his firearm. "Sir, we are not here to arrest you. Our use of weapons is purely for our own protection."

Wearily, Brandon glanced at Tyler and Belinda, and then back to Crane. "I don't understand. I'm on America's most wanted list."

"I understand your confusion, but there's the possibility of a presidential pardon in this for you if you cooperate with us." Crane took out his identification. "We're with SDT. Homeland Security."

Brandon couldn't help looking at Wilmot. It was driving him to distraction not knowing where he'd seen him before. "Why would you be offering me a presidential pardon?"

"It's very complicated, sir," Crane said, "and I will explain it all to you. But I'm going to seriously advise you come with us."

Brandon held Crane's gaze for a prolonged moment. Despite his reservations, there was something about this man that seemed sincere and trustworthy. "All right, I'll go with you. But please, let my brother and Belinda go."

"There are no warrants out for either of them, and we have no powers of arrest, so that's not even an issue." Crane turned to Belinda and Tyler. "I don't want either of you to worry about anything. Brandon *is* going to be fine."

Reluctantly, Tyler nodded.

Crane slowly came toward Brandon with a look of assurance. "It'll be fine, sir."

All resistance had left Brandon, and Crane's compassionate demeanor was compelling. Finally, he stepped forward.

Wilmot shook his head at how easy taking Drake in had been. Crane's diplomacy and Drake's apparent ill health had made for the perfect combination of advantages. It was clear that, despite his initial annoyance, bringing Crane along had paid off profoundly.

His cell phone beeped, and he took it out. "Wilmot."

"Agent Wilmot, you need to return to D.C. immediately. There's been a tragedy." Deborah Beaumont said.

Wilmot turned away in order that nobody would see his shrewd smile.

"Director Wolfe was found hanged in his home. There was also a suicide note."

Garrett, you're such a goddamn genius. "Oh, my God. I can't believe it. We'll get back immediately." Ending the call, he stepped over to Rhodes, and whispered, "There's been an event at Langley. We've got to get back right away."

"What's happened?"

"The moment we've been waiting for. Drake should go with Crane. He seems to trust him, and we don't want him blowing a gasket."

"I agree."

Wilmot called across the street to Crane. "Drake goes with you."

Crane escorted Brandon into the back of his car.

Wilmot silently rejoiced knowing he was about to be appointed director of SDT, and he had his only remaining problem in his clutches.

Brandon climbed into the back of Crane's Camaro. The door closed, locking him in.

Wilmot hurried over to Crane. "There's been an incident at Langley. I'm gonna phone in an emergency flight from North Las Vegas Airport."

"All right, you go on ahead," Crane said. "I'll be right behind you."

The four cars turned around, blocking traffic in the process. Crane's was the last car in the convoy.

As they moved forward, Brandon looked out the car window at Belinda and Tyler. They returned his gaze with the same grief-tainted stare.

Belinda turned to Tyler and asked him something, but he shook his head. She was obviously appealing to him for suggestions about what they were going to do, and Tyler clearly had no answers. None of them did.

Crane's car moved past them and they disappeared from view within seconds.

Brandon continued to shiver, and Crane couldn't fail to notice. "Sir, you have to tell me. Are you sick? Do you need medical attention?"

"Not exactly s-sick."

"So, what is it?"

"It's real embarrassing is what it is."

Crane glanced in his rear-view mirror, somewhat astounded by what Drake was alluding to. "Sir, is it a narcotics issue?"

"C-close. I've got a real bad case of alcohol w-withdrawal."

Crane was silent as he tried to process the shocking revelation. Brandon Drake—the one many thought of as a national hero, bordering on the superhuman—had a drinking problem. Conversely, it wasn't so difficult to understand. He'd been incarcerated for two years, only to have escaped to a life on the run. Who wouldn't have been drawn to the bottle under such circumstances?

"I don't know what to suggest for that, sir. But you're clearly unwell, so I'll have to call it in."

Brandon looked away despondently. "Whatever."

Crane pressed auto-dial on his cell phone and awaited a response through his blu-tooth earpiece. Deborah Beaumont came on the line immediately. "Hi Deborah, this is Jed Crane. I need to know of any rapid solutions for alcohol withdrawal symptoms." He waited for a few moments while Deborah looked it up. Finally, she came back with a response and Crane relayed her question to Brandon. "How long have you been drinking?"

"About four weeks."

Crane repeated Brandon's answer to Deborah and received a fairly banal response. "She said Alka Selzer to bring your salt levels back, and about four liters of water. That's the best we can do for now."

"Thank you."

With the conversation continuing through Crane's ear piece, the agent's jaw dropped. "What . . . ? Deborah, are you absolutely sure . . . ? No, he didn't say a word. He just said there'd been an incident back at Langley . . . OK . . . No, I don't know what I'm going to do." The call ended.

"What's wrong?" Brandon said.

Deep in thought, Crane didn't answer. He knew his career as he knew it had just come to an end. What was he going to do? How was he going to handle the situation now that Wolfe was dead? For long moments his mind was overwrought with multiple possibilities, each of which were riddled with peril. As was doing nothing at all. Finally, he realized he had to bring Brandon into the fold. "Sir, there's something I have to tell you."

"What's that?"

"I've wanted to meet you for a long time. I'm sympathetic to you, OK? I might work for SDT, but something fishy is going on, I just know it."

Brandon leaned forward. "Seriously?"

"The entire point of us coming out here for you is because our superior, Director Wolfe, needed your help with an investigation."

"What investigation?"

Crane explained the story of how, after Treadwell's death, Wilmot and Agent Martyn McKay were assigned to track down Agent Payne. Soon after Brandon killed Payne, McKay committed suicide, and Wilmot was quickly appointed Wolfe's second-in-command. However, McKay's brother had leveled a number of accusations against SDT, claiming his brother wasn't the suicidal type. That led to a Congress investigation into whether there were remnants of Treadwell's rogue cell still active within the intelligence community.

"And this guy Wolfe thinks I know something?" Brandon said.

"He did. I've just received word that now *he* has committed suicide too, and I don't buy it. The guy was a patriot and as tough as steel. He was the most unlikely man on earth to do something like that."

Brandon wrapped his arms around himself as another bout of shivering took hold. "I-I'm really s-sorry to hear that, but you should've saved yourselves the trouble. I don't know anything. Anything at all."

"You might not, but I think I do. They thought Wilmot was just an innocent who followed Treadwell's orders, believing he had no knowledge of what he was doing."

"And you don't?"

"I think Wilmot was Treadwell's back-up plan all along. I think he murdered McKay, and that he's responsible for Director Wolfe's death. I believe he's the new leader of Treadwell's cell, and the bastard's about to take Wolfe's place in SDT."

Brandon exhaled and wiped his brow. "Look, man, I'm real sorry about what's going on, but it's none of my business. I can't help you. Now, you've got to let me go. When you found us outside that bar we'd just found out—" He shuddered as another withdrawal shiver gripped him. "W-we just found out our sister has b-been k-kidnapped by some human trafficking gang in L.A. Now, please. You've got to help us."

"But how? You're shivering like crazy. You're in no shape to run. I could pull over and let you cold-cock me, but that'd just add another assault charge to your resume."

"You've got a point."

"Yeah, I do, and we're also following three men I believe to be a part this conspiracy. No matter which way we turn, Brandon, we're screwed."

Twenty-Three

Captives

Emily's smile glowed as she stepped inside a stunning Wilshire Boulevard condominium. In spite of that, every time she caught sight of her reflection, her smile faded with a twinge of guilt. Wearing a layer of make-up and lipstick for the first time in her life, and a flowing, white, knee-length dress, her conscience at appearing so worldly tore at her.

Fabian removed his sunglasses and summoned the elevator. He turned to Emily again and smiled. "You look absolutely beautiful."

Shaking her head, she smiled awkwardly. "Stop teasing me."

"I'm not. I'm being truthful."

The elevator arrived, and he gestured for her to step inside.

As the doors closed, her mind was awash with thoughts she couldn't process. Two days ago she'd been an unhappy nun living under the stifling authority of the convent. Now, she was riding an elevator in Los Angeles, the city of dreams, looking more radiant than she'd ever imagined, and with a most dashing man by her side. *Surely, it isn't real. It has to be a dream.*

The elevator doors opened, and they stepped out into a plush corridor.

"It's just down here," Fabian said, and led the way.

With each step, Emily's heart quickened a little more. Her mind became an amalgam of emotions: excitement, confusion, guilt, and just a twinge of fear. She had no idea where her life was taking her.

They came to a door at the end of the corridor. Fabian took out a key, opened it, and led Emily inside.

At first glance, she was awestruck. The apartment was lavish and almost alien to her inexperienced eyes. It was the very antithesis of where her previous travels had taken her—to poverty, hunger, dereliction, and destruction. The highly-polished wooden flooring, a circular glass table, and cream leather chair set, offered a startling contrast.

Placed against the rear windows to the side was a leather sofa behind a spotless coffee table. On the opposite side of the room, she noticed a lavish kitchen unit. The view of the city through the windows was breathtaking.

Unfortunately, it was marred by the sudden appearance of two huge oriental males who stepped out from a side room.

Emily smiled politely but couldn't help feeling uncomfortable. She instinctively knew these men were not benevolent, as evidenced by their cold, intimidating stares. They were so tall and broad, she felt dwarfed by their presence.

"What the fuck took you so long?" the man on the right snarled at Fabian.

Fabian simply shrugged his shoulders. "We had a long lunch." Pushing past the two men, he led Emily into the room from which they had emerged.

She entered with him to discover it was a luxurious office with the same spectacular view of the city.

Sitting behind the desk was a fierce-looking woman whom Emily estimated was in her early forties. Her short, jet black hair seemed to give her a slightly masculine appearance, further enhanced by a dark gray business suit with trousers. Her features suggested oriental origin.

The woman stood and smiled, breaking her otherwise stern visage. "You were right, as usual, Fabian. She *is* beautiful. Perfect, in fact."

Emily noticed the woman's authoritative tone was an octave lower than the average American female. Perturbed, she looked to Fabian for clarification. "I don't understand. If I am to be helping poor people, why is my appearance relevant?"

The woman laughed. "I could say I was simply admiring your looks in passing, my dear. But, alas, such is not the case. Your appearance is very relevant." Her smile faded and she gave Fabian a sinister nod.

Emily's heart pounded as Fabian seized her shoulders and dug his fingers deeply into her flesh. "Please. You're hurting me."

"Let's see what she's got," the woman said.

Fabian tore Emily's dress open and pulled it down below her knees.

"What are you doing?" she screamed.

The woman stood before her and gazed upon her almost-naked body, admiringly. "Remove her bra and panties."

"No!"

Fabian tore away her remaining garments within the space of a heartbeat, and braced Emily's hands behind her back.

The woman came closer to her. "I understand you were a nun. That's very interesting. Unfortunately, you will have to be taught a few things before we can make use of you."

"W-why, are you doing this to me? Fabian, you said I would be helping people. The poor." Emily wept with terror, but the cold, heartless cruelty continued.

"Oh, you'll be helping people, all right," the woman said. "You'll be helping many men along the road to whatever it is they wish from you. And they are *poor* men. Fabian was telling you the truth." She reached out her hand and caressed Emily between her thighs. "Poor in spirit."

Fabian stretched out Emily's right arm as the woman took out a hypodermic needle from her jacket pocket. "This will help you to see the situation more favorably." After removing the sheath, she expelled the air from the syringe.

Emily's terrified gaze locked on the needle. She instinctively recoiled, but was held fast by Fabian.

The woman inserted the tip of the needle into a vein in the crook of Emily's arm. Very quickly, her panic and terror became a feeling of floating.

Emily's final thought before the drug completely clouded her mind was that she'd died. Her heart told her this terrible ordeal was the wrath of God being poured out upon her for abandoning her calling. She couldn't justify pleading for mercy, for in her belief, all that was happening was so very just.

***

Brandon guzzled a bottle of water that Crane had in the glove compartment. "Damn," he said. "My jeans are getting tighter by the minute."

"Why's that?" Crane said.

"Water retention, I guess. I'm dehydrated from the alcohol."

"All right just hang in there."

Crane had been following Wilmot, Kerwin, and Rhodes for forty-five minutes. Then something appeared in the distance. He noticed a long line of stationary vehicles on the narrow desert road leading to the town of Blair Creek, fifty miles south of Vegas. There had been a number of signs along the way advertising an evangelical revival in the town. With a number of cars behind him, Jed knew that if he was going to act, now was his chance.

But by doing so, his career would be over. He would become a fugitive. He would be hunted, just like Brandon, and for exactly the same reasons. His life would be in danger, and he would lose everything, including his relationship with his fiancée. He would have no choice but to simply disappear.

However, the alternative was something he couldn't live with. He would be turning a freedom fighter over to his colleagues, whom he knew to be corrupt, merciless killers. He'd be compelled to serve under Wilmot, who was a traitor to his own country.

There was always the possibility of his remaining in SDT and doing whatever he could to expose them from within. But he knew there was very little likelihood of him surviving if he attempted something like that, singlehandedly.

His brow and palms became damp, his breathing was shallow, and he was stricken with an intense attack of anxiety. Intentionally slowing down, he created a distance between himself and Kerwin and Rhodes.

The driver behind sounded his horn, clearly impatient, but Crane remained frustratingly slow. Before long it overtook him, followed by another, and then another. Within moments, there was a line of cars between Crane, Kerwin and Rhodes.

"What are you doing?" Brandon said.

The line of cars came to a standstill as they hit the gridlock. The last car overtook Crane to join the queue, the primal instinct to be before the guy in front, always dominant.

"OK, what's goin' on? You gonna fill me in?" Brandon said.

Crane checked behind one last time. The road was clear, and there were several hundred yards between him and the queue.

He gunned the car forward, then stepped on the brakes and twisted the wheel. The car spun around, accompanied by the sound of screeching tires.

In response to Brandon's question, he said, "I just quit Homeland Security."

Wilmot watched Crane's car speeding away in the rear view mirror and knew Crane had figured it all out. He realized that as long as they were blocked in the gridlock, they could do nothing to stop him. Overcome with rage and frustration, he punched his steering wheel. "Fuck!"

Twenty-Four

Relentless

"So, you're telling me Treadwell altered your memories?" Crane said as he raced along the dusty highway.

"That's what I'm telling you," Brandon replied. "Seems he wanted to use me for something, but my natural personality was too volatile for him to control. Apparently, they called me The Scorpion."

"I see."

"Why are you doing this for me?"

"Because it's right."

"But don't you realize what you've just done?"

"Only too well." Crane pressed down on the accelerator, his instincts propelling him to get away from his colleagues as quickly as possible. "I joined SDT just over two years ago. I was introduced to scumbags like Ogilsby and Woodford and never liked them. I always knew something was wrong."

"Who?"

"Ogilsby and Woodford. Those two agents you took down at the TV studio a couple of years back. They were with Payne."

"Oh, yeah. Those guys. I never caught their names."

"Just after I arrived at Langley, you put that video exposing Treadwell on the TV. Treadwell was in and out of Wolfe's office all the time, and then he disappeared. With Payne, Ogilsby, and Woodford gone, we thought we were clear of Treadwell's faction."

"What do you think about that now?"

"Wilmot was trusted. Everyone believed he was just an innocent Wolfe had assigned to occasionally assist the senator. Like I said before, I believe he was Treadwell's protégé all along. He's been running this cell from within, and he thinks you know something."

Brandon frowned. "But I don't."

"Wilmot doesn't know that, so if I'm right, he sees you as a serious threat. He wants to put you away."

"This is crazy. You're saying he wants to kill me because he doesn't know that I don't know?"

"Basically, yes. There would also have been a revenge element to it too."

"Revenge for what?"

"Two years ago you beat the crap out of him in Wyoming."

Brandon shook his head, confused. "In Wyoming?"

"Yes, didn't you recognize him?"

"There was something vaguely familiar about him, but I couldn't quite place him."

"It happened in the woods, apparently. He was trying to take your girlfriend in, and you went wild. You really did a number on him. I remember when he came back to Langley. I'd never seen him look so good." Crane chuckled.

"Oh, my God, it was him," Brandon said with wide-eyed realization. "He was accosting Belinda, and I just lost it completely."

"Yeah, you did."

"Whatever, we've got to get back to Crispin Rock. We've got to find Belinda and Tyler. With what's happened to my sister, I can't afford to lose them too."

"I'm going as fast as I can. We'll be there in about thirty minutes, hopefully sooner."

Weakened by withdrawal, Brandon sat back enduring his plight as they sped along the highway.

***

"You two look like you could use a couple of really stiff drinks."

Tyler looked at Bill from his seat at the bar. "Tempting, but no thanks. Coffee will be fine. We need to keep our wits about us while we figure this out."

Bill went over to the percolator and returned with two coffees. "I'm so sorry for you people, I really am. I swear to you, if it were up to me I would've intervened. But I've got my family and the families of every man who was in here to consider."

Tyler tried to appear sympathetic but it was difficult. "Is there anything else you can tell us about this guy, Fabian Rodriguez? I mean, how often does he come in here?"

"Hard to say. Sometimes we've seen him in here twice in one week. Other times it's a couple of months between visits. The son of a bitch patrols desert towns looking for vulnerable girls. This ain't the only state he trolls around in, I can assure you."

Tyler lowered his head despairingly. It was just him and Belinda now. How were they going to go after Emily without Brandon? He was the fighter. The soldier. He was the one with wartime experience and knowledge of battle strategy. But now he was gone and desperately sick. What was going to happen to him?

Tyler noticed the same empty sense of hopelessness overwhelming Belinda as she sat in silence beside him. She gazed aimlessly into her coffee.

"I pleaded with him not to go ahead with this," she said. "We had our freedom and happiness in our hands, but he just couldn't let go of the idea of restoring himself to a family."

Tyler couldn't offer any response. He'd been just as eager for them to be reunited with Emily as Brandon had.

"So, who was it that took your brother in?" Bill said. "Police? FBI?"

Tyler glanced up at him again, not feeling particularly sociable. "I'm not sure. Homeland Security, I think they said."

"When he came in here, I had no idea he was Brandon Drake. He looked so different. On the night he broke out of Leavenworth, we had one hell of a bash in here. Busiest night I've had in years." Bill chortled, but stopped the moment he saw the humorless glare in Tyler's eyes.

"Hey, wait a second," Tyler said. "You said this guy . . . *Sapphire*, is it?"

"That's his nickname," Bill said. "I have no idea what his real name is. Nobody does."

"You said they operate from the Avenue Nineteen area—"

"No, no. They control all of the prostitutes around that area. It's not where they'd be located. For that, I supposed you'd be lookin' closer to Beverly Hills."

"OK, have—?"

"No idea. Honestly."

"OK, but I think I have a way of finding out."

Belinda's head shot up. "You do?"

"Yeah. Alex."

"Alex?"

"He used to live in L.A., and he's been around." Tyler turned back to Bill. "You said this Sapphire sells these girls to the highest bidder."

"That's right."

"What kind of people are these buyers?"

Bill shrugged. "Rich ones, I guess. Business guys. Foreigners."

Calculation filled Tyler's mind. Perhaps he didn't need Brandon's brawn after all.

Bill placed his hand on Tyler's shoulder. "Please. Whatever you're thinking of doing, don't."

"Too late." Tyler finished his coffee and stood. "Belinda, we should get moving." He turned to Bill again. "How much do I owe you?"

"It's on the house." Bill said despondently.

"Thanks."

Tyler made his way out the bar with Belinda. On the steps outside they paused for a moment, concerned they were going to run into the authorities again. However, the road was clear. Hurriedly, they continued on.

Belinda struggled to keep up with the stride of Tyler's considerably longer legs. "Tyler, slow down."

"I'm sorry. I'm just really anxious."

They stepped onto the sidewalk and headed in the direction of the van.

"Are you gonna tell me what you've got planned?" she said breathlessly.

"I'm gonna get Alex to talk to some of his buddies in L.A. to see what information they can pick up off the street about this Sapphire character. Then I'm gonna see if I can infiltrate the organization."

"And do what?"

He stopped in his stride and turned to her with undeniable conviction in his eyes. "I'm gonna buy my sister."

Belinda looked at him in disbelief. "You're not serious."

"Can you think of a safer way to get her out of there?"

She didn't answer.

"Now, come on. Let's go."

They continued along the walkway and two side streets. Before long, they saw the van parked in the distance along the desert roadside.

Belinda's mind was still on Brandon. The fear of what the authorities were going to do to him continued to eat away at her. The 'not knowing' was the worst part. Everything about his being taken was immersed in the excruciating unknown.

As they came upon the van, Tyler took the keys out of his pocket.

The driver's side door came open.

Tyler and Belinda came to a halt. They recognized old Earl instantly, with his shotgun trained on them.

"I knew I'd find you assholes sooner or later," Earl said. "Nice to see you left my rifle under the seat. Looks like we hit ourselves the jackpot this time."

The passenger's side door opened and his son, Bobby, climbed out.

Tyler instinctively went for his pistol, but he'd left it in the van.

"You lookin' for this?" Bobby held up the Super Carry Ultra HD. "It's amazing what you can find under other folks' seats. A gun like this looks mighty expensive."

Earl shot them a gloating grimace. "You guys picked the wrong boys to mess with. This time we brought along some reinforcements."

The rear doors of the van sprung open and four heavies with shotguns leaped out.

Tyler and Belinda stepped back fearfully.

Earl made his way around to the back of the van to join his cohorts, and gestured inside at the Turbo Swan. "Now, what'n the hell is that thing? I'm willin' to bet it's worth an arm and a leg."

"Oh, Jesus," Tyler said. "This is relentless."

Twenty-Five

Separate Ways

"It's just around here. Next left," Brandon said as Crane sped the car into Crispin Rock.

"OK, just hang in there."

Brandon gripped the back of Crane's seat anxiously. During the time they'd been away, there was every chance Tyler and Belinda had left the area. If so, he had no idea how he would locate them again.

With another screech of the tires, Crane turned onto the desert road just before the main town area. Brandon exhaled with relief at the sight of the van.

And then his heart sank again just as quickly.

"Something's going down," Crane said.

Brandon immediately processed the scene: Tyler and Belinda at gunpoint facing Earl, Bobby, and four heavies. "I remember now. The young guy and the older one tried to steal the van from us yesterday. Looks like they came back with help."

Crane lowered the electric side window and drew his pistol. He aimed at two of the henchmen and took them down with two clean shots.

Tyler and Belinda snapped their heads to the left. Bobby aimed at the oncoming vehicle, but Crane gunned the car into him, knocking him into his father. Both men were hurled across the gravel. Tyler's .45 flew from Bobby's hand.

Belinda threw herself to the ground and grasped the pistol. The remaining two thugs were almost upon her. Darting back, she scrambled to her feet, firing aimlessly at the feet of the two assailants. A geyser of sand and stone exploded before them, forcing them to turn and run.

Tyler seized Earl's rifle and trained it on him and Bobby. "If I were you I'd stay put, assholes."

Crane switched off the engine and exited the car with Brandon.

Belinda hurried over to Brandon and threw her arms around him. "Oh, baby. I've been so worried about you. What happened?"

"It's complicated."

Crane approached the two guys he'd shot. One had taken a bullet in the stomach, and the other a shot to his chest, just below the heart. Crane walked briskly over to Earl and Bobby. "I'd get your two friends to the hospital."

Earl nodded in defeat. Both he and Bobby appeared to be severely bruised. Earl had also sustained a fractured leg, as was clear from the fact that he couldn't bend it. Bobby took out his cell phone and called for an ambulance.

Tyler turned to Crane finally. "What's going on, man? You just took off with my brother, and now you come back with him, racing to the rescue."

"I'm not your enemy, Mr. Faraday," Crane said. "I am so sorry for everything you people have been through."

Brandon and Belinda joined them. "He's telling the truth, Ty," Brandon said. "This is Jed, by the way. He may have just saved my life."

Tyler shook Crane's hand. "Good to meet you, Jed. What happens now?"

"Now, you three need to get as far away from this town as you can."

"What are *you* gonna do?"

Crane hesitated for a moment, and then replied, "Whatever I can to stay alive."

"Is there anything we can do for you?" Brandon said.

Crane shook his head. "The best thing we can do now is split up and go our separate ways. I'll have to lay low until I can figure this out. Chances are Wilmot will have Garrett on my tail by tonight, and that's not likely to end well."

"Who's Garrett?"

"One of SDT's finest trackers. An assassin with a zero-percent failure rate."

Brandon, Tyler, and Belinda glanced at one another with concern.

Brandon extended his hand to Crane. "Thank you for everything, Jed. I really hope we can get together again someday, under better circumstances."

Jed had doubt in his eyes, along with a hint of sadness. "I hope so too." He broke the handshake and made his way back to his car.

"Come on, let's get outta here," Tyler said.

Brandon and Tyler closed the back doors of the van. Belinda climbed in the front.

From his driver's seat, Jed Crane held Brandon's gaze for an ominous moment. He then turned the car around and headed back out, away from the town.

Belinda realized she was still holding Tyler's pistol. Although firing it had been a disturbing experience, she couldn't deny the sense of security it gave her. Almost unconsciously, she slipped it inside the rim of her jeans, and sat back in preparation for another long journey.

Tyler took the driver's seat, and Brandon climbed in next to Belinda.

"How are you feeling, babe?" she said.

"Not good. Very sleepy."

"OK, let's hit the road and find another hotel somewhere, but a long ways from here," Tyler said.

The van backed up, meandered around the remaining hijackers, and drove on into the horizon.

***

Wilmot, Kerwin, and Rhodes pulled up outside the car rental office at North Las Vegas airport.

Wilmot angrily slammed the car door shut behind him.

"Take it easy," Kerwin said. "Let's not make a spectacle of ourselves here."

Wilmot inhaled deeply and let it out slowly. "So, Crane knows. That's not good."

"Crane and Drake together is a serious problem for all of us," Rhodes said. "We have to stay calm and figure out how we're going to neutralize them."

"I think I have."

"What?"

"Crane and Drake will split up. Drake will almost certainly resume his search for his sister. Chances are he was in that bar with Reese and Faraday asking questions."

"That's obvious enough," Rhodes said.

"I need to get back to D.C. I have no choice. You two go back to that bar and see if you can find out where Drake might be headed, even a clue."

"You got it," Rhodes said. "What are you going to do about Crane?"

Wilmot turned to him darkly. "Garrett."

"Garrett?"

"No offense, gentlemen. You are damn good at your jobs, nobody's going to argue with that. But when it comes to hunting and tracking, Garrett's the best."

"Agreed," Kerwin said.

"Find out what you can, and take the late flight back," Wilmot said. "Call me as soon as you learn anything."

The two men nodded, climbed into the car, and fired up the engine.

Wilmot turned away toward the airport check-in, eager to embrace his new position of power.

***

Bill looked up from behind the bar to see two men in dark suits entering. His attractive, brunette assistant gave him a worried glance. He knew immediately that the two new arrivals were with the authorities, and why they had come to his bar. "Good evening, gentlemen," he said. "I'll be with you in a minute."

"Agents Rhodes and Kerwin. Homeland Security," Rhodes said. "Can we talk in private?"

After a moment's hesitation, Bill caught the attention of his barmaid. "Can you mind the fort for me, Jenny?" He turned back to the two agents. "Follow me."

Kerwin and Rhodes followed him into his office in the back.

Rhodes closed the door behind them and stood beside Kerwin in the disarranged room. They quickly took out their identifications.

Bill swallowed hard.

Rhodes began. "Three people were in your bar earlier today, and—"

"Brandon Drake," Bill said.

"He escaped."

Bill didn't respond, at a loss as to what to say. *I'm glad to hear it?* Or, *Oh, my God, they're going ahead with their trip to L.A.* Ultimately, he decided leading these guys to them was preferable to them dying a grisly death at the hands a ruthless human trafficking organization. "All right, guys. Please take a seat." He gestured to two molded plastic seats scattered at non-specific positions in the room, and then perched himself on the edge of his paper-cluttered desk.

Kerwin pulled up a chair. "OK, what can you tell us about Brandon Drake and his two companions? Do you have any idea where they might be headed?"

"Only roughly," Bill said.

"What's that supposed to mean?"

"It's a long story. A young woman stopped by the bar yesterday. Turns out it was Drake's sister. She was apparently a nun who'd run away from the convent over the ways there."

"We know all about that."

"She got picked up in the bar by a scumbag named Fabian Rodriguez."

"Who's that?"

"A Puerto Rican scout for a sex slavery outfit based in L.A."

Rhodes took out a pen and a small notepad. "Is there anything you can tell us about these people?"

"Sapphire. That's all I know. That's what I told Drake and his brother."

Rhodes scribbled down the name.

"You have no idea what this person's real name is?" Kerwin said.

"No. I don't think anybody does. But if those kids are heading out there to break the nun out, they're gonna be comin' home in body bags."

Rhodes held up the notepad. "I'll have this run through the system and see what turns up."

"For what it's worth," Bill said, "I sure as hell hope you guys get to them before they get to Sapphire."

Kerwin took out his card and placed it on the desk next to Bill. "If you see anything of this Rodriguez guy, I want you to call me."

Rhodes and Kerwin stood and exited the office.

Bill remained seated on the desk staring at Kerwin's card, his mind flooded with thoughts of the last two days' events.

Twenty-Six

Director Wilmot

Wilmot entered his new office. *Wolfe's office*. Surveying the room as a victor would relish the spoils of war, he smiled with gloating self-adoration, despite his fatigue. He'd spent the night performing his duties, including accepting his new appointment from the CIA director, and handling hordes of journalists over Wolfe's death.

He turned to the desk and savored the moment from the seat of his new directorship. Now, finally, he was in a position of considerable authority, with access to information he had long been denied.

He recalled how, after being an officer of SDT since he was twenty-one, the sense of pride that had come over him at twenty-eight. Wolfe had assigned him to assist Senator Garrison Treadwell with an investigation into a well-concealed al-Qaeda cell, which had been plotting to initiate an attack against Langley itself. The perpetrators were soon apprehended, by which time, Wilmot and Treadwell had developed a close mentor/apprentice relationship.

Slowly, and with great caution, Treadwell had probed the young agent's mindset, and manipulated his desire for power, his pride, and his hubris. As far as Wilmot knew, he'd been the first recruit in Treadwell's plot to elevate the status of America and its economy, no matter the cost. Treason was a word he'd forced into the deepest recesses of his subconscious, in deference to ambition, and his own newfound sense of purpose.

That was five years ago.

Treadwell's covert faction had grown considerably over the following three years. It had all been enabled by the senator's ability to procure, manipulate, and offer extraordinary wealth to those who joined him. He never revealed his agenda to any of whom he wasn't completely certain.

Wilmot's involvement had always been kept secret from the others, forcing him to swallow his pride, and act as a mere agent who occasionally helped Treadwell. Operatives such as Payne, Ogilsby, Woodford, Kerwin, and Rhodes, had performed all of Treadwell's dirty work, while Wilmot remained in the shadows.

However, there were secrets that Treadwell had, without doubt, kept from him. He was now in a position to finally uncover those secrets. Wolfe had access to high-level security clearance files that, hitherto, Wilmot had not—specifically, anything relating to Brandon Drake.

With his new clearance, Wilmot entered the codes and passwords into the desk keypad. The computer monitor displayed a small search bar in the top right hand corner, into which he typed in 'Brandon Drake.'

Multiple links to files relating to Drake's history appeared. He scanned through them, bypassing details of Drake's past army exploits, and reinstated reports of his frequent convictions for military misconduct. It seemed Treadwell had erased them all from the official record.

He finally discovered a file bearing the title *Project: Scorpion.* Clicking on it, he found it led to a recovered Treadwell file that required further clearance. After entering a second username and password he'd only been provided with the day before, the file opened:

```
Subject: Brandon Drake, Sergeant. 82nd
Airborne Division
Condition: Stable (Head injury, with
indeterminate amnesia)
Memory revision specialist: Dr.
Frederick DeSouza, Neurobiologist,
Keene, Cheshire County, New Hampshire.
```

Wilmot stared at the screen in bewilderment. What was the meaning of the term *revision* with regards to Drake's memory? Why didn't it say *restoration*? Surely calling in a neurobiologist to treat an amnesia patient would have been for the purpose of restoring his memory.

Why hadn't Treadwell told him what his plans had been for Drake? He'd been his right hand man, and yet the senator had kept key information from him. He couldn't deny his bitterness and the affront to his pride.

He was alerted to a knock on the door. "Come in."

Deborah Beaumont stepped inside with a hostile expression. She was clearly perturbed by Wolfe's death, and the subsequent reality that she was now subservient to a man she despised. "Dr. Steven McKay to see you, *sir*."

Wilmot stood, eager to bring an end to an irritating investigation. "Please, send him in."

Moments later, a man in his late thirties entered the office. Wilmot had been taken aback by the resemblance between his visitor and his late partner, Martyn McKay, when he'd first met him at Martyn's funeral. Aside from the thinning hair and the man being several inches shorter, the similarity between him and his deceased brother was notable. "Dr. McKay. It's good to see you again."

"Steven, please."

"Very well. Take a seat, Steven."

"This investigation has been going on for two years, and Wolfe was handling it. Now you're telling me he was the one who murdered my brother?"

"He was found hanged in his home. He left a suicide note confessing to the murder." Wilmot took a photocopy from the desk and slid it across the table. "This is why I called you over. The original is still with forensics, but we have verification that Wolfe's fingerprints and DNA are all over it. I'll forward a report to you as soon as it's finalized."

McKay looked at the photocopy, shaking his head. "It was him all along. That certainly explains why there had been no developments in the investigation all these months. Where the hell is this country going when we have corrupt frauds like that in positions of authority?"

"It's disturbing, all right," Wilmot said with convincing faux sincerity. "Your brother and I were up to our necks in it with the investigation into Treadwell. We thought it was all over, and now this. Wolfe and Treadwell were at the top of this conspiracy from day one, it seems."

"You've certainly done well out of it," McKay said sardonically.

Wilmot leaned forward. "Steven, not an hour has gone by since Wolfe's death that I haven't played that night over in my head. Martyn and I had been interviewing two of Treadwell's assassins, and we were both highly-strung. We went back to Martyn's place to get drunk, and when I'd had my fill, I left. If I'd had a stronger stomach, I wouldn't be here today. Wolfe would have shot me as sure as he shot your brother."

"I suppose that's one way of looking at it."

"Ten more minutes. That's all it would have taken, from what I've worked out."

McKay stood again. "Count your blessings then."

Wilmot moved around the table and outstretched his hand. McKay took it, albeit with a strained expression. Wilmot could detect the man's trust in intelligence personnel had been deeply scarred by the turn of events.

"I think that's all I need for now," Steven said. "But I'll be expecting that full report."

"You have my word. It's good to see you again. I'm so sorry about what happened to Martyn. He was a fine operative and a good friend."

"Thank you."

The moment McKay closed the door behind him, Wilmot's eyes assumed a sinister glare. It was unlikely McKay was going to leave it at that, and there was a possibility he might become a considerable inconvenience to SDT. There was also the immediate threat posed by Jed Crane.

With haste, Wilmot returned to his desk, took out his unlawfully-smuggled cell phone, and selected his contact. The reply came quickly. "Garrett, I need you to get out to Nevada and track down Crane. He's already had a day's head start . . . No, Kerwin and Rhodes called in last night. They're on their way back. Drake's heading to Los Angeles, apparently, so I've got some planning to do . . .

Yeah, I need to meet up with you too, but it'll have to wait. First, I have some business to attend to in New Hampshire. You just take care of Jed Crane. When you find him, you know what to do."

Twenty-Seven

Fallen Hero

Brandon covered his face with his cap and low-hanging hair. He followed Belinda and Tyler into the Days Inn South Lenwood Hotel, in Barstow, California. Night had fallen, and they had no choice but to stop. Brandon was in need of rest, and they knew it was pointless continuing on to Los Angeles with no information on Sapphire's whereabouts.

As Tyler checked them in under assumed names, Brandon subtly concealed himself under an alcove. His spaced-out gaze fell onto the restaurant, and shiver went through him. He didn't know why, but presumed it was just another glitch in his withdrawal recovery.

Belinda approached him and stood across his path to provide additional shielding. "Are you OK?" she said.

"Just tired."

She placed her hand on his shoulder. "As soon as Tyler's checked us in, you can get some sleep."

As if on cue, Tyler joined them and handed Brandon a key. "Room one-oh-six. Go get some sleep, bro."

Brandon smiled wearily. "Thanks." He took Belinda's hand, and they made their way to the elevator.

Tyler squeezed between them and placed his arms around their shoulders. "Hey, listen up, guys. You have yourselves a restful night. I'll work on finding a possible location for Sapphire, OK?"

"OK," Brandon grunted.

"You got the Alka Seltzer?"

Brandon tapped his jacket pocket as they stepped into the elevator.

"Good. Keep taking them. We need you in full form, A.S.A.F.P."

The elevator doors opened, and Tyler stepped out first. "I'm in one-oh-nine, so we're gonna be pretty close."

They walked along the corridor of rooms. Belinda found room 106 first. "This is ours, babe."

"I'll see you two in the morning," Tyler said.

Tyler entered his room and closed the door behind him. He braced his back up against the door, overcome with exhaustion. Nevertheless, he still had work to do.

Reaching into his inside pockets, he took out two cell phones: one, his own, and the other, Brandon's sat-scrambler phone. After searching through the numbers in his own phone, he came to a number marked: Alex Home. Using the sat-scrambler, he punched in Alex's number, and waited for the reply. "Alex? Hey, how're you doing, bud?"

Alex Dalton stumbled out of bed to answer the phone, and took it with him into the living room. He made his way toward his sofa, taking in the neon splendor of the city of Dallas through the window. "Ty?" he said, slightly annoyed. "Jesus, man. It's past midnight."

"Actually, it's only past ten here," Tyler said, as though it made any difference.

"Where the hell are you? Your dad's been real worried about you."

"Yeah. I've been real worried about me too. Look man, I really need your help."

"Sure, what's going on? Where are you?"

"I can't tell you that. Don't worry. Nobody's gonna pinpoint me with the phone I'm using. How much do you know about the underground scene in L.A.?"

Alex looked at his phone, puzzled. "What do you mean? Gangs? Drugs?"

"Prostitutes."

Alex thought about it for a moment and cringed. There was only one person he knew who was even remotely connected to that world, and they didn't see eye to eye. The woman in question had particular personality traits he'd never been comfortable with. Those traits had led to a rather emotional end to their former relationship.

But Tyler was his best friend, and he sounded desperate. "Well, maybe one, but not exactly prostitution in the street sense."

"OK, let me explain. Somewhere in L.A., there's a prostitution and human trafficking outfit led by some clown named Sapphire. These guys are killers, bud. I just need word on where we can talk to someone who'd know anything about them."

Alex swallowed hard. "Human trafficking? Are you serious?"

"Deadly."

Alex reached for a pen and paper on his glass living room table and scribbled down 'Sapphire.' "But Ty, why are you looking for these people?"

"They have my sister."

The moments ticked by in painful silence.

"Alex? You still there?"

"Y-yeah, I'm here."

"Look man, I need you to promise me not to say a word to my dad about this."

"No, of course I won't. I'll get on this Sapphire business right away."

"Thanks. There's another name to check out too. A Fabian Rodriguez. He's tied up with this shit, and they apparently have some involvement with what goes on around Avenue Nineteen."

Alex wrote down the name and details. "OK. Leave it to me."

"Thanks, Alex. I really appreciate this."

"No problem, bud."

The call ended.

Alex immediately dialed out again. Within moments, a familiar voice answered. "Hey, Miranda. It's Alex. Long time no speak, babe. How are you doing?"

***

Belinda lay beside Brandon with deep concern. He had yet to fall asleep, and she felt an emotional need to talk to him. So much needed to be discussed. "Brandon?"

He merely grunted a response.

"What's happening to us?"

With minimal energy, he turned over to face her. "We both have issues, and we both messed up. Big time. We can't take it all back. All we can do is move on and deal with it the best we can."

She could see he was having difficulty keeping his eyes open and decided to accept his answer as best she could for now. "All right, let's get some sleep."

He sank his head back onto the pillow.

Belinda held him and closed her eyes, her thoughts dominated by the desperate hope that he would return to his former greatness. But in her heart, she doubted it would happen any time soon. Memories of the many months she'd dreamed of being reunited with him, and the hope that they could recapture what they once had, tormented her. The dynamic, romantic hero of two years ago was gone. All that now remained was a shell of a man.

***

Emily sat at a bureau in a bedroom with no windows. She presumed she was still in the high rise apartment on Wilshire Boulevard. Her senses were hopelessly disoriented by the drug Fabian and the woman had injected into her. She felt they might have administered further shots to her, but she couldn't be certain. She didn't even know how long she'd been in captivity. Was it a day? Two days? A week? She'd lost all sense of time.

She would've considered the room comfortable, even luxurious, if it wasn't for the circumstances. The bed was delicious, and the master bathroom was plush and spotless.

She looked into her tear-stained eyes in the mirror above the bureau, constantly filled with regret about leaving the convent. She'd been unhappy there, but she'd always known where she stood. At least it had been safe. Now, she was lost in every conceivable way. She was lost to the world, to her sisters, to everything she had ever known—and to her god.

She thought of Father Henry, the closest she'd ever had to a male friend. He'd always been so warm and kind. She'd often fantasized he might have been her long-lost older brother, whom God had led into the priesthood to secretly watch over her.

Her mind frequently roamed into the realms of myriad possibilities. She was an orphan. Did she really have siblings? Or was she an only child? Did she have a sister? Or a brother? If so, how many? Where were they now? Did they ever wonder about her, and who she might be? It was all just a fantasy, but she needed her imaginary family so desperately in that moment. The dream—the merest possibility—brought her the slightest of comforts.

Placing her elbows on the bureau, she clasped her hands together. "Heavenly Father, Blessed Mother, I beseech thee. Forgive me my sins. Deliver me from the evil that has taken me. Whomever you may appoint, send them, in your mercy, to liberate me from the wretchedness of my damnation. Oh, Lord, I know that I am unworthy and undeserving of your favor. But I beg of you that you may grant that this chalice be taken from me."

The door clicked open. She snapped her head to it with a start. Her heart raced and her hands trembled.

The oriental woman entered first. Her eyes were as cold as ever, with a predatory glare.

Fabian followed behind her with a tall, rugged-looking man who appeared to be perhaps Greek or Italian. His hair was jet black, and his skin tone was a light shade of bronze. The hardness in his face was threatening.

"We will be moving you to another location tomorrow, Emily," the woman said. "Before that, there are a number of basic skills for you to learn." She snapped her fingers.

Fabian stepped forward and took a syringe out of his pocket.

Emily looked with horror as he removed the sheath from the needle. "Oh, no. No, no, no."

"Just take it easy. This is to help you," he said.

"Help me to what?"

"To not find it so terrible. It's for your own good."

He grasped her arm. Too terrified to resist, her heart sank into the pits of dread. "Why are you doing this to me, Fabian?"

He inserted the needle into the vein. "It's nothing personal. It's just business."

The woman turned to the other man with a commanding demeanor. "Just remember, you don't take it any farther than we discussed. You don't touch her where it counts. Are we clear?"

He nodded.

"If you do anything to affect her value, I'll see to it that something similar happens to you."

Emily closed her eyes and began to mutter in prayer. She knew she was going to be violated, but she had no idea to what extent.

Fabian rejoined the woman and they exited the room, closing the door behind them.

As the drugs began to take effect, Emily felt like she was dreaming. The fear was leaving her, and the feeling of floating took over her senses. The man before her no longer seemed so threatening. He came closer to her, but somehow, she didn't seem to care.

Twenty-Eight

The Memory Man

Andrew Wilmot settled up with the cab driver. He stepped out onto the drive of a nineteenth-century colonial house in one of the more secluded areas of Keene, New Hampshire. Never having visited New England before, it took a moment for his city-acclimatized eyes to adjust to the rural, affluent, historical ambiance of the state.

The cab drove away as he stared, filled with the anticipation, at the sizable, million dollar property.

After pressing the doorbell, he surveyed the well-maintained garden and surrounding grounds while he waited.

The door opened, and he turned to see a man in his mid-sixties. He was shorter than Wilmot's six feet, the top of his head stopping at the bottom of Wilmot's chin. His thinning gray hair and circular-rimmed spectacles seemed to give him a harmless appearance. A cream cashmere sweater, and the house slippers on his feet, conveyed the message he was a man of leisure. It was clear he'd earned his wealth and had settled into life enjoying the fruits of his labor.

Wilmot smiled cordially. "Doctor DeSouza? Frederick DeSouza?"

"Yes, Agent Wilmot," DeSouza said in a polished British accent. He offered his hand.

"You know me?"

DeSouza smiled. "Not really. Please, come inside."

193

Wilmot followed the older man into the house.

"Let's go into my study, shall we?" DeSouza said. "May I offer you a drink? Tea? Coffee? A glass of sherry, perhaps?"

"Do you have any bourbon?"

"Certainly. Come in and take a seat." DeSouza entered his small, homely study, and approached the drinks cabinet. "We met once, rather fleetingly, in Senator Treadwell's office on Capitol Hill, five years ago. I was just leaving as you were coming in."

"I don't recall, sir." Wilmot sat in the guest chair at the doctor's desk, and took a crystal cut glass with a double shot of bourbon from his host. "Thank you."

"So, what can I do for you?"

"What can you tell me about Brandon Drake?"

The doctor's brow furrowed. "I don't understand. If you don't know what my connection to Brandon Drake is, what brought you here?"

"Two days ago, I was appointed director of SDT. Since then, I've had access to Senator Treadwell's files, and I came across your name."

"Well, this might sound strange, but I never actually met Brandon Drake."

"But I found your name on—"

"Oh, indeed you did, and I was responsible for his reconditioning. But I was never in his presence when he was conscious."

"How's that?"

"Drake had received a head injury in Afghanistan. Before Garrison brought me to him, it had been established that he was stricken with amnesia as a result of the trauma.

I had no doubt his condition was temporary, but it made what I had to do so much easier."

Wilmot edged closer to the man eagerly. "What did you mean when you said 'reconditioning'?"

"My hypotheses and papers were utilized by the CIA during the Cold War. Memory is my field of expertise. It has long been established that the human mind is malleable. Fictional experiences and incidents can be assimilated by the brain, and recalled as true memories."

Wilmot sipped his bourbon thoughtfully. "And this is what you did to Brandon Drake? You're saying he's not who he thinks he is?"

"That's correct. I had a long-standing friendship with Garrison Treadwell. He employed my expertise on a project he referred to as *Project: Scorpion*. The CIA wanted me to revise Brandon Drake's persona because he was unmanageable. My task was to neutralize his violent temperament in order to dispatch him on covert operations. It was nothing new. I'd been involved in a similar project in the seventies."

Wilmot's eyebrows rose as all of the mysteries were beginning to fall into place. Treadwell had arranged for Drake to have a new personality, which he thought he could manage in order to use him for his own purposes. DeSouza believed he'd been working for a legitimate CIA operation because of his long-standing friendship with Treadwell, whom he evidently trusted. And then there was his obvious penchant for money.

He turned back to the doctor. "Well, this time, it didn't quite work out. Drake is a maniac on the loose right now."

DeSouza looked away with disappointment in his eyes. "So I gather from the recent turn of events on the news. You see, the techniques I used are not perfect. Using electro-chemical stimulus and oral, subliminal induction can only affect the memories of the conscious mind. The inherent persona remains within the subconscious. Pre-existing skills, intellect, and habits will still be apparent after the memory revision has been performed."

Wilmot's mind was awash with possibilities he hadn't previously contemplated. DeSouza had just provided him with an option where he could use Drake for his own ends. He marveled at the irony. Within minutes, he'd made the transition from wanting Drake dead, to wanting him very much alive. Drake had always been Treadwell's secret, which he'd kept from him. Now, he wanted Drake, and to succeed where Treadwell failed.

He also knew that having Drake under his control would ease his sense of humiliation after suffering the most severe beating of his life at Drake's hands. With such considerations, DeSouza was sure to make an invaluable ally. "Can the procedure be performed a second time on the same subject?"

"Once a person has manufactured memories, and subsequent experiences following them, they remain with him for life. Brandon Drake's true persona still resides within his subconscious. Moving a conflicting persona into that subconscious alongside the original could have serious consequences."

"Like what?"

"Complete cerebral shutdown. There is a strong possibility he could become irretrievably catatonic."

Wilmot sought his words carefully. "Drake is unstable. He's out there right now somewhere, and we are doing everything we can to bring him in."

"I see."

"When that happens, sir, I need your help. We will cover the costs to make him viable again."

The doctor's eyes widened. "I can only try. But as I said, there are no guarantees."

"Don't worry about it. I'll take full responsibility. This will be an official intelligence operation, and your cover will be protected."

DeSouza looked at him suspiciously. "Not protected enough, judging from the fact that you are here, sitting in my office. I was also investigated after Treadwell died. No action was taken, but it was enough to tell me *Project: Scorpion* wasn't as official as I was led to believe."

Wilmot finished his bourbon and stood. "I'll take care of everything. We're on the same team, doctor, and America needs your help."

DeSouza stood. "I'll be waiting for your call, Ag— *Director* Wilmot."

"First we have to catch him." Wilmot turned and headed out toward the front door.

"I'll await your call," DeSouza said.

"Indeed. Goodbye, sir."

The door closed. Wilmot processed what DeSouza had told him, and the implications that came with it. Wolfe had obviously known about the mind control operation, but kept a tight lid on it for fear of it getting out. If the information had found its way to the press, there would have been a national panic.

He took out his cell phone and called for a cab. Immediately afterwards, he punched in the number of his favorite contact. "Garrett? Any word on Crane?" Listening intently to the response, a broad smile spread across his face.

***

Jed Crane sat on the bed in a hotel room off a remote, rural highway, just outside the small border village of Stanton, Utah. He felt it was obscure enough for him to conceal himself for the night. Two days' stubble had produced a shadow on his face. The suit he'd been wearing when he fled from Crispin Rock remained his only clothing.

The room was basic and simple. It was clean, and offered the essentials with a shower, toilet, toothpaste and brush, and a television set. There was no window to the outside, only a plasterboard and wooden wall, which created a claustrophobic, but strangely secure atmosphere.

Now into his second night on the run, he was no closer toward formulating his next move. He struggled to come to terms with how quickly his life had fallen apart. The constant fear that Wilmot had already managed to track him was debilitating.

It was approaching one o'clock in the morning, and weariness overcame him. After stripping down to his shorts, he climbed into bed and switched off the light.

With difficulty, he finally fell asleep, although subconsciously retaining a degree of awareness.

In the midst of his half-sleep, at just past 3:00 a.m., he was awoken by the sound of his door clicking shut, followed by a snapping sound.

And then, he became aware of the faint-but-unmistakable odor of pitch. His eyes snapped open, his heart racing. Throwing the sheets off him, he bolted for the door in one swift move. It was locked.

He ran across to the bedside cabinet, picked up the room key, and noticed a faint red glow coming from underneath the bed. Peering under it, he saw a digital C4 explosive time bomb counting down in minutes and seconds, reading: 1:32.

Bolting upright again, he hurried over to the door and inserted the key, but it wouldn't penetrate the lock. He then realized the snapping sound he'd heard was a duplicate or skeleton key being broken off after being inserted on the other side.

His immediate thought was to take his pistol out of his jacket and blow the lock. But there were occupied rooms on either side of him. Whoever was in them would die in the explosion. He couldn't simply run and leave them, but there wasn't enough time to warn them. The bomb was timed to facilitate the escape of the assassin, who obviously didn't want to attract witnesses with the sound of a gunshot to his head.

Rage took over his reason. He couldn't accept the concept that human beings, whom he'd actually been associated with, were merciless, wanton killers. They had no regard for the lives of innocents. It didn't matter to them whether they were men, women, or children.

Pounding his fist despairingly into the door, he roared, "Garrett!"

Coming back to his senses, he rapidly spun around again, and stared at the bomb as the countdown continued.

0:46—0:45—0:44—0:43—

Twenty-Nine

The One That Got Away

Jed pulled the bedside drawer open and took out his car keys. Hooked on the ring was a circular disc with four small rectangular protrusions of varying dimensions—perfect miniature screwdrivers. He knelt down again, and frantically placed the smallest of them into the screws on top of the explosive device. He twisted them out with life and death speed.

As he came to the last screw, he noticed the timer reading: 0:23.

His heart pounded so fiercely it was affecting his vision, and his hyperventilation almost caused him to black out.

As the cover of the bomb came away, he looked down to see a series of wires connected to the timer. Removal of the wires in the wrong sequence would cause an immediate detonation.

0:20.

Oh, sweet Jesus. Stay calm, Jed. Keep a clear head. It's just a standard C4. Perspiration poured from his brow. His trembling fingers gripped a blue wire and disconnected it. Nothing happened.

0:17.

Next, he took the yellow wire out safely, but the countdown continued. *Green one and green two next. But which is one and which is two?*

He suffered a violent start at the sound of a knock on the door.

"What's goin' on in there? We heard a shout," a male voice said.

"J-just a second." Jed chanced removing the green wire on the right first. He had a gut feeling Garrett would've arranged green one and two the wrong way around just to trick him. *Oh, please God.*

Removing the second green wire and then the first didn't result in detonation, proving his suspicion correct.

0:05.

Grasping the red wire last, he closed his eyes. With his teeth chattering, he removed it to the heavenly sound of a faint beep.

He glanced down to catch the terrifying sight of '0:01' for a microsecond before the digits disappeared completely.

Slumping back against the bedside cabinet, he let out a deep breath, consumed with relief.

"Sir?" the voice at the door pressed.

Jed remembered the other problem Garrett had left him with. It seemed the solution was standing on the other side of the door. Still shaking, he hurried across the room. "Hey, there, buddy. I really could use your help."

"What's that?"

"Some asshole broke a key in my door, so I can't get out. Do you think you could tell the janitor?"

"Sure will. But we heard what sounded like screaming, and a banging noise. Are you OK?"

"Oh, that. Don't worry about it. I was having a nightmare and fell out of bed."

"Right. Gotcha. Just hang in there. I'll get some help with the door."

"Thank you, bud. You're a life saver."

Jed waited until he heard the man walking away. Finally, he returned to the bed.

Sitting on the edge, he rubbed his damp face with his palm, and lightly chuckled. "Nice try, Garrett. Guess your zero-percent failure rate just went right down the crapper."

After a few moments, he collected himself, and took the diffused explosive device from under the bed. He looked at it hopelessly, affirming his belief that wherever he went, they would find him. He wouldn't be safe anywhere.

Then he remembered Brandon, Belinda, and Tyler were heading into L.A. to find information on a human trafficking organization. Wilmot, Kerwin, and Rhodes would undoubtedly be aware of that by now, and were most likely in pursuit of them. He would be just as wise to step directly into the fray rather than run from it. After all, attack had long been recognized as the most effective form of defense.

He took his backpack from the cupboard and concealed the bomb inside it.

***

Tamara Quinn approached a seemingly-normal residence in San Fernando. To the unenlightened eye, it appeared as a standard urban house in a regular built-up area, north of Hollywood. However, the area was well-known for its innocent-looking homes actually being used as studios for the production of countless adult movies.

At twenty-six, Tamara knew the traces of hardship were apparent in her visage. Nevertheless, attired in a respectable three-quarter-length blue skirt and white blouse, she appeared convincing as a corporate executive. Her short blonde hair completed her image of a hardened survivor, who'd made the transition from street hooker to acquisitions manager for a record label.

She rang the doorbell and waited. She hadn't seen her friend, Miranda Curtis, in over a year.

The door opened, and she smiled at the tall, stern-faced young woman before her. It was a surprise for her to see Miranda without her usual, gothic, white face makeup. The dyed, raven-black hair and black lipstick remained, along with a black, leather lace-up bodice, tight-fitting leather trousers, high-heeled leather boots, and a spike-studded collar. "Hi, Mir."

"Come on in."

Tamara followed her inside and immediately noticed the hallway lined with candles in holders on the black walls. Whips, canes, and shackles hooked on the wall acted as bizarre decorations. Above were rows of candles, and an oppressive, gloss black ceiling.

As they came to a closed living room door at the end of the corridor, Tamara glanced at an open doorway to her immediate left. She grinned, knowing the stairwell, with its archaic, faux-stone walls, led to Miranda's play-dungeon.

"I always keep the door to the living area closed," Miranda said. "I don't want the subs to see anything domestic in here."

'Subs' being a shortened term for *submissives*, Tamara understood perfectly. "I taught you well, it seems."

"You better believe it. I get a lot of repeat business."

They stepped into a regular-looking living room, fully carpeted with sofas, armchairs, and a widescreen television fixed to the wall.

Miranda sat down on the edge of her sofa. "I asked you over here because I had a call from an ex-boyfriend of mine."

"Oh? Who's that?"

"Alex Dalton. Gorgeous son of a bitch, playboy, and high-flying corporate whiz. He works for a major corporation in Dallas."

"I see. So, what can I do for you?"

"Sapphire."

Tamara sat opposite Miranda and felt the color draining from her face. "Are you serious?"

"I don't know. All I know is what Alex told me. He needs to know about Sapphire, and where he's holed up."

"Forget it. Sapphire isn't a subject anyone should be asking about."

"Why?"

"I was working the street five years ago, remember?"

"Yeah, that's why I'm asking you. You're the only one I know who would even have a clue about this guy. Who is he?"

"Sapphire came to town and took over most of the street vice. I managed to escape from that life before he could take me, as he did so many of the others."

"What I think Alex wants to know is, where does this Sapphire take people after he's kidnapped them?"

Tamara shook her head in a warning manner. "I don't know. And even if I did, I wouldn't like to say. There's no way anybody could survive trying a stunt like a rescue, if that's what he's thinking. Sapphire practically runs Los Angeles from the shadows."

"You want me to tell you who's been taken?" Miranda said. "And who's trying to break her out?"

"No, and it doesn't matter. Even the LAPD won't go anywhere near them. It would take an army to pull it off, and I doubt it's a battalion that wants to do this."

Miranda looked away coyly, and Tamara noticed. "It isn't an army, is it?"

"Not exactly. But it's not far off."

Tamara's intrigue peaked. "OK, who?"

"It's Brandon Drake. Sapphire has his sister."

"Brandon Drake? The soldier who escaped from Leavenworth?"

"Yes, and he's not alone."

"Oh, boy." Tamara was quiet for a moment as she considered the possibilities.

Miranda moved across the room and knelt before her friend. "Tam, we've known each other for years. Isn't there anything you can tell me? Isn't there someone who would know?"

"Not really. I mean, there's an urban legend, but nothing real."

"What urban legend?"

"Siren. But, it's just a crazy story that was going around at about the time I got off the streets."

"So, what's the story?"

Tamara sighed. "I wish I hadn't said anything now. I can't take it seriously, and I think it's a waste of time."

"Humor me."

Tamara looked at her curiously. "You're going to a lot of trouble for this Alex guy. Wanna tell me why?"

"He . . . He still means a lot to me, all right? He couldn't accept my sexual preferences, but—"

"You're still burning a candle for him, right?"

"Something like that."

Awkwardly, Tamara said, "OK. It was in the early days, when Sapphire first arrived. It was only ever spoken of in hushed whispers. A story about a beautiful young girl. She was a backpacker who was picked up by Sapphire's scouts in Tucson, and taken to the place where he sells women to the highest bidder. According to the legend, she escaped."

"So, where is she?"

"I'm not even convinced she ever existed. Street girls spin tall yarns. Helps to keep up their morale. She's referred to as Siren. Rumor has it she set herself up in another state. New life, new name. Someone once suggested even a new face. It's absurd."

"Maybe not."

"On the street, they used to whisper about it. 'The one that got away,' they'd say. But I just used to roll my eyes at it. Typical street bullshit."

"But what if it isn't?" Miranda said. "What if there's a woman out there who is the only one outside of Sapphire's members, or whatever they're called, who actually knows where this shit goes down? If it's true, how do we get in contact with her?"

"If she actually exists, she's not gonna want to talk to anyone. People disappear for a reason."

Miranda sat back in deflation.

Tamara softened a little. "All right, I'll try, OK?"

"Try what?"

"I think it's a complete waste of time, but . . ."

"But?"

"But just on the chance there's anything to this, I'm still in touch with a girl I used to work with on Avenue Nineteen. But I have to be so damn careful. She's being watched almost twenty-four-seven. They all are. This will just be the first step. It'll take one lead to lead to another, and another, until I can communicate with someone who knows how to contact Siren, who is most likely a myth. Don't get your hopes up."

Concern appeared in Miranda's eyes. "Tamara, don't do anything, please. We'll find another way. Don't go anywhere near Avenue Nineteen. I just wanted to help Alex."

Tamara stood and smiled reassuringly. "I won't be going anywhere near there, I promise. I wouldn't risk being seen talking to any one of them. What you're looking for is an email address, if it even exists. I know how to play the cyber-anonymity game."

Miranda gave her a peck on the cheek. "Thank you, Tam."

"I'll do my best."

Tamara parked her new Lexus outside an internet café on Palm Canyon Drive in Palm Springs.

She stepped out of the car, entered the building, and walked through rows of people conducting their business at the screens.

She approached the refreshments bar at the end, purchased a cappuccino. After buying an access shield for thirty minutes of internet usage, she then made her way across to a secluded corner of the room.

Sitting down behind a monitor screen, she inserted her shield into the scanner. The screen flashed up a welcome message, allowing her to open up an internet connection.

Her mind became filled with apprehension and hope. If there was even a chance of Sapphire being taken down, she knew she had to do whatever she could to make it happen.

She proceeded to log onto an exclusive ghost blog where she would be completely unidentifiable, except to the one she was attempting to contact. The account had been set up at another internet café in Mexico, where she'd created her username *Firebird*. There was no name, no IP address, and no other form of identification that could be linked to her. Such was the nature of the extreme risk. Never before had she felt as anxious.

A box appeared on screen bearing the invitation:

```
Enter your comment here: -
```

Tamara typed in her message:

```
Firebird: Contact me as soon as you
can. There are people who need your
help, and they're not regular folks. I
think these are the ones you've been
praying for.
```

She checked the message and once she was satisfied, pressed 'send.' Sitting back, she finished her cappuccino.

As she was about to log off and collect her credit shield, a response appeared on the screen:

```
Siren: Tell me more.
```

Thirty

Interceptor

Extremely frustrated, Tyler strolled along the aisle of a convenience store in Barstow with a basket of provisions. It was the morning of the third day he'd been stranded with his brother and Belinda in the hotel awaiting word from Alex. Brandon couldn't leave the hotel room for fear of being identified, yet again placing him in a type of prison. A 'do not disturb' sign affixed to the room's door handle prevented even the cleaning staff from entering. Tyler had generously paid the manager not to be concerned, lightly laughing it off as a long weekend for two friends 'doing what lovers do.' However, as the days rolled by, it was beginning to wear a little thin.

Moving along the newspaper and magazine aisle, he scanned the pages to see if he could find any articles about Brandon, but there wasn't anything. As far as the media was concerned, he'd become old news already, which was certainly an advantage.

To his left, he noticed a comic book bearing the illustration of a man wearing the exact outfit he'd worn when he'd rescued Belinda in Denver. Brandon's outfit.

He picked up the copy of *Interceptor* #1, flicked through the pages, and quickly came to stylishly-illustrated panels of a man gliding a woman on a zip-line between two skyscrapers. Then they were in a blue sports car flying out of an exploding van. On the following page, it devolved into complete fiction as the flying car arrived in a cave-like underground hideout.

Regardless, it was abundantly clear his brother had been turned into a comic book superhero. As outlandish as the idea was, there was something about it that brought a smile to his persistently tense expression. He decided it was something Brandon had to see and took the comic to the checkout.

While carrying his provisions out to the parking lot, his cell phone buzzed in his pants pocket. He rested the two shopping bags next to the van, took out the phone, and answered. "Hello? Oh, hey Alex. What's happening?"

As he listened to Alex, he was seized with urgency. Quickly opening the van with his free hand, he threw the shopping bags into the footwell.

***

Brandon was finally coming through his period of alcohol withdrawal, surprised by how being confined to a hotel room had helped. There was no exposure to alcohol, no temptations, and Belinda was with him every step of the way.

Her support had grown since they arrived. She'd watched him drink gallons of water, and resume his physical training regime, confident the man he'd once been was very close to making a return.

He'd begun training on the day following their arrival, albeit with great difficulty, due to a dense head and reduced energy levels. By the second day, he was feeling livelier and able to attempt more vigorous workouts. Their love-making had also resumed with energy and passion.

Brandon had practically rearranged the room by taking away the bedside tables and pushing the bed into the far corner. The wide space that was left provided an ample environment for him to perform push-ups, then push-ups on his knuckles with his feet on the bed, sit-ups, crunches, and leg stretches. He pushed himself beyond the pain barrier, driven by an obsessive need to redeem himself and exorcise the booze from his system.

He practiced his karate kata moves within the space he'd created. It mystified Belinda how he knew the punches, blocks, and kicks when he had no recollection of ever learning them. They seemed to come to him by instinct.

She watched him joyously. As every hour of practice passed, his balance and precision improved, with a combination of sharp strikes to the air and graceful sweeping movements.

He completed his morning workout and stepped into the bathroom to freshen up.

Belinda stood up from the bed and a sudden nausea came over her. It was the second time she'd felt it since arriving at the hotel, although it passed quickly. She thought it was perhaps because she hadn't eaten. Hopefully, Tyler would be back soon with some food, or maybe he'd arrange something with room service again.

After half an hour, Brandon came out of the bathroom, clean and shaved. His long, damp hair hung in his eyes. He swiftly combed it back with his fingers.

Belinda looked at him with a hopeful stare. "Are you feeling better?"

"Much," he said. "I feel awake, alive, and like every last drop of that goddamn poison is finally out of my system."

She moved toward him amorously. "I can't tell you how happy I am to hear you say that." She held his affectionate gaze for a prolonged moment. "Come here."

He came toward her and put his arms around her. She immersing herself in his embrace, and owned the moment of her lover's long-awaited return. "I love you so much."

They were halted by a rapid knock on the door.

"Hey, guys. It's me," Tyler said.

"Yeah, hold on, bro. I'll be right with you." Brandon broke the embrace and opened the door.

Tyler hurried inside breathlessly with his two bags of provisions. "I'd have ordered something from downstairs, but we're gonna have to start on what I've got here."

"Why? What's going on?"

"I just had a call from Alex."

Brandon's eyes widened. "What's he say?"

"Just that everything with regards to Sapphire is 'in hand.' We should get to L.A. right away. I've got the address and details of the person we're supposed to contact."

"Who is it?"

Tyler rummaged around the inside pockets of his denim jacket and took out a hand-scrawled note. "Someone named Miranda Curtis. San Fernando."

"Who's that?"

"She's an ex-girlfriend of Alex's. Apparently, she has a contact who stands a chance of finding something out."

"OK, let's have a bite to eat and get packed."

Brandon took the provisions bags, and Tyler took out the rolled copy of *Interceptor* #1 from his inside pocket. "I thought maybe you'd like to see this too."

"What is it? You started reading comic books now?"

"No, but I think you're gonna want to read this one."

Brandon took the comic and scanned the cover and first few pages. "What the f—!"

Belinda looked over his shoulder, instantly deducing the story in the comic began with the Carringby attack and Brandon rescuing her. When all material from the newspaper reports and cell phone camera photos were exhausted, it became a completely fictional narrative. "No way."

Brandon finally broke into the unique laughter that could only come with the realization that he was now, officially, a comic book. It seemed like an eternity since any of them had laughed. Caught up in the contagion, Tyler and Belinda followed. The comic book seemed to add yet another dimension to the effect his story was having upon society.

After the levity died down, Brandon said, "Come on. Let's get ready."

"Sure." Tyler edged closer to his brother. "Hey, you sure you're OK? I mean—"

"I'm fine, Ty. Trust me. There's gonna be no more bullshit." He looked down repentantly. "I can't tell you how sorry I am."

Tyler smiled and tapped him on the shoulder. "All right, let's get moving."

Thirty-One

From the Shadows

Wilmot walked out of the elevator into his office floor, and made his way through the hustle and bustle of a regular day at Langley Headquarters. Several employees acknowledged him as he moved through the crowd with his brand new leather briefcase, but he was too preoccupied to reciprocate.

Arriving at Deborah Beaumont's office, he opened the door without knocking. Deborah turned to him, startled. The anger on her face was unmistakable. Wilmot ignored the contemptuous stare from behind the spectacles resting on the tip of her nose. "Tell Kerwin and Rhodes I want to see them immediately." He turned and exited the room, slamming the door behind him.

After entering his office, he placed the briefcase on his desk and sat down. He'd only been made aware during the last hour that Crane had survived, marking Garrett's first failure. And Crane was too dangerous to be still living.

The awaited knock on his door came within minutes. "Come in."

Kerwin stepped inside, followed by Rhodes.

"How did it go in New Hampshire?" Rhodes said.

"Very revealing, as it happens. We have a change of plans. I want Drake taken alive. There are options I never suspected, but we still need to find him. What'd you find out about this skin trade outfit?"

"Nothing," Kerwin said. "We've run a complete check on Sapphire, including the LAPD database and all vice arrest records. There's nothing on the guy."

Wilmot's brow crumpled. "Are you sure that bartender was telling you the truth? Is there any chance he was selling you a line of bullshit?"

Rhodes said, "No chance. If you'd have seen the look in his eyes, you'd know he was convinced. If none of it's true, he sure as hell believes it is, and so do the patrons in that bar. If it's bullshit, who took the nun? We spoke to everyone who saw her ride off with this Fabian Rodriguez."

"The bartender was afraid for his life," Kerwin said. "You don't fake fear like what we saw."

Wilmot tapped his lips pensively. "Something's going down, that's for sure, but we need to know what we're dealing with." He stood and paced the office, mentally formulating the best method of approach. "Get out to Los Angeles and do an initial investigation with the LAPD. Keep it low key. No overkill."

"Maybe you should come along," Rhodes said. "The director of SDT is likely to have more clout than we have."

"I intend to. I have to make a stop en route, so I'm giving you a head start."

"You got it."

Wilmot came closer to them with an intense glare. "I have a gut feeling this is a hell of a lot bigger than you guys suspect. We might need contingencies."

"What do you have in mind?" Kerwin said.

"I'm going to try to persuade Drake's old unit to assist us in bringing him in."

"You're thinking of calling in the Eighty-Second?"

"Just to have them on stand-by. It's their boy we're after. They've got more of a chance of talking him round and avoiding any unnecessary conflict. If I call the FBI in on this, all hell could break loose."

The two agents nodded in concurrence.

"OK, let's get to it," Kerwin said, turned, and exited the room with Rhodes.

Wilmot returned to his desk, picked up his desk phone and made a call. It was quickly answered by a professional-sounding female. "This is Director Andrew Wilmot at SDT. I'd like you to put me through to General Thaddeus Grant."

***

Buck Weston took in the fresh air as he walked through the stables of his lifelong home, Rolling Hills Ranch. The view surrounding the property, a vast spectacle of hills and greenery for as far as the eye could see, conveyed the pinnacle of majestic scenery in Southern Oregon.

A third generation cattle rancher, Buck had just turned forty-nine. He'd been divorced for five years, and was beginning to notice the signs of age in his face. His Stetson kept the rapid spread of gray in his hair concealed.

The news he'd just received from his ranch foreman had not been welcome. With some sadness, he approached the ranch hands' cabins, situated one hundred yards away from the main house.

He came to the end and gingerly knocked on the door of the last cabin. He could hear scuffling around inside, and his sadness deepened.

The door opened finally. He looked upon a woman in her late twenties wearing a red shirt tied off beneath her bust, leaving her abdomen exposed. Her denim shorts showed off her smooth, slender legs above her ankle boots. Her flowing, dark brown hair failed to disguise her blonde roots. Buck had always been curious about it. Didn't women usually choose to disguise their dark hair with blonde, and not the other way around?

"Hi, Buck," she said.

"Ralph told me you were leaving."

She looked behind her and gestured to an open suitcase. "I was just packing."

He stepped inside. "May I ask why?"

She turned away from him and resumed packing. "Some urgent personal business came up. I have to go to L.A. for awhile."

"Are you coming back?"

"Maybe."

He placed his hand on her shoulder, and she froze. He knew there was no chance of her returning, and could almost feel her pangs of conscience. He'd given her a job working with the horses, and providing her with a home. He also suspected she knew he was in love with her.

She turned around again, and he looked into her intensely dark brown eyes. They seemed to bear the spirit of a survivor, yet were graced with such gentle femininity. "You wanna talk about it?" he said.

"Nothing much to talk about. It's just personal stuff, nothing exciting."

He nodded in reluctant acceptance. "You just won't let anybody in, will you, Jodie?"

She threw another t-shirt in the case and turned back to him. "Buck, I really appreciate everything you've done for me. The job, a place to stay, but—"

"It's OK. It's none of my business, I know. But I sure am gonna miss you. You're the best damn stable hand I've ever had. I'd make you a partner in a heartbeat, if you'd let me. Till death do us part, even."

She threw her arms around him and kissed him tenderly on the cheek.

Buck couldn't figure it out. He knew his credentials. It wasn't every day that a girl met a successful, single, rugged, millionaire who was just crazy about her. Could it have been the fact he was almost twenty years her senior? She knew he'd been completely committed to his ex-wife. His marriage only ended when he discovered she was a predatory opportunist who'd attempted to financially defraud him. *Why won't she just take a chance on me?*

"I'm gonna miss you, Buck," she said.

"Yeah. Touché. You've been like one of the family. Three years is a long time. It's not gonna be the same around here without you."

Breaking the embrace, she returned to her suitcase. "Thank you. You don't know what that means to me."

"How are you traveling?"

"Catching a bus in two hours. It's a ten hour ride."

"Can I give you a ride to the station?"

"I'll be fine."

He turned away in exasperation. "You won't even let me give you a ride?"

She threw her laptop onto her clothes and zipped up the suitcase. "It's better this way. I really hate long goodbyes."

"I just want you to know you've got a home here whenever you want it." He took a wad of bills out of his pocket and handed them to her. "Please take this. It's just to tide you over."

With a reluctant expression, she took the money, and then picked up her suitcase. She followed him out and closed the door behind her. "Goodbye, Buck."

"Goodbye, Jodie."

Standing beside the cabin, he watched as she walked across the dusty yard, finally permitting his tears to come. He always knew this day would come, just as he'd always known she was running. From what, he had no idea. But expecting her to leave and actually facing it were worlds apart. "I'll always love you," he whispered.

Jodie succumbed to sadness and regret. Her stoicism made way for a rare show of tears when she reached the end of the stables. She'd developed a bond with the horses as she'd tended to them over the many months. She tried not to look at them as she departed.

Making her way around the sprawling grounds to the mile-long entrance, she recalled the summer's day when she'd arrived three years earlier. She'd already spent two years concealing herself by moving from one menial job to another. Before arriving in Jackson County, she'd traveled across Idaho and Wyoming, using countless aliases. She'd felt more at home and safer with Buck than anywhere else.

The other ranch hands had grown to accept and love her. She knew most of them harbored a secret desire to sleep with her, but she'd always maintained the boundaries.

If only she hadn't had to lie every single day. 'Jodie Madison' had been her most enduring pseudonym. She knew she couldn't have entered into a relationship with Buck when all she could offer him was a falsehood. She hadn't been able to connect with any of them beyond the occasional frivolous laugh and casual conversation.

Fear gripped her at the thought of emerging from the shadows to set foot in Los Angeles again.

But there was more than just herself at stake. If she could make contact with people who might be able to bring an end to the demons that plagued her, she could live free again, securing the freedoms of many others in the process.

And for the first time in five years, she would finally hear her true name again.

Thirty-Two

Hidden

Emily stared at her face in the mirror but didn't see herself. The woman in the reflection was a stranger to her. Wearing a delicate application of makeup, her complexion had been given a flawless appearance. Her hair had been lightened to a dark shade of blonde, and straightened from her slightly-wavy natural look. It fell shining and smelling of lilacs, onto her shoulders.

Barely aware she was under the effects of euphoria-inducing compounds and tranquilizers, she was constantly uncertain if she was dreaming. She was hardly aware of the brush stroking her hair from behind, or of the woman brushing it. The attendant had very dark hair and looked to be in her early twenties. Emily thought she was perhaps Chinese or Japanese.

Remotely conscious of the room she'd been confined to, she deduced it was a large bedroom with no windows. The thick, cream-colored carpet and the oriental décor of the walls suggested opulence.

Several men had been sent to her room. They'd forced her to perform unspeakable acts upon them, but she found it difficult to remember. It had all occurred in a haze, like a distorted vision. Her life as a nun had become a vague recollection, indistinguishable from a dream. She no longer had any sense of identity or being.

Her vacant gaze fell upon a surveillance camera trained on her at all times from the top left hand corner of the ceiling.

Fabian Rodriguez stood behind his employer watching Emily on her office desk monitor. "Well?"

"She's beautiful."

"Yeah, she sure is."

The woman turned her chair around and looked up at him sternly with dark, piercing eyes. Her expression oozed icy opportunism, with no hint of love or morality. "Just make sure the men only instruct her in the basics. Under no circumstances are they to take her virginity."

"They're not gonna do something as stupid as that, Mae Ling. Her virginity will triple her bids. And that's far more than any of those assholes will be able to cover."

She stood and straightened her black business jacket, her fingers lightly brushing a golden dragon broach on her lapel. "I want her ready for the auction next Friday."

"You got it. I'll make sure everything goes according to plan. I think you forget I've got a stake in this too."

She smiled seductively and gently caressed his cheek. Despite his lustful infatuation for her, he knew she was unreservedly ruthless. There was also the far greater danger of Sapphire's vengeance should a sexual relationship develop between them.

"How could I forget that?" she said throatily. "I just want to make sure those animals don't violate her completely. They have their uses, but their cocks often override their reason."

"I'm aware of that, and I have it under control."

She turned back to the monitor and watched the oriental girl attending to Emily. "I want maximum security next week. Every buyer is to be double and triple checked, including those who are regulars. No mishaps. No oversights."

Fabian gripped Mae Ling lightly by the shoulders and held her gaze. "Now, what could possibly go wrong?"

The concern in her face showed she wasn't as confident as usual. He didn't know why. Was she paranoid? Nevertheless, he knew she would spare no expense to thwart whatever threat might be forthcoming.

***

Tyler pulled up the van outside Miranda Curtis' home in San Fernando, with Brandon and Belinda by his side.

"Looks homey enough," Brandon said.

Tyler turned to him. "Yeah, look, I think you guys should stay put while I go check it out."

"OK."

Tyler stepped out of the van. He paused momentarily in preparation for what he was going to say. Miranda didn't know him, and the only information he had about her was from a brief conversation with Alex. He moved forward and approached the front door.

As he came to thirty feet away, he was startled as the door opened. A middle-aged man in a business suit stepped out with his head lowered and his hands lightly grasping his buttocks.

Immediately, Miranda appeared with her spiked collar, and a full rubber body-suit. "Can I help you?" she said in a stern voice.

The man in the business suit hurried past Tyler and quickened his pace along the walkway, clearly embarrassed. It was blatantly obvious what his business in the house had been.

Tyler had difficulty suppressing an amused chuckle. "S-sorry to bother you, ma'am. I'm looking for Miranda Curtis. Do you know her?"

She looked at him with a suspicious glint in her eyes. "Who are you?"

"My name is Tyler Faraday. Alex Dalton sent me here."

The van door closed, and Brandon and Belinda walked up the driveway. Brandon's face was heavily shrouded by large Ray-Bans and a baseball cap.

Miranda's gaze moved over Tyler's shoulder. Her demeanor relaxed into a look of awe, as though she was staring at a man for whom she'd harbored a quiet admiration. "Come on, get inside. Hurry."

They followed her into the house, and she closed the door behind them.

Tyler took a moment to come to terms with the strange regalia of whips and crops decorating Miranda's hallway. Brandon slowly removed his sunglasses in a manner that suggested, 'What the hell?'

"You never let me down, do you, Alex?" Tyler mumbled with a chuckle.

"Come into the living room," Miranda said.

They stepped inside, and Miranda removed her spiked collar.

226

"Ma'am? Miranda, is it?" Tyler said.

"Yes, I do apologize."

"OK. Miranda, I'm Tyler. This is my brother Brandon, and his girlfriend, Belinda."

"I know. You're quite the celebrities."

"Alex sent us here. I hope you don't mind, but we need to know what's happening."

"Of course," she said in a chirpy, cooperative tone. "Let me get us all some coffee, and then we can go over it."

"Sounds good."

They removed their jackets and sat while Miranda made her way over to the kitchen.

She quickly returned with their coffees. "So," she said, "let me tell you where we're at. Alex called me and said your sister has been taken by someone called Sapphire. He also wanted any information we could find on some guy named Fabian Rodriguez."

"Yeah, that's about it," Tyler said. "Alex never misses a thing."

"Well, I've got somebody working on it."

Their gazes shot up in eager anticipation. "Who?" Brandon said.

"A friend of mine. Tamara Quinn. She has contacts in the Avenue Nineteen area. There's some kind of a story about a woman called Siren, who escaped from Sapphire and went into hiding. Tamara's trying to find a way of contacting her, but it's going to take time."

"How come?" Tyler said.

"We're not even sure this person exists. And if she does, it's gonna take a lot of networking. It's a nightmare."

Brandon gave his leg a frustrated slap. "Is there any way we can meet Tamara?"

"Of course. But for now, I really think you should all stay here. I've got a spare room upstairs. I think this will be the safest place for you with everything that's going on."

"We can't ask that of you," Brandon said. "I'm a wanted man, and you would be harboring a fugitive."

She smiled at him warmly. "I've been doing that since the moment you stepped through the front door. You're a hero, Brandon. I have a lot of admiration for you. So do many others."

Brandon looked away with a shameful expression.

"We'd love to stay, Miranda, and *we* can't thank you enough." Tyler shot Brandon an insistent glance. His sister's life was in serious danger. The authorities went to the bottom of his list of priorities as long as she remained in jeopardy.

However, Brandon didn't share his viewpoint. "Are you crazy?"

"You don't know the half of it. I've got a plan to get Emily out as safely as possible, and I'm gonna do everything I can to make that happen."

"What plan?"

Belinda slapped her forehead. "Oh, hell. I never told you, did I?"

"Tell me what?"

"I'm so sorry, sweetheart. We had so much going on with you being ill and all, it just slipped my mind."

Miranda frowned. "Brandon? Have you been unwell?"

"It's fine. I got over it." He turned back to Tyler. "What's this plan?"

"I had an idea of infiltrating these guys, and . . ."

"And what?"

"I intend to buy Emily."

"You what?"

"Look, can you think of a better idea? I've got the money, the connections, and no warrant out for my arrest. All I'll have to do is play the role. But first I need to know which slime balls to hook up with."

Brandon shook his head. "I don't like this, Ty. It's twisted."

"It's the only way, bro."

"It's insane."

"Well, what the hell would you do, *Interceptor*? Bust in there with guns blazing, and just hope she doesn't get caught in the crossfire?"

Brandon stood rapidly, fists clenched, and the scar on his forehead deepened.

Tyler looked into his brother's maniacal eyes and swallowed hard. He knew of Brandon's condition, The Scorpion. He'd borne witness to it once before during his trial at Fort Bragg. He'd seen him take out five military police officers within seconds under the effects of a Scorpion attack. He knew that if Brandon was to set upon him, he wouldn't stand a chance. Gripped with fear, he shivered.

Thirty-Three

Meltdown

Belinda and Miranda raced up to Brandon vocalizing a chorus of "No, Brandon. He's your brother!"

Belinda held him by the shoulders. He looked into her pleading eyes, her panic instantly bringing him back from the edge of the abyss. It was as though he could see the horror of what he was about to become through her eyes.

He shook his head, and the scar faded again as his moment of meltdown abated. "Oh, my God, Ty. I–I'm so sorry. I didn't mean to . . ."

Tyler exhaled and rested a shaking hand on Brandon's shoulder. "D-don't worry about it. Let's just get this sorted out."

Miranda moved to the far corner of the room and opened the door to the stairwell. "Look guys, I really think you have things to discuss, so I'm going to point you to the spare room. Top of the stairs, second on the right. There's a double bed and a spare mattress in the closet."

Tyler turned to her regretfully. "I am so sorry for what just happened. It was my fault. I really do appreciate everything you're doing for us."

She smiled with forgiving eyes. "It's my pleasure. I'll call Tamara right now and ask her to come over."

"Thank you."

"I've got a client coming in an hour. Just keep quiet up there, and nobody'll know you're here."

"Client?" Belinda said.

"Yeah. You'll probably hear some strange noises coming from below. Just ignore it."

Having their own issues on their minds, they left their host to her own devices, and climbed the stairs.

Once they'd reached the landing, Brandon touched Tyler's arm with a look of disgrace.

"You all right now?"

Brandon looked down at the floor. "I can't believe what just happened. I'm so sorry, Ty. You've done so much for me. For all of us. And I just went and blew up at you like that. What the hell is wrong with me?"

Belinda stood beside them with a worried expression.

"They messed with your mind, bro," Tyler said. "I don't know how you're gonna deal with this. But what I just saw downstairs was terrifying. Your eyes changed, your face changed, and something happened to that scar between your eyes. It was like you weren't *you*, anymore."

"That's the problem," Brandon said gravely. "It *was* me, Ty. The real me. Who I am most of the time isn't true. I'm a fake. An illusion."

Tyler looked at him pensively. "I think you're whoever you want to be, Brandon. You can choose your identity, just as I choose mine, and just as Belinda chooses hers."

"He's right," she said.

"You can deal with this, bro. It was just a glitch, like a chink in your armor. You're strong and you can handle this. I know you can."

Brandon recalled the moment the rage took control of him, and he wasn't as confident as Belinda and Tyler. The scene played over in his head. He was overcome with doubt and the crushing bane of depression. It was followed immediately by a need for a drink that he couldn't even consider permitting himself. The urge simply wouldn't leave him.

Miranda's words, when she'd called him a hero, repeated in his mind. It was the last term in the world he would've chosen to describe himself. His recent bout with alcohol, and his rage episode made him feel more of a villain than anything else. A sense of gross unworthiness came over him.

After a moment, he somberly headed for the bedroom.

***

Tamara Quinn settled into her apartment for the evening after a long day at the office. Having secured the transfer of a popular dance group from an indie label, she felt particularly satisfied by the day's events. She knew that under A & Z Records, the band would soar to heights they'd never dreamed possible.

Living alone, single by choice, she couldn't feel trusting enough toward a man to commit to him.

However, always body and diet-conscious, she stood at the kitchen sideboard preparing a chicken salad.

She heard a knock at the door. Setting her knife and cutting board aside, she wiped her hands and exited the kitchen.

She opened the front door ajar with a chain bracing it and peered into the gap. Who she saw on the other side caused her heart to quicken. "Nicole? Is it really you?"

The young woman on the other side raised her head, concealed under a straw hat, sunglasses, and dyed brunette hair.

Tamara slid the chain away and ushered her visitor inside. The woman put down her suitcase, removed her sunglasses and hat, and embraced her.

"Oh, Nicole. Thank God you made it. You're staying here. Agreed?"

The woman nodded, but appeared profoundly emotional.

"What's wrong?" Tamara said.

"It's been five years since I've heard anyone speak my real name. I've been called 'Jodie Madison' for so long I'd almost come to believe it."

"Jodie Madison? Oh, sweetheart. Where have you been hiding all this time?"

"Oregon for the last three years. I've been raising horses on a ranch."

"Sounds great. You know, you really do look different now."

"That was the intention."

Tamara gestured to the couch. "Rest for awhile. I'll get you something to eat. Would you like a drink?"

"Do you have any beer? I've kinda developed a taste for it."

"Sure."

"When am I gonna meet these people?"

"Soon. So far, they think you're a myth. I had to lie to them. I told them I'd keep searching until I found someone who knew how to contact you."

Nicole nodded in approval. "Do you trust them?"

"It's impossible to trust anybody. Anybody at all. But let's just say I have no reason to *distrust* them."

The telephone rang. Tamara hurried into the kitchen and answered it. "Hello? Oh, hi, Miranda . . . Not quite, but I'm getting pretty close . . . They are? OK, I don't think this is gonna take as long as we thought."

Nicole entered the kitchen and fixed her gaze on Tamara as she was ending the call.

"In fact, things are looking pretty good. Wait for my call. Bye. "

"That was them?" Nicole said.

"Yes. Brandon Drake and his brother have arrived, and they're just itching for information about you."

Nicole's expression was deadpan. "If my sister had been taken in by Sapphire, I'd be pretty damn eager to get some answers too."

"What do you think we should do?"

Nicole paced the kitchen thoughtfully. "We play it cautiously. Set up a meeting, and we'll go to them. From there, I'll weigh up the situation to see if I can trust them. My instincts are pretty good."

"OK."

"This is so dangerous, Tam, but what else can I do?" Nicole came closer to her, and the fear in her was undeniable. "You saved my life five years ago, and I have to do what I can to help someone else escape, but I'm so damn scared. I really hope Brandon Drake is as formidable as so many believe, because he's gonna need to be."

"You'll be safe if you hide out in here. First thing tomorrow, we'll go see them."

"I want Sapphire taken down so badly. I just want my life back."

Tamara shot her an encouraging smile. "Maybe this time you will."

"There is no 'maybe'," Nicole said with conviction. "Sapphire has to be stopped. The lives of countless innocent women and children are at stake. Failure is not an option."

Thirty-Four

The Other Cabin

Andrew Wilmot drove a rented, black, Jeep Wrangler through the rocky terrain of Arizona's Sonoran Desert. The intense heat was made bearable only by the wind blowing through his hair. The legendary high temperatures of the area demanded the best open-air form of transport to his location—advice provided, most helpfully, by Treadwell.

The vast, flat plains spread across to every horizon. Only scatterings of cacti, and the occasional giant saguaro, broke up the vision of the sun-baked, rust-colored wasteland.

He continued, following his destination direction via GPS. Despite numerous visits to the place, the location was so remote it was impossible for him to get there from memory. There were no roads, landmarks, or directions anywhere.

After four hours, he saw the mesa in the distance and smiled, knowing the end of his arduous trek was in sight.

He often wondered how Treadwell had managed to find such a contender for the most remote spot in the United States. It wasn't a part of any national preserve, Native American or military reservation, as was much of the Sonoran.

The closer he came to his destination, the more his anticipation gripped him. There was so much ground to cover in his forthcoming discussion.

He finally came to the base of the mesa and slowed the jeep. After parking beside an identical model on his immediate right, he stepped out with a two-liter bottle of unavoidably-warm water.

Looking around him, he took in the barren landscape as the sun beat down on him. Even his white t-shirt and jeans were too much for this climate. The dry heat struck him with an oppressive, claustrophobic grip.

He walked ahead slowly so as not to exhaust himself in the infernal environment. He kept within a narrow shadow at the base of the mesa until he reached the end.

Turning the corner, he saw a wooden cabin and marveled at how effectively Treadwell had concealed it at the base of the mesa. It was hidden away from any roads or routes where it could be seen. The top of the mountain hung overhead, obscuring it even from the air.

He saw the front door was ajar and made his way up onto the porch to push it open.

"Thought you'd never get here," a raspy female voice said.

He stepped inside and smiled at the sight of a striking woman wearing sawn-off, high-cut jeans, and a blue t-shirt. Her blonde hair was cut harshly short in an almost-militaristic style. Her defined, angular jaw complemented her piercing blue eyes.

He walked across the spacious living room and glanced inside the small kitchen through a door at the end. He noticed the oak floor was polished, and a circular cream rug in the center of the room had been recently vacuumed. The top-of-the-line, high-definition television set on the wall above the mantelpiece was spotless, as was the digital

MP3 music system positioned to the side. "You've been busy," he said.

He stood beneath four electric fans whirring overhead. The installed air conditioning alone didn't alleviate the heat effectively enough.

The woman walked into the kitchen and immediately returned with two glasses and a chilled bottle of chardonnay. "Care to join me?" she said in a sultry voice.

Wilmot placed the water bottle on the living room table and exhaled with outstretched arms, absorbing the refreshing breeze of the fans. "You have no idea how much I would. I can't get used to this damn heat."

She handed him a glass of wine. "I love it. It makes me horny."

"What doesn't?"

"How was your trip to New Hampshire? You never told me."

"Surprisingly enlightening. It seems our Mr. Drake is not who he thinks he is. At least not entirely."

"I don't understand."

"It seems Treadwell subjected him to some kind of memory-altering procedure in an attempt to make him more manageable. In my opinion, he made a mistake."

"Why do you think that?"

"I think it's the morality and compassion he planted into him that led to him attacking us. Treadwell couldn't see the bigger picture, but it's given me a change of plans."

"What's that?"

"I want him alive."

"Do you know if Kerwin and Rhodes have managed to acquire a lead on his whereabouts?"

"Not yet. They're in L.A. trying to find information on this Sapphire organization. Something about this just doesn't sit right with me." He took the sofa and sank into its cushioned embrace.

"What doesn't sit right with you?" she said.

"I'm not sure. They said the people in the bar were absolutely terrified of Sapphire. You don't get a reaction like that if there's no official trace of him. So what the hell is going on?"

"As with all mysteries, there's always an explanation," she said with a wily grin.

"It'd be a hell of a lot easier if I could bring in more reinforcements on this, but the time isn't right. I'm still running Treadwell's operation under the radar. I just need Drake, and then we can introduce *Nemesis* in an official capacity. There are genuine threats we can apply it to now."

"And then?"

"Then I'll have options that will enable me to propose it to congress and eliminate the need for cover."

"Are you serious?"

"Very."

"What about Jed Crane?"

"Right now, I have no idea. That lucky son of a bitch could be anywhere." He paused and gave himself a moment to survey the cabin. "You know, as many times as I've been here, it never ceases to amaze me. Treadwell thought of everything. Self-contained electricity and its own filtered water supply. It's remarkable. He must've suspected his days were numbered."

"He got real unlucky with the helicopter crash, that's all."

Wilmot shook his head. "I'm not so sure. Before he died, he sent me a letter detailing his entire plans, and directions to this cabin hideout. He knew he was going to die. There's more to his death than meets the eye." The thought that had tormented him for days returned. "So, why didn't he tell me about Drake?"

Calculation appeared in the woman's eyes, as though a computer was registering behind them. "I think he was convinced Payne would kill him. There's no other explanation."

"Maybe. But nobody has ever been able to pin Drake down. He disappears for months on end. Two years ago, he'd show up, stir a little trouble, and just vanish without a trace. Where the hell did he go after Leavenworth? No sightings anywhere for two months, until his idiot girlfriend punched out a priest. How do you figure that?"

She looked around the cabin intently, and then her jaw dropped. "Oh, my God."

"What?"

"There's another cabin."

His head snapped toward her. "What do you mean?"

"Think about it. You said Treadwell had Drake's memories altered, right?"

"Right."

"OK. He was clearly a test subject, and one that Treadwell would've needed to keep track of. I'm telling you. Somewhere, there's another cabin like this one. It's remote and hidden away just like this place. I'd bet my bottom dollar it has exactly the same design as this one too."

"Why?"

"Human beings are habitual. If they build two houses in different locations, the two properties usually have parallel designs. The design of this place is very simplistic. There's not much of a margin for variation."

"But where?"

"I have no idea. Studying Drake's past itinerary might provide a clue. We could also search for any information on who built *this* cabin, but it's unlikely the two cabins share the same builders. And Treadwell wouldn't have allowed himself to be known as the vendor. He was too shrewd for that."

"You're right, but it's a moot point. Drake's hidden away in Los Angeles right now, and that's where I'm headed first thing tomorrow."

"And he just might disappear again. Take me with you."

He looked into her eyes, awed by her keen mind. Leaning across, he kissed her deeply. "I wonder if Treadwell ever imagined this place would be used for our secret liaisons."

"More than likely," she said, grinning.

"I know relationships between operatives are encouraged, but with what we're doing, I think it's best we keep our relationship to ourselves. At least for now, Cynthia."

"I agree. I ask only one thing."

"What's that?"

"Call me by my other name. You know how much it turns me on."

He smiled at her familiar-but-unusual sexual quirks. "Of course . . . *Agent Garrett.*"

***

Brandon lay in the double bed in Miranda's spare bedroom. Belinda slept soundly beside him. Tyler rested comfortably on a makeshift bed on the floor next to them.

Brandon looked around the basic room, but could see only dim shadows reflected by moonlight through the drapes. He estimated it was past midnight, but he couldn't sleep. His mind was awash with tortured questions. What was happening to him? He pondered how he'd fallen so far into the depths of what he now feared was alcoholism. His natural father had been an alcoholic, and there was a genetic predisposition to the disease. What could've possessed him to have allowed it to happen? What if it couldn't be overcome?

His liberation from Leavenworth had been fraught with turmoil. He'd been seriously injured and almost lost his life. Then there had been the following weeks it had taken him to recover from the bullet wound. Even now, almost two months later, he still suffered pain from it. His two year wish to be reunited with Belinda in the cabin, with harmony, peace, love, and serenity, had been hampered by so very much.

He recalled the first time he'd helped himself to the liquor cabinet, thinking nothing of it. He was free. He could do as he wished. It was only a relaxing drink.

But then he'd realized how enjoyable it was. Enjoyment was something that had eluded him, seemingly forever.

He'd subconsciously decided to take his share, night after night.

Before long, seven o'clock in the evening would arrive, and his heart would quicken. It was excitement he found irresistible, and yet it wasn't a problem. He wasn't hurting anyone. If anything, it made him easier to be around. It took away his intensity and concern about the persona that was constantly lurking inside him, waiting for any opportunity to erupt.

By the time the alcohol had taken hold of him, all care had been pushed to the back of his mind. When he became barely conscious of it becoming a little excessive, he didn't want to confront it. He simply drank the concern away.

Gradually, he became increasingly dysfunctional. He'd jeopardized their mission to be reunited with Emily, failing her in her darkest hour. Then he'd been forced to confront the horrors of withdrawal.

Now he was coming through it, but one disagreement with the one to whom he owed so very much, and his killer instinct returned. He had never felt so torn. He was damned if he drank and damned if he didn't. A question pounded in his mind: what was it going to take for him to defeat both the bottle, *and* his inner demon?

The first rays of daylight coursed into the bedroom. Brandon had been asleep for several hours, fatigued by his own tumultuous thoughts. He started to stir, alerted by movement on the bed beside him—and whispering.

He turned over and opened his eyes, blinking a few times as he adjusted to the light. Belinda was sitting on the edge of the bed. Tyler sat next to her holding her hand looking concerned.

"Good morning," Brandon said, and yawned. "Is everything all right?"

"Hey, bro," Tyler said. "I'm not sure. Belinda's not looking too great."

Instantly awoken by his brother's words, he sat up. He moved around the bed to see her face was pallid. "Baby, what's wrong?"

"I don't think anything's really *wrong*," she said. "I've felt like this for the last few mornings, and now I'm pretty sure."

"Pretty sure what?"

She touched his cheek tenderly and smiled with a hint of sadness. "I love you so much, sweetheart."

"Baby, what's wrong?"

"Brandon . . . I think I'm pregnant."

Tyler's mouth dropped open in shock. "Oh, my God."

Brandon held her other hand, her words having struck him like a thunderbolt. The one thought that went through his mind was the last question he'd asked himself before he'd finally fallen asleep. What would it take for him to overcome his issues?

In an instant, he knew he'd just been provided with the answer.

Thirty-Five

Siren

Brandon, Belinda, and Tyler sat at Miranda's kitchen table eating a basic breakfast of cereal and coffee. The morning's revelation had shaken them all.

Miranda returned to the table with a fresh pot of coffee.

"Thank you," Tyler said. "I can't tell you how much we appreciate this, Miranda."

"It's a pleasure. Is there anything I can do for you, Belinda? Pregnancy isn't something I've had much experience with."

Belinda looked up at her with an appreciative smile. "Me neither."

Brandon turned to Belinda. "I want you to take it easy. Ty and I will do what needs to be done. You just lay low, and don't do anything to exert yourself."

"I'm a few weeks pregnant at best," she said. "I'm not an invalid, so quit treating me like one. I'm more concerned about the future, with everything that's going on right now. What the hell kind of a world are we bringing this baby into?"

Brandon opened his mouth to respond, but was interrupted by the doorbell.

"Just give me a moment." Miranda placed the fresh coffee on the table and briskly left the room.

She opened the front door, surprised to see Tamara and a stranger. She could tell the other woman was extremely attractive, even underneath a straw hat and sunglasses.

Instinctively, she knew this was the news her guests had been waiting for. "Tam. What a surprise. Come on in. Who's your friend?"

The young brunette removed the sunglasses and hat, and held her hand out for Miranda. "Hi. I'm Nicole. *Nikki* to my friends."

"Well, it's good to meet you."

Miranda led the two women along the corridor.

Nicole gestured at the curious décor. "You're a dominatrix?"

Miranda shrugged, unabashed. "It pays the rent and beats working for a living."

"Interesting."

They entered the living room. "They're in the kitchen," Miranda said.

Brandon stood in the kitchen doorway facing them.

Nicole froze. "Oh, my God." She slowly moved toward him, almost as an adoring fan would approach a rock star. It was clear from the look in her eyes that he represented the closest thing to hope she'd ever known. She glanced back at Miranda. "Is it really him?"

Brandon seemed overawed by her reaction. There was discomfort apparent in him, as though he didn't feel her optimism was founded. "Ma'am, I'm Brandon."

"I know. I just can't believe it."

"What's your name?"

Tears came to her eyes. "Nikki. Nikki Hawke."

Brandon walked over to her and instinctively held her. "Hey, hey. It's OK."

Belinda and Tyler entered the living room from the kitchen. Belinda stopped in her tracks at the sight of Brandon holding another woman. The memory of how she'd broken down in his arms in the cabin after he'd rescued her on that first night, flashed before her. No matter how irrational her feelings might be, she was stricken with a stab of jealousy.

Nikki broke the embrace and stepped back. "I'm sorry," she said, wiping her eyes with her denim sleeve.

"Look, everybody take a seat," Miranda said. "I just made a fresh pot of coffee, but we're gonna need more. Just give me a minute."

"Thank you, Mir." Tamara turned to Brandon. "Mr. Drake, I'm Tamara Quinn."

"Yeah, Miranda told us all about you. It's good to meet you, and we really appreciate you helping us."

Tyler stepped in and introduced himself to Tamara and Nikki. Belinda did likewise before they all sat down in the living room.

"Tamara," Brandon said, "Miranda told us you may be able to get a lead on where we can locate someone who knows the location of Sapphire's organization."

"What kind of arsenal do you have?" Nikki said with an assertive tone.

"We have the arsenal, but we're hoping we won't have to use it," Tyler said. "I have a plan to do it more subtly. We just need certain information first."

"What do you have planned?"

"We'll get to that. But first we need you to help us find this Siren character. Does she really exist?"

Nikki held herself still for a moment. She then looked to Tamara who gave her an affirmative nod. Finally, she turned back to Tyler. "I am Siren."

Miranda almost dropped the pot of coffee as she re-entered the room. "What?"

"I'm Siren."

Miranda turned to Tamara, clearly vexed. "And after all that bullshit you spun to me about her being a myth? After looking me in the eye and telling me you'd have to email one person after another?"

Tamara held up her hand passively. "Calm down, Mir. I promised Nikki I'd keep her secret and not tell a soul. You've got to understand, her life is in danger. If Sapphire had an inkling of where she was, he'd have her killed. Hell, if they knew that I knew, they'd take me out too."

"All right, already," Tyler said. "Nikki, the floor is yours. Why don't you tell us what you know?"

Nikki exhaled and collected herself. "Five years ago, I was a singer. I was raised in Minnesota, but I wanted to make a name for myself, so I headed for L.A. I met a guy in a bar in Tucson. He was attractive and charming. He said he wanted to help me because he had friends in the music business. I guess I believed him because I wanted to. I was a fool."

"What was his name?"

"Fabian. Fabian Rodriguez."

Tyler, Brandon, and Belinda looked at one another ominously.

"Go on," Tyler said.

"He took me to L.A. with him." Nikki closed her eyes, stifling her tears. "They kept me drugged. I think I was raped countless times, but it's a haze. I was doped up most of the time. And then, the day of the auction came."

Belinda gasped at the thought of what Nikki must have suffered, recalling her experience with Payne. He'd been a mere micro-second away from raping her before Brandon returned to save her.

"What happened at the auction, Nikki?" Tyler said.

"Sapphire appeared from an unknown location on a screen behind the stage. He was hosting the auction like a TV game show. He's black, probably of Afro-Caribbean origin, but definitely American judging from his accent. He had dreadlocked hair and a sapphire in place of one of his upper front teeth. I suppose that's how he got his nickname."

Belinda noticed Nikki's hands trembling as she described him.

"Somebody bought you?" Brandon said.

"Yes. I was sold for one hundred thousand dollars to a Libyan nationalist. That's when I got my lucky break."

"What do you mean?"

"I was driven away in a limousine with the buyer. Sapphire had only recently taken over the L.A. underground, but the rival drug lords and pimps were hungry to regain their territory. About two miles from Sapphire's base, the limo was attacked. Machine-gun fire, the whole nine yards. The driver and the asshole who bought me were killed instantly, and the car overturned."

Tyler's eyebrows rose. "How did you get out?"

"It was a miracle I survived, but there was a lot of commotion. The door on my side of the limo was open so I tried to crawl out. The pimps and drug lords must've thought there were no survivors and headed past the limo to intercept the next car."

Finally, Tamara spoke. "It was my only chance too."

"*Your* only chance?" Brandon said.

"Yes. I was a street hooker."

Nikki placed an affectionate hand on Tamara's. "The limo was already on fire, and Tamara pulled me out. Together, we escaped just before it exploded. Me from Sapphire, and Tam from her pimp."

"Oh, my God, Tam," Miranda said. "You were involved in this? Isn't your pimp still looking for you?"

Tamara shook her head. "He's dead. Immediately after the ambush, all of the pimps in that area were massacred by Sapphire's goons."

Nikki continued. "I've been on the run ever since that day, moving from state to state. Another town, another name. Anything to keep myself hidden. They know my name because they took all my identification. I can't even contact my family to tell them I'm all right. As far as my mom and dad are concerned, I just disappeared." Her eyes welled up again. "Sapphire took everything from me. My whole life."

"We're going to put a stop to this, Nikki," Brandon said. "But we need your help."

"I know they have your sister. What are you gonna do?"

"I'm gonna try to infiltrate the organization and buy my sister," Tyler said. "But I need to know who to hook up with."

"That's impossible. It would cost you a fortune."

He smiled. "I have a fortune."

"How so?"

"My father is the founder of a multi-national conglomerate, and I'm his chief investment specialist. We're talking billions of dollars. It's the perfect cover."

"I'll be handling the strong-arm stuff if anything goes wrong," Brandon said.

Nikki looked at him with uncertainty. "You alone?"

"Trust me, I know what I'm doing. I have access to tech and weaponry these guys couldn't even imagine."

"Well, after seeing the stories about you on the news, I'm inclined to believe you. But what about the others?"

"Others?"

"The other victims. It's not just young women in there, but little children too. They sell kids to international perverts."

Tyler swallowed hard. "Once I've been there, I'll have all the information I need to take to the authorities. That's why it's essential I look like the real deal to them. We can't afford for anybody to suspect anything."

Nikki turned away with devastation in her eyes. "The authorities aren't going to do anything. Sapphire has been in L.A. for over five years, and they haven't lifted a finger."

"One way or another, we're going to take them down, Nikki," Brandon said.

"So, how would I get close to them?" Tyler said. "Do you have any ideas?"

"Nobody joins the auctions on a whim," she said. "You have to be invited into the fold."

"So, where do I go to get noticed?"

"During the three weeks I was being held at Sapphire's base, I heard one word repeatedly. *Citadel*."

"What's that?"

"It's a high-stakes card room in L.A. I'm pretty sure the guy who owns it has connections to Sapphire."

A wry smile crept from Tyler's mouth.

"Did I say something amusing?" Nikki said.

"Very. Casinos and card rooms are where I'm in my element. I have a long history with them around the globe. Poker, Baccarat, Blackjack, you name it. I play them all. This is already panning out better than I expected."

"That's lucky," Miranda said.

"Alrighty, it's settled. I'll get on it right away."

Belinda noticed Nikki's gaze lingering on Tyler, and the glint in his eyes showed her attraction to him was reciprocated.

"We've got to keep our minds on what we're doing," Brandon said, dampening the moment. "Nikki, I need you to tell me—where is Sapphire's base?"

"Do you have a map?"

"I've got a map upstairs. I'll go get it," Miranda said.

"I'll point it out to you," Nikki said. "It's on the docks. From the outside, it looks like a deserted fish factory, but on the inside, on the lower floors, it's lavish."

As Brandon watched Miranda scale the steps, he pondered the information Nikki had provided, and was already gaining an insight into what he might be facing. He was fully aware it was going to be one of the most hazardous missions he'd ever embarked upon.

Nevertheless, he needed to know more about the location and the security measures Sapphire had in place.

One troubling thought played over in his mind. *Why haven't the police made a move on this outfit?*

Thirty-Six

City of Angels

Andrew Wilmot and Cynthia Garrett made their way up the front entrance to the Los Angeles Police Department.

Wilmot's cell phone rang. Noting the caller's ID, he wasn't pleased to be bothered at that precise moment, but answered it, nonetheless. "Yeah, what is it?"

Deborah Beaumont's professional tone came through the earpiece. "I received an email from Director Brenham. He was asking about your whereabouts. You've been away from Langley for three days. What should I tell him?"

"Tell him the truth. It's believed Brandon Drake may be in Los Angeles, and I'm looking into it. Garrett's with me at LAPD headquarters."

"I've been trying to reach you all day. I'll send the director an email."

"You do that." Abruptly ending the call, he placed the palm of his hand in the small of Garrett's back. "Come on. Let's see what we can find out."

They stepped inside the basketball-court-sized reception area and approached the front desk.

A balding, middle-aged desk sergeant greeted them. "Yes, sir? Ma'am?"

Wilmot and Garrett produced their identification cards. "SDT Director Wilmot and Agent Cynthia Garrett to see Commissioner Landis," Wilmot said.

A smartly-suited, bespectacled man in his early fifties emerged from a long corridor to their right. "Yes, Director Wilmot. I'm Jason Landis. We spoke on the phone."

"It's a pleasure to meet you." Wilmot offered his hand.

"Please, follow me."

Landis led them through the main processing area and X-ray detection unit. A spattering of officers walked across the area in pursuit of their tasks. Others escorted suspects in handcuffs toward the custody area.

Wilmot and Garrett followed Landis along a corridor and into an elevator.

Arriving at the third floor, they walked along another sprawling corridor until they came to Landis' office door.

They entered a spacious room, which was in somewhat of a disarray. Pages spread across the desk showed Landis was overcome with paperwork.

Wilmot had done his homework on the commissioner prior to leaving for L.A. Landis had risen through the ranks of the police since joining the LAPD at the age of twenty, leading to a further twenty years of dedicated service. It ultimately led to him becoming the Chief of Police, until seven years ago when he was appointed to the position of commissioner. Now, at fifty-six, the years were clearly beginning to take their toll on him, as evidenced by the deep bags under his eyes.

"So, Director Wilmot. What can I do for you? And please, take a seat." Landis gestured to the two chairs in front of his desk.

"Thank you," Wilmot said. "Recently, two of my operatives, Agents Kerwin and Rhodes, had a discussion with your Chief of Police, Jarred Tepper, about a human trafficking organization, and a character known as Sapphire."

Landis loosened his collar and sat down. "I'm aware of that, and there's really nothing more I can say to you on the matter. This department is fully aware of the major vice in this town, where it operates, and who operates it. We have no reason to believe Sapphire is anything more than myth."

"What makes you so sure of that?"

"If a powerful sex slavery outfit was operating on our own doorstep, we'd know about it."

Wilmot smiled condescendingly. "Our interest in this is related to another matter altogether. We're gathering intelligence on one particular individual, and we believe if we can locate Sapphire, we can locate our quarry."

Landis leaned forward, showing a curious degree of enthusiasm. "May I ask who it is you're investigating?"

"I'm sorry. It's a highly sensitive, highly classified case."

Garrett's eyes squinted almost unnoticeably, although Wilmot was fully aware of what was going through her mind. He could detect discomfort in Landis, and Garrett had an even keener eye than he had. He sensed her straightening her blue suit jacket as a highly practiced misdirection. With Landis distracted by Wilmot's intimidating stare, she subtly slipped the fingers of her left hand into her pocket for a fleeting second.

"Well," Landis said, "I don't know how far you're going to get chasing phantoms. It's nothing but an urban legend."

"Not according to the people we've interviewed," Wilmot said.

"Yes, I know. Your agents told Chief Tepper about the people they'd spoken to in Nevada. I'm telling you, you're wasting your time."

Garrett gripped the sides of her seat and pulled it forward a fraction of an inch. "We believe there's more to it than that."

Wilmot glanced at Cynthia for a brief moment, and she gave him a barely detectable nod of the head.

Turning back to Landis, he smiled and stood. "We'll be in touch, Commissioner. It's been a pleasure."

After the customary handshakes, Landis cordially led them out of the office and escorted them out of the building.

Wilmot smiled smugly. "Good work, Cynthia."

She smiled gloatingly. "The trap is set."

With calculating grins, they came to the end of the street, and hailed another cab.

Landis hurried back into his office and took a 35ml bottle of whiskey from a desk drawer. Heavy perspiration and hyperventilation punctuated generous gulps. Had it not been for his anxiety, he knew he would've been quite taken by Agent Garrett's sophisticated beauty. However, the distress he'd tried so earnestly to disguise had impaired his attentions.

Shaking, he sat down, took out his cell phone, and punched in a number he'd committed to memory. "Mae Ling?" he said. "I know my calling you is dangerous, but what we're facing is much more so. I've kept you clear of police investigations for five goddamn years, but now it's becoming problematic. I've just had a visit from the director of SDT, a Homeland Security sub-division. This is their second visit to the department. They're looking for Sapphire . . . No, no, of course I didn't tell them anything. But I'm telling you, something's going down, and you should watch your back."

***

Jed Crane sat at a coffee table in one of the less expensive motels in Santa Monica staring at his laptop screen. He knew he was testing his luck. Low on funds, he'd been forced to continue traveling in the car he'd been driving since escaping with Brandon in Nevada. It was unlikely he was going to succeed in concealing himself for much longer. His greatest fear was being captured before he found Brandon. However, finding him would be futile if he didn't have any information for him.

With a standard SDT issue laptop, Jed had the skills to tap into the email accounts of many departments, although not high-ranking offices such as Wilmot's.

But Deborah Beaumont's was not a problem. During his time with the SDT, they'd sent countless emails to one another. With her email address in his contacts file, hacking into it was child's play.

He'd been checking her inbox and sent box for most of the day, but no email headings seemed to be concerned with Wilmot. He was familiar with the operations in their headings, which affirmed the information contained therein was of no use to him.

A new message, addressed to Director Brenham, appeared in Deborah's sent box entitled: 'Director Wilmot'.

With an attack of conscience he opened the message. "I'm sorry, Deborah. But under the circumstances, I don't think you'd disapprove."

The email opened:

```
I've contacted Director Wilmot, and
he's in Los Angeles investigating
Brandon Drake with the Los Angeles
Police Department. I will keep you
informed of further developments.
```

With a shrewd smile, Jed closed down Deborah's email account, and exhaled with satisfaction. "So, you're working with the LAPD are you, asshole?"

Thirty-Seven

The Citadel

Seated at a Blackjack table, Tyler looked down at his cards with a deadpan expression. A four of diamonds, a seven of clubs, a five of hearts, and a four of spades—four cards totaling twenty. The dealer's face up card was a queen of clubs.

Tyler's hand lightly brushed the subtle, black button cover fixed to his collar, exposing a $90,000, gold Rolex watch. Wearing a newly-purchased designer tuxedo and his hair slicked back, his image conveyed the epitome of wealth and self-assurance.

"Mr. Faraday?" the stunning blonde dealer said.

"I stand."

An Italian sitting at the table failed to disguise his disappointment as he glanced at the three cards in front of him—a two of clubs, a ten of diamonds, and an ace of hearts. After a tense moment, he said, "Hit me." He glanced at the three of spades the dealer put down. "Hit me again." The dealer dealt him the king of clubs.

"Bust," the dealer said, and scooped up the cards.

As she drew a six of hearts, Tyler held his breath. She had sixteen showing. With the usual dealer's luck, her hole card would be a five, giving her twenty-one. However, she turned over a jack of spades.

Tyler let out a small sigh of relief, and the dealer paid him.

The Italian smiled. Accepting his loss of $200,000, he graciously departed the blackjack table, and disappeared into the crowd.

Earlier, Tyler had won $300,000 at the poker table. In a mere two hours, he'd attracted great attention to himself, just as he'd intended.

Located on the east side of Hollywood, The Citadel was one of the most prestigious card room hotels in L.A. A golden fountain surrounded by limousines on the outside, marble floors and pillars, decorative statues, a luxurious bar area with the finest-quality leather couches, and impeccable, hospitable service, demonstrated opulence. The gaming arena offered a sprawling spectacle of international clientele. It had required most of the day for Tyler to verify his financial means in order to prove his eligibility.

He looked up at the dealer with a cocky glint in his eyes. The dealer waited for two women to join the table before she dealt the next hand.

The two attractive women, one blonde, and the other brunette, sat down on either side of Tyler. Both flirted with him outrageously. At any other time, he would've reciprocated. However, with his true agenda at the forefront of his mind, his sexual interests were dampened considerably, and Nikki had captured him in a way that overshadowed other temptations.

Han Fong sat at the desk in his office. A bathroom and kitchen were annexed to it via oak doors on either side of the entrance. The walls displayed a strong adherence to

Chinese tradition. Images of Chinese settings, along with dragon emblems, adorned the red wallpaper.

Fong studied a folder before him, occasionally glancing at the monitor screen on his desk. The camera in the card room focused closely upon Tyler.

"That's what we've managed to come up with on Mr. Faraday," a young Chinese executive said in Mandarin.

Fong looked up at him. "Quite a catch. A most interesting young man, indeed."

"How would you like us to proceed, Mr. Fong? Shall we bring him up here?"

"Certainly not. We should extend to him the greatest hospitality. I'll go down and introduce myself." Fong stood, took his tailor-made suit jacket from his coat stand, and made his way to the door.

Tyler turned over a hand of five cards consisting of an ace of spades, a five of hearts, a six of clubs, a four of clubs, and a five of diamonds—five cards totaling twenty-one exactly.

"You have extraordinary luck, Mr. Faraday."

Tyler's breathing quickened. He sensed his brow becoming slightly damp at the sound of his name being uttered in a Chinese accent. Switching to his role in a heartbeat, he turned and looked up to see Fong smiling down at him. He studied the man's mature features, which seemed to ooze confidence, authority, and command. His combed back hair revealed the widow's peak of temporal recession, enhancing a sinister darkness in his deep-set eyes. "Thank you, sir." Tyler offered his hand. "And you are?"

"I am Han Fong, the owner and founder of The Citadel."

I know who you are, you evil prick. "Well, it's an honor to meet you. Everything here is a contender for the most impressive I've seen."

"Coming from such a highly-experienced connoisseur as yourself, I consider that quite a compliment."

Tyler smiled, feigning flattery. "I wasn't aware I was such a celebrity."

"Well, I don't want to take you away from your game. I would just like to extend an invitation for you to join me in a drink."

Damn, I'm good. "You know what? I've been at this for a few hours. That sounds great, Mr. Fong. Thank you."

Tyler stood and followed his host across the room, a dark sensation gripping him as he struggled to maintain his humorous, confident demeanor. This time, he knew he was walking into the lion's den. If he faltered even once, his entire plan would be forfeit. As would his very life.

En route to the office, his mind became lost in a tempest of uncertainty. That very doubt, the cause of his distress, presented the paradox of a potentially-fatal problem actually creating itself.

In the elevator, he smiled cordially at Fong, who reciprocated. That, at least, helped to ease his mind. So far, he was pulling it off.

The elevator arrived at Fong's floor. They stepped out together and made their way to the office.

Tyler silently rehearsed his act and focused upon portraying a persona of absolute narcissism and callousness. Everything depended upon him being believable as a predatory opportunist.

Fong unlocked his office door. "Please, come in, Mr. Faraday."

Tyler quickly surveyed the interior and decided a brief, almost-flippant compliment, would be the most appropriate for his role. "Nice place you got."

"Thank you." Fong took two glasses and a bottle of vintage Cognac from his liquor cabinet. "Brandy?"

Tyler's immediate reaction was to say 'yes', but he quickly changed his mind. An arrogant personality would probably be more demanding. "Actually, I prefer bourbon."

"Of course."

Fong took out a bottle of bourbon, poured Tyler a shot, and handed both bottle and glass to him.

Once they were both seated, Fong took out Tyler's folder. "I do hope you don't mind. We have to run a check on all our new members. The Citadel is an exclusive organization, and we must ensure that our guests meet our requirements."

Tyler feigned a chuckle. "And do I check out?"

Fong's grin beamed down at the file. "You most certainly do. The son and heir of Charlton Faraday, the founder of the Faraday Corporation. Investment specialist with a taste for the finer things in life, an avid gambler, and member of the most prestigious casinos in the world, including the Venetian Macao." He looked up again. "You certainly get around, don't you?"

"It's the only way to be."

The conversation continued for another thirty minutes, with the two men discussing people and places they had in common. They marveled at the small world they lived in, and other considerations of the six degrees of separation.

Finally, Fong said, "So, what brings you to Los Angeles?"

"Oh, just a little business in Beverly Hills. A particular celebrity, I can't say who, is looking to buy a couple of helicopters from my dad."

"I see. Are you alone?"

"Yes, why?"

"According to your résumé, you usually have an escort. Always an extremely attractive escort." Fong shot him a sly grin.

This is it. "It gets boring after a time," Tyler said. "Pussies are like frogs. You've seen one, you've seen 'em all. I'm looking around for something more . . . I don't know. *Kinky*, maybe?" *I can't believe I just said that.*

"Oh, I completely understand."

"Know anywhere in town that stretches the boundaries?"

Fong stared at him for a moment, and Tyler wasn't sure he'd been a little too hasty in asking such questions.

"I just might," Fong said. "But it could be highly expensive."

Tyler laughed in a manner that conveyed money was no object. Fong followed in the mirth.

After a moment, and with a faux-beaming smile, Tyler drummed his fingertips on the desk. "So, c'mon. You gonna tell me?"

"All in good time, Mr. Faraday. Do you plan to be in town on Friday?"

"I could be."

"Good. I'll see what I can do. There is a particular event that takes place every six weeks that I think you will find most stimulating."

Tyler took a sip of his bourbon. "So, can you tell me what to expect?"

"There is a procedure that needs to be followed first, but I will arrange it."

Tyler realized a sociopath would be concerned for his own well-being and promptly assumed the role. "Hey, there's not a chance of me getting busted for something, is there?"

"No. That's what the procedure is all about. Just leave it to me. I assume you have offshore bank accounts?"

"Yeah, several."

"Good. Meet me here at six p.m. on Friday, and we'll discuss it further. For now, let us drink and discuss life."

With a painted grin, Tyler poured himself a generous shot of bourbon and raised his glass with a wink. "You got it."

Tyler was becoming noticeably intoxicated by the early hours, and decided it was time for him to call a cab. On highly amicable terms as far as Fong was concerned, they parted company and awaited their next meeting on Friday evening.

In the privacy of his office once again, Fong took out his cell phone and made a call. "Mae Ling, I may have a highly-lucrative customer for Friday's auction. An

266

extremely wealthy young man with exotic tastes . . . Yes, all of his credentials check out. I will explain the first time procedure to him on Friday. He will have no idea where he is when he arrives." With a satisfied grin, Fong ended the call.

Thirty-Eight

On the Take

Nikki Hawke entered Miranda Curtis' living room at just past 3:00 a.m. Brandon sat on the sofa, deeply focused on a tiny device wedged between his fingers. With his other hand, he held a pin, which he used to carefully bore a slender hole through the center of the device's thin casing.

Beside him on the coffee table, his open silver attaché case rested, displaying an array of sophisticated gadgets positioned in sponge, cut-out compartments.

"Miranda and Belinda are sleeping soundly," Nikki said. "What's that you're doing?"

"It's a transmitter."

"A transmitter for what?"

He finally looked up at her. "You said this organization scans everyone who goes into the auctions for bugs, right?"

"Yes."

He held up the tiny gadget. "This is for Tyler. It's the core from a very sophisticated bugging device. It contains a jamming chip that'll bypass any sensor equipment these clowns have. This technology still hasn't been made available to the public yet."

Nikki sat beside him. "What's Tyler going to do with it?"

"When he goes in there, he'll have this attached to his scalp. I'm creating a hole in it to weave a few of his hairs through." He gestured to a slick, silver, pocket-sized radio receiver on the table. "When he's inside, I'll be close by on

268

the outside listening to everything that goes on in there. First sign of a problem, I'm going in."

"It's good to know you've got this covered and you're thinking everything through. But I have no idea how you think you're gonna take on all that manpower in there."

"Leave that to me."

She stood and moved over to the open attaché case. "Is this all of your weaponry?"

"What you're looking at is just the first layer," he said. "There are three more beneath it. I used to have two cases, but the other was destroyed in a car explosion, two years ago."

There was a knock at the front door. "I'll get it," Nikki said, and exited the room.

She opened the door to see Tyler standing in his tuxedo. His button cover was removed and the top two buttons of his dress shirt were open. His bleary eyes gave away his intoxication.

"Hi," he said without concealing his attraction to her. His inhibitions were clearly lowered.

However, far from concerned, Nikki returned his amorous glare with the same enthusiasm. "How did it go?"

"Well, let's just say I'm in the club." He stepped inside and staggered into the living room.

Brandon stood abruptly with an intensely serious expression. "What did you find out? And keep your voice down. Belinda's asleep."

"Nice to see you too, bro," Tyler said, slurring.

Brandon's brow furrowed. "Hey, are you drunk?"

"Yeah, look, I'm sorry. I didn't want to cause you any anxiety, but I had no choice. I think the son of a bitch

269

wanted to adopt me. I had to suck up to him to get in with him over a bottle of bourbon."

"How do you know you weren't followed?"

"Don't worry, bro. A cab took me from The Citadel to The Four Seasons. I booked a room there earlier in case they checked me out. From there I called another cab from the men's room to meet me round the back and bring me here. I kept my head down the whole time."

"So, what's happening?"

"I'm meeting them at six on Friday night." He paused for a moment. "Actually, that'll be tomorrow night. This is Thursday morning. One way or another, this goes down tomorrow night."

"And?"

"They're taking me to the auction. I did it, Brandon. I actually did it. Fong said they have these auctions every six weeks, and Emily hasn't been with 'em for two months. She has to be there."

Brandon sat down again. "All right. You did great, Ty."

Tyler collapsed onto the couch. "Damn, I need a coffee."

"I'll get it." Nikki stepped into the kitchen. A sudden attack of panic gripped her. What they were planning was positively lethal, and she couldn't conceive of any way they were going to succeed.

***

"Director Wilmot, I'm telling you, you're wasting your time. There is no *Sapphire*. There's nothing more that I, or anybody in this department, can say."

Wilmot stared at Commissioner Landis with Garrett by his side. The agents' gazes were typically intimidating and accusatory, enhanced further by their unresponsiveness.

Unable to cope with the silence anymore, Landis began to perspire. He couldn't be certain if they knew something, or if they were trying to psyche him out. "So, is there anything else I can do for you? Because I've got a busy schedule."

Garrett took a slender digital recorder from her pocket and placed it on Landis' desk. Wilmot stepped forward and pressed the play button. Immediately, the echoed, tinny sound of their conversation the day before came through the small speakers.

Landis shivered at the first two words that came from the recorder.

"I'm just going to zoom this along a little," Wilmot said, and watched the rapidly advancing digital timeline on the LCD. He stopped it and smiled. "This is the best part."

Landis sank back into his chair feeling his face become ashen as his own voice came through the speaker:

Mae Ling? I know my calling you is dangerous, but what we're facing is much more so . . . I've kept you clear of police investigations for five goddamn years, but now it's becoming problematic. I've just had a visit from the director of SDT, a Homeland Security sub-division. This is their second visit to the department. They're looking for Sapphire . . . No, no, of course I didn't tell them anything, but I'm telling you, something's going down, and you should watch your back.

Wilmot stopped the recorder. "That was recorded at thirteen thirty-six hours yesterday, which would be approximately five minutes after we left." He pulled up a chair and smiled gloatingly. "Now, are you sure you don't want to revise your bullshit story, Landis?"

Garrett moved across to the chair besides Wilmot's. She reached under the left underside, peeled away her adhesive-backed, thumbnail-sized transmitter, and held it up with a contemptuous expression.

Landis trembled as his life seemed to be collapsing around him. "Y-you bugged my office?"

Wilmot chuckled. "That's right. It was obvious we weren't going to get any answers out of you voluntarily."

"What do you want from me?"

Garrett sat down beside Wilmot. "We want answers, Commissioner. Who is Sapphire, and where is his organization?"

"P-please, I can't. They'll kill me."

"The alternative could be even worse," Wilmot said. "A police commissioner spending the rest of his life in a federal penitentiary for aiding and abetting a human trafficking outfit, profiting from it, and perverting the course of justice? Just think about it, Landis. They'd have to put your ass in solitary just to keep you alive. After a few weeks of your own company, you'd become a dribbling vegetable."

Landis wept. "P-please—"

"Hey, hey. Don't get all bent out of shape. We can make all of this go away. All we need is information. So far, we've got that you're on the take, and you've enabled this organization to evade police detection from the beginning. What we want to know is—who, and where are they?"

"I don't know."

"What do you mean, you don't know? Who's Mae Ling?"

"S-she's the one who came to me in the beginning. She seduced me and got everything on film. She threatened to expose me. My marriage, my position in the community. . . I could've lost everything."

Wilmot's eyebrows rose. "She's been paying you off too, hasn't she?"

Landis nodded.

"Who is Sapphire? And who is Mae Ling?"

"I've never actually seen Sapphire," Landis said. "Nobody has, except for on a screen. He's African-American, mid-forties, well-dressed, and he broadcasts to the auctions from God-knows-where. Mae Ling is Chinese, and she's his . . . I don't know what you'd call her."

"Where and when do these auctions take place?"

Landis buried his head in his hands, knowing he was damned if he told them, and damned if he didn't. Ultimately, he decided to disclose the location. "It's on the docks."

"OK, here's what's going to happen," Wilmot said. "You're going to tell us exactly where on the docks it is and when the next auction is going to take place."

"It's tomorrow night."

"Well, here's the good news," Garrett said. "We're not here looking for Sapphire, or Mae Ling. We're after someone we're expecting to be at this place imminently."

"Nobody finds it without being a part of it," Landis said.

"Yeah, well, this particular person is extremely resourceful and not to be underestimated."

"Who?"

"No, no, no. We ask the questions, Landis," Wilmot said. "You answer them, and do as you are told. We'll take care of everything else." He turned to Garrett. "If this auction is taking place tomorrow, we'd better get going. We've got a lot of work to do."

Landis stood in desperation. "Hey, wait a minute—"

"Sit down!" Wilmot snapped. "We'll meet you here tomorrow. If you try to warn them, if you try to interfere with this investigation in any way, you're finished, you understand?"

"Yes, I understand. But these people are extremely well-funded, and heavily armed. They're killers."

Garrett turned to Landis with a sly grin. "So are we."

They closed the door behind them, leaving the commissioner to his thoughts with his hands trembling and perspiration dripping from his face.

Wilmot hurriedly exited the LAPD building with Garrett and immediately took out his cell phone.

"So, what's the plan, *Director*?" Garrett said with a wink.

"If this auction is happening tomorrow, and Sapphire has Drake's sister, there's as good a chance as any he's going to be there, *if* he's managed to nail down the location."

"I agree."

Wilmot switched on the phone. "I've already set this up. It took a little persuading, but it's a matter of mutual interest. He's an escaped soldier, and he's their boy."

"*Their* boy?"

"Drake's own comrades. The Eighty-Second."

"You're bringing in the military?"

"No, not simply the military. Drake's own unit. They've got more of a chance of taking him in alive than anybody. They've got the skill, the training, and he's one of them."

"*Was* one of them. He was discharged after he was sent down."

"Doesn't matter. They have battlefield history with him, and the jury did everything possible to let him go free. He's the one who screwed it up for himself."

"You've got a point."

"Yeah, I do. They'll help us to capture Drake, and when it's over, we'll throw the book at Landis. It'll be a beautiful collection for our résumé."

Garrett smirked in agreement.

Wilmot punched in the contact and held the phone to his ear. "This is Director Andrew Wilmot at SDT. Patch me through to General Grant. This is an emergency."

Jed Crane braced his hand against the side wall of the precinct and peered around to see Wilmot and Garrett disappearing into the crowd. "Gotcha."

Thirty-Nine

Playing with Fire

Fabian Rodriguez swaggered across a parking lot toward a bare, warehouse-type environment. Approaching a door at the far end with a smug grin, he recalled, with pride, how far his journey in life had taken him.

Six years earlier, he'd been working the streets of Baja for one of Mexicali's drug cartels since he was fourteen. The day came when he'd been assigned to traffic a consignment of cocaine for Mae Ling Cheung, one of the most fearsome characters he'd ever encountered.

However, Mae Ling had taken to him warmly. She'd offered him a vocational opportunity that would pay him, in one month, more money than he could earn in a year. After eagerly accepting, he relocated to Los Angeles with her, and became her favored scout.

His own survival instincts had long since annihilated any sense of morality. Selling drugs, the kidnapping of children, and seducing women into human cattle auctions, had become a way of life to him. Using his experience, looks, and charm, he developed the ability to spot vulnerable females from a considerable distance, and manipulate them to their doom. Seeing them as nothing more than acquisitions, he never gave a thought to the horrendous torment into which he was leading them. He'd lost sight of the fact that they might have families who would spend their lives grieving. Should his victims lose their lives at the hands of those who purchased them—it was simply business.

He took out a key and inserted it into the door lock. Instantly, the environment changed. He stepped into an ornate corridor with a plush red carpet, leading to a spiral stairwell.

He stood for a moment and beheld the auditorium and catwalk. As many times as he'd seen it, it never failed to fill him with excitement. It had become the source of hundreds of thousands of dollars in commissions. But he was becoming greedier, and today was his day for negotiations.

He turned left, walked through a vacant bar area, and came to another carpeted stairwell. After climbing two flights, he made his way along another corridor. He stopped at the last door, and knocked.

"Come in, Fabian."

Smiling, he entered to see Mae Ling sitting behind her desk filing her talon-like nails.

"Are you ready for tomorrow night?" she said without looking up.

He pulled up a seat opposite her. "You bet I am. This is gonna be our most profitable event yet."

"What makes you say that?"

"Are you kidding me? When have you ever had a virgin nun on the table?"

She finally looked up, and he noticed her studying his cocky expression derisively.

"You still have much to learn, my boy," she said. "Blessed is he who expecteth nothing, for verily he shall not be disappointed."

"What's that? Buddhism?"

She rolled her eyes. "No, Fabian. I'm just trying to keep your feet on the ground."

"Yeah, well, my feet are itchin' to *leave* the ground. I've been at this for six years, and you've been paying me five percent in all that time. I'm the one who does all the leg work."

"Oh?"

"From now on, I want ten percent."

"Do you, now?"

A sense of affront welled up in him, a stark contrast to the arrogant, grinning confidence with which he'd entered. "Hey, come on, lady. Without me, these events wouldn't even be happening. Show a little respect here."

For a fleeting moment, a flash of anger appeared in her eyes. However, she reined it in just as quickly, replacing it with her sultry smile. "I'll talk to Sapphire."

"Yeah, well, when am I gonna meet him? I've been working for the guy all this time, and—"

"He's overseas, as you know. Just leave it to me."

They stared at one another for a tense moment. Even when Mae Ling appeared to be amicable and supportive, she never failed to cause him a slight shiver.

"All right. Thanks." He stood, and made his way to the door.

He looked back at her for a brief moment. Then, without a word, he exited the office and closed the door behind him.

Mae Ling pondered the conversation with rage swelling in her. Fabian was an expendable convenience, at best.

Recruiting scouts was a simplistic task. There were so many other opportunistic, greedy hoodlums on offer. She was not about to be dictated to by one of them, neither was she willing to share any more with Fabian than she already had.

She took out her cell phone and selected a contact. "Jin? I want to see you in my office right now."

Within minutes, a tall, slightly-overweight, oriental male wearing a dark suit entered. His shaved head and stature complemented his cold, hard features.

"Fabian was just here," she said.

"I saw him."

"He's become a problem."

Jin smiled with a hint of sadism.

"You know what to do," she said. "Make sure you leave no trace."

As he left the office, Mae Ling sat back, linking her talon-nailed fingers with no hint of regret.

Fabian stepped back into the parking lot feeling particularly happy, certain he would receive what he'd demanded. With a smile, he continued toward the entrance.

Halfway across, he spotted a silver Mercedes speeding into the lot. It stopped only inches from mowing him down.

Darting back instinctively, he stumbled into Jin who'd come up behind him. Jin grasped his shoulders, and Fabian immediately knew. *Oh, shit.*

Four Chinese goons exited the Mercedes and made slow, daunting steps toward him.

"H-hey, hey, guys. Look, let's talk about this," he said. "You know me. I was just kidding. You know. Kid—"

Cut off mid-sentence by a blow to his solar plexus, he fell to the floor in agony. With one hand braced on the ground, he grasped his stomach with the other. The blade of a hard shoe collided with his elbow, breaking the bone. He collapsed with an ear-piercing shriek.

But it didn't stop.

He felt his jaw shatter under the impact of a heavy boot, followed by another. Stars appeared before his eyes and a veil came over him, as though it wasn't really happening.

The heavies kicked Fabian senseless within seconds, until his face was unrecognizable and bloodied. Wasting no time, two of them grasped him under his arms and dragged his limp form across to the Mercedes. Jin opened up the trunk and hurled Fabian inside.

They closed the trunk again, climbed into the car, and sped out of the parking lot. Jin spun the car around, accelerated along the dockside, and drove on into the night.

Fabian began to stir as the car came to a halt, unaware of how long he'd been unconscious. The pain in his right arm was excruciating. His face stung severely and felt three times its actual size.

He tried to twist around but couldn't. Fear gripped him despite his disorientation. Cramped up in total darkness, he suspected he'd been buried alive.

The car doors closed and vibrated through to the trunk. The back of his head knocked against something that felt like a tin container.

The trunk opened. He looked up to see Jin and his four cronies gazing down upon him, smiling.

Strong hands gripped his lapels and pulled him from the trunk. The pain in what was left of his elbow screamed through his body. He roared under the effects of a torture he'd never before imagined. "Please. Please, no more." His cry came out as a muffled drone, his speech severely impaired by his broken jaw.

They emptied his pockets and took his wallet. He knew they were ensuring there wasn't a trace of identification on him.

They cast him to the floor again, and he looked around to see they'd brought him to the middle of the desert. There was nothing other than rock and cacti for as far as the eye could see. In that moment, he knew they were going to kill him.

Two of them gripped him under his arms again and pulled him along farther into the desert.

"Guys, don't do this," he said with a pleading tone. "I'll do anything. I'm sorry, all right? I'll work for free, I swear. I'll catch you the hottest bitches you've ever seen."

Cold, cruel laughter was their only response.

Finally, they released him and cast him down again. He looked behind to see the Mercedes was at least a hundred yards away.

Jin walked slowly toward him holding a gasoline canister. Fabian realized it must have been what his head had knocked against in the trunk and became blind with terror. "Oh, my God. I'm begging you. Please, Jin. Don't do this!"

Jin continued toward him, grinning. He was quickly upon him, unscrewing the canister. He looked down at him for a prolonged, intimidating moment.

Without warning, he hurled a large splash of gasoline onto Fabian's face. Fabian screamed as the flammable liquid burned into his skin and open lacerations. Jin paused for a moment before pouring more across his body, soaking his jacket and jeans.

Fabian attempted to stand in order to run, but accidentally put pressure onto his broken elbow. The shocking pain almost caused him to lose consciousness again.

Jin poured a short trail away from Fabian on a line of rock and took a cigarette lighter from his pocket.

Only now, at the end, did Fabian experience a moment of repentance. The faces of the women he'd brought into slavery came to his mind as a legion of specters. The looks of terror in their eyes at the moment they'd realized they'd been duped by him, flashed across his mind.

Especially the nun.

"Oh, God. Sweet Jesus. Holy Mary, forgive me."

Jin flicked the lighter and the flame appeared.

"No!"

Jin threw the lighter into the gasoline trail, and Fabian was instantly consumed. His screams echoed across the desert in response to the most horrific, torturous agony a man could experience. He attempted to roll around to extinguish the fire, but found he was too weak, further hampered by his broken elbow.

The flames seared his flesh as his howls continued to echo into the night. Every moment seemed like an eternity to him, an infinity of indescribable, blazing horror.

After almost a minute, he cried out his last. His final thought—the realization that during his life, he had always been playing with fire.

Jin and the others waited until there was no sign of life. Satisfied, they returned to the car, leaving a faint, flickering glow illuminating the Arizona desert night.

Forty

Nexus

Brandon and Nikki stepped out of the van onto the sidewalk of a back street, close to the harbor. With a pair of infrared binoculars in his hand, he followed her to a mesh fence.

"OK, right here," she said.

Brandon followed her gaze to a row of warehouses in the distance. The 9:00 p.m. darkness wasn't helping his visibility. "Which one is it?"

"It's the one at the front, set apart from the rest. Do you see it? It's an old fish factory."

He raised the binoculars and focused in on the building. The infrared revealed it clearly enough, although he was concerned she wasn't remembering correctly. "There's nothing there, Nikki. You sure we've got the right place?"

Looking away, she shivered. "You'd better believe it. I was drugged when I was driven away from there, five years ago, but I saw enough and I remember everything. Every detail, every brick, every sound. Trust me, that's the place."

He lowered the binoculars. "All right, I believe you."

"In five years, the nightmares haven't stopped," she said. "I still wake up in a cold sweat from dreaming I'm still in there."

"Well, tonight, we take this place down forever. Do you think the captives are in there right now?"

"I know they are. All the time I was there I was never moved. Down below are rooms where they kept us confined and groomed us. Your sister is in there right now, I guarantee it."

Brandon snapped his attention back to the building as an urgent need to get inside gripped him. But he knew he had to wait and allow Tyler to do his part. "Come on. Let's get back to the van."

Nikki followed him. "So, what's the deal with you and Belinda?"

"She wanted to come with us, but I told her to stay with Miranda. We think she's pregnant."

"Seriously?"

"Yeah. It's imperative she stays out of harm's way."

They arrived back at the van and climbed in. Brandon took the radio receiver out of the glove compartment and switched it on. "They should be leaving The Citadel any minute. The transmitter I planted in Ty's hair has a range of a hundred miles."

Nikki closed the door and stared intently at the receiver. "I know I don't know Tyler that well, but I'm really scared for him. The butterflies in my stomach are going into overdrive."

Before Brandon could respond, white noise emanated from the receiver as he searched for the frequency. Once he'd found it, he listened intently.

***

Tyler walked across the rear parking lot of The Citadel attired in a new, charcoal-gray, Armani suit. Fong walked alongside him. Ahead was a pristine, black limousine with the rear doors held open by a security guard and a chauffeur. Tyler and Fong climbed in.

"I like the décor you've used in here," Tyler said, gently touching the extravagant, wooden, inside panels.

"Thank you, Mr. Faraday. It's nothing you're not familiar with, I'm sure."

"That's for sure. I've always had a thing for limos, though. There's just something sexy about 'em. Being in control of a sleek babe that can really *drive*, know what I mean?" He winked.

"I know exactly what you mean, Mr. Faraday."

The doors closed, and Fong handed Tyler a blindfold. "I do apologize, but this is part of the first-time security procedure I told you about."

Tyler looked at him, concerned for the briefest moment, but quickly conceded. "You're the boss." He put the blindfold on, always conscious that Brandon needed to know what was happening. He came up with an excuse to speak again. "Do you think you could tie the back of it for me? I don't have much experience with blindfolds."

"Certainly."

Once they were set, the limousine moved.

"Well, it works. Can't see a damn thing," Tyler said.

Fong laughed. "I'm sure you'll feel it was all worth it. There's just one more security procedure when we arrive, and then the night is yours."

"Can't wait."

With his feigned-relaxed attitude convincingly concealing the fear in his pounding heart, Tyler sat back in total darkness. The limousine's engine started, and his journey into the unknown began.

***

Wilmot and Garrett studied a map of Los Angeles Harbor on Commissioner Landis' desk.

Landis placed his index finger on the precise spot. "That's where it is. The old Hamlin fish factory."

"And you're sure this auction is taking place tonight?" Wilmot said.

Landis closed his eyes in shame. "Positive."

"All right, tell Chief Tepper to have a couple of helicopters on standby."

Landis looked up sharply, his eyes filled with worry. "Why? You said this was a private operation."

"There's no such thing, you idiot. Not with something as big as this. The guy we're after has his hands on a particularly impressive piece of hardware. At the very least, we need aerial support. The Eighty-Second are handling it on the ground."

Landis' hands trembled uncontrollably. "T-the Eighty-Second?"

"That's right. The Eighty-Second Airborne Division."

Landis fell back into his chair. "Oh, my God. What have I done?"

"You screwed up major league, Landis, that's what. And we're going to put it right. Now make that goddamn call. It's not going to look too good for this department when a major intelligence operation kicks off in L.A. and the police are nowhere to be seen. With the possibility of human traffickers getting in the way, this is for added credibility as much as anything." Wilmot tapped Garrett's arm. "Come on, let's get to it."

Sergeant Major David Spicer entered the LAPD precinct from the rear corridor, fully clad in a khaki field uniform.

Wilmot and Garrett exited an elevator. Spicer noticed Wilmot immediately.

"Spicer—" Wilmot caught sight of Chief Tepper coming toward them from the other end of the corridor, and then turned back to Spicer. "Just give me a moment."

Tepper approached Wilmot and Garrett looking somewhat bewildered.

"Chief Tepper?" Wilmot said.

"Yes."

"Andrew Wilmot, director of SDT, Langley. This is my associate, Agent Cynthia Garrett." The two men shook hands. Tepper acknowledged Garrett with a nod.

"What's going on?" Tepper said. "I just had a call from Landis. He said you wanted a couple of helicopters deployed to the harbor."

"It's just a precautionary measure," Garrett said. "It might not be necessary. Just wait for our call."

Wilmot turned back to Spicer. "Well, Sergeant Major. It's been a long time."

"Two years."

Tepper turned away to attend to his task.

"The men are out back. I have five troopers and a Humvee," Spicer said. "We're keeping it as low-key as possible. I want Drake brought in peacefully."

"To get to him, you may have to engage armed killers," Wilmot said.

"I'm aware of that. We've all been briefed. But it's not our job to take out human traffickers."

"They're incidental, but they might get in the way of you doing your job. One way or another, Drake must be arrested and brought in."

Darkness came across Spicer's eyes. He didn't care for Wilmot's attitude, and he knew more about Brandon Drake than he could disclose to anyone. Drake wasn't the battle-happy psychopath the other soldiers remembered. He was no longer The Scorpion. His last encounter with Drake had revealed Brandon was a man of integrity, courage, and compassion, albeit as a result of a covert mind-control operation. He could only take him as he found him, and loathed the thought of having to turn in a man he now knew to be a hero. In the case at hand, Drake was taking on a human slavery ring in an attempt at a rescue. All particulars considered, he was following his orders with great reluctance. "My men know their jobs, Director Wilmot." His tone brooked no argument.

"Good. You're his buddies. He'll listen to you."

Wilmot and Garrett turned away and continued along the corridor to greet the military unit.

Uneasily, Spicer followed.

***

The police helicopter unit was alerted by Tepper and communications were conveyed via radio throughout the department. The information relayed was scant—back-up for an intelligence operation involving the army at the old Hamlin fish factory at L.A. harbor.

And that was all Jed Crane needed to know. Parked in a lot on West Second Street behind the LAPD, he'd been listening in on communications in the department for almost two days. Knowing the LAPD radio frequency, the task of intercepting the information with an SDT radio had been relatively simple. There was no doubt the messages he'd just heard were concerned with Wilmot and Garrett's plan to capture Brandon Drake. Brandon had to be alerted if he too had discovered the location.

Jed knew he was risking his own life by doing what he was going to do. He kept reminding himself of the C4 explosive he'd discovered under the bed in his motel room. Running had made no difference. He had nothing to lose by helping a man who was in the same predicament.

He looked at the satchel on the seat next to him. He then glanced behind him, almost obsessively, to ensure his bullet-proof vest was still on the back seat. He opened the glove compartment and took out his pistol and two spare cartridges. Satisfied he had as much protection as possible, he started the car and drove forward.

***

Brandon and Nikki sat in silence listening to the receiver. The van had become mostly concealed by shadows created by a spattering of street lamps in the distance.

Several hundred yards ahead, they heard a car engine and looked up. It was another limousine passing their street. They'd seen around twenty during the past hour. Tyler could have been in any one of them.

Nikki trembled with the realization of what was happening.

"Just hang in there, Nikki. It's almost over," Brandon said.

"Oh, God, Brandon. What if it isn't? What if you and Ty can't stop them?"

"I can't give any guarantees. All we can do is our best. Please understand that. Tyler's a shrewd guy, and I've got the equipment and the experience. That's what we're bringing to this."

She looked ahead without a word as the fluttering in the pit of her stomach continued.

***

The limo finally stopped. Tyler heard the front doors open and assumed the chauffeur and security guard had exited the car. The rear door opened. Tyler felt himself being helped out of the car and very carefully found his footing, unable to see a thing.

"Easy, sir. If you'll just walk slowly ahead, I'll guide you," someone said in an Italian accent.

"Hey, thanks, bud," Ty said, successfully keeping up his 'unconcerned' act.

He was led inside what he assumed was a building and heard the doors close behind him. Dance music echoed in the distance, and he felt sickened. These monsters actually regarded selling innocent women and children as a party. It was just a social occasion to them, like a nightclub.

"Let me relieve you of this, Mr. Faraday," Fong said, and removed the blindfold.

Tyler squinted a few times and took in the overpowering radiant red of the entrance carpet. *Keep it together, Ty. Keep it together.* "Hey, well, I guess you got me."

"What's that?"

"I haven't got a goddamn clue where I am," he said with feigned laughter.

Fong reciprocated his joviality. "I will buy you a drink. But first, there is one more security measure."

"You lead the way." A lump formed in Tyler's throat, but he held it until his head was turned to an angle where he could swallow unseen.

"This way, sir," the Italian said.

Tyler followed them a little farther along the corridor until they came to a door. The Italian opened it, and he followed them inside.

The room was unnervingly bare. There were no tables, chairs, windows, or décor. The walls were simply gray concrete with no wallpaper or plastering.

"Wow," Tyler said. "I think you need to get a decorator firm in."

Fong smiled. "I agree."

"If you would stretch your arms out, please, sir," the Italian said.

Tyler complied, and they quickly frisked him. His skin crawled as the man's hands slid along his legs, waist, and then he patted down his jacket.

"That's fine, sir. We're almost done." The Italian took a small detector and retractable wand from his pocket. After connecting the wand's wire to the socket in the detector, he pulled the sensor out to its full length. "Just stand still, sir. This will only take a moment."

The smile faded from Tyler's face involuntarily as his legs were scanned. Slowly, the wand swept upwards along his body, and then finally came up to his head. *Oh, shit, bro. That transmitter had better be everything you said.*

Forty-One

Heart of Darkness

Tyler held his breath as the probe-wand swept over his head. He watched the Italian glance at the detector. Nothing happened. The light was static green.

As silently as possible, Tyler exhaled through his teeth. Trying to appear calm with his heart pounding in his chest was almost beyond his ability.

The wand sailed along the left side of his body, and finally, it was over. "That's fine, Mr. Faraday. Thank you," the Italian said.

Fong placed his palm in the small of Tyler's back. "Now, let's have a drink, shall we?"

"You lead the way." Tyler accompanied his host out of the room and down a spiral staircase.

Fong approached the bar, and a beautiful young oriental girl, no older than eighteen, greeted him with a smile. "What can I get for you, Mr. Fong?"

"A double brandy, and a double bourbon for my guest."

Tyler's eyes darted around the bar area. It was lavish, with marble pillars, deep burgundy carpeting, and European art-deco fittings. In contrast, the lighting was provided by two exquisite, crystalline chandeliers. Dance music played through four barely-visible, digital speakers positioned at the top four corners of the room. The puzzling factor for Tyler was that the place was empty.

Fong handed him his bourbon.

"Thanks," Tyler said. "So, where is everybody?"

"All of the guests are in the auditorium. We're a little late. It took longer to set up your debit details than we expected, but the auction won't begin for another ten minutes."

"Yeah, about that. If I make a . . . what do you call it? Purchase?"

"Yes?"

"What's gonna show up on my account statement."

Fong smiled reassuringly. "That's what took the time. We've set up a company name for your dealings with us. All of our guests have one. Any transactions will appear on your statement as Pearl, Incorporated."

Tyler considered the name for a moment. "OK, that sounds legit."

Fong gestured to the door on the right. "Shall we go in?"

"Sure."

As they entered the auditorium, Tyler took a sip of his bourbon to help calm his nerves. Once the doors were closed, the dance music was silenced, heightening his anxiety yet again.

He could see two security guards standing at the far side of the walkway at the top of the auditorium. Both were dark-haired males who looked like they'd been hired from a modeling agency.

Spotlights beamed down onto the catwalk, hiding the faces of the audience in shadow.

Fong led Tyler down the steps until they came to their designated seats. Two digital screens were positioned on a small table a few inches in front of them.

Fong directed Tyler to his seat, and then took his own beside him. "This touch screen is linked to your account," he whispered. "When you see something that catches your interest, simply type in your bid here." He pointed to the digital bidding bar on the screen above a zero-to-nine number display. "It's very simple, just like eBay."

"Thanks."

Tyler glanced all around him. From lower down the auditorium, he could make out a few faces through the dim light. He saw a gray-haired man wearing a suit who must've been in his sixties. There was another who looked around fifty. It sickened Tyler to his core. They were older men who were paying to sexually abuse young women and innocent children.

And then he caught a glimpse of the greatest shock of all. Two rows down across the stairwell aisle, he could clearly see the blonde hair of a female customer.

His attention was distracted by the screen at the back of the stage becoming brighter. Within moments, the image of a smiling black man appeared. He was broad-shouldered and attired in a white suit, black silk shirt, and a black tie with a huge diamond studded into the middle. His dreadlocked hair fell onto the tips of his shoulders. His eyes were concealed by sunglasses, conducive with the tropical setting behind him. Tyler guessed it was perhaps the Seychelles or the Maldives, judging from the white sands and crystal blue waters. The man's smile revealed a blue jewel in place of his left upper front tooth. *Sapphire*.

"Ladies and gentlemen," Sapphire said in a deep, baritone voice, and the presentation of sports announcer.

"Welcome to *The Scramble*. This time, we have spared no expense to bring you the very best of the very best."

Whispered mumblings of anticipation filled the room, only to be silenced by Sapphire's continuation. Extending his hands in an offering manner, he revealed gold and jewel-encrusted fingers.

A small girl in a pink dress appeared at the back of the stage. Slowly, she made her way forward along the catwalk.

Tyler gritted his teeth as he fought to curb his rage. The girl looked no older than ten or eleven and Caucasian, with mousy blonde hair. As she came farther into the light, he could see her fear had been anesthetized by some kind of soporific drug. She moved along as though she was in a trance, not fully aware of where she was, or what was happening.

"Show your appreciation for young Tiffany," Sapphire said. "She's ten years old, and yours to do with as you please. Place your bids."

Tyler lowered his head to the bidding screen and watched as the price escalated—five thousand dollars, then six, seven, and eight. His stomach turned over with a feeling of helplessness. Could he save them all by buying them? Was there enough money in his Swiss account? He had around $3 million. But if he tried something like that, he would not only risk losing the funds he needed to buy Emily, he would surely expose his true agenda. Even the thought of purchasing a child chilled him to the bone. He knew, beyond any shadow of a doubt, that of all the places he had encountered during his worldly travels, this was truly the heart of darkness. *There has to be another way to save them. There just has to be another way.*

"Are you not placing a bid, Mr. Faraday?" Fong whispered in his ear.

Note to self: pull it together, NOW! Tyler shrugged his shoulders. "Not my scene. I like 'em younger." He tapped Fong's shoulder and laughed convincingly. "Just kidding. Let me see what's on offer. I need to know what kind of competition I've got. Let's see what she goes for."

"Of course. Take all the time you need, and enjoy the evening."

"You bet."

The final bid for Tiffany flashed up on Tyler's screen at $10,720.

"Congratulations to that high bidder," Sapphire said.

Tyler watched as two tuxedoed men approached the girl, took her by her hands, and led her off the catwalk. He gripped the armrests of his seat tightly in order to hide his trembling hands.

Nine more children appeared on the catwalk—seven girls, and three boys, aged between eight and thirteen. Their prices ended at bids between $8,500 and $9,600 for one of the boys.

Tyler's resolve was wearing down. He didn't know how much more he could endure.

Almost forty-five minutes had elapsed. After the last child had been escorted from the stage, *The Scramble* moved on to the next phase.

"And now, ladies and gentlemen," Sapphire said, "I proudly present a selection of beauties to satisfy even the most discerning. First up is Robin. She's twenty-one years old, a keen athlete, and also trained to fulfill your wildest fantasies."

Tyler watched a beautiful young woman step onto the catwalk. Her black, Lycra body glove accentuated every curve of her lean, toned physique. Her tanned, olive complexion complemented her flowing, raven black hair. Her stunning blue eyes appeared lifeless under the effects of drugs.

Tyler still couldn't bring himself to touch the bidding screen and watched in horror as Robin sold for $75,600.

And so it continued.

Thirteen more women appeared on the catwalk. After the seventh, Tyler became anxious. What if Emily wasn't going to be among them? What if, down to that one possibility, his elaborate plan to save his sister had been in vain?

He was also conscious of Fong's eyes on him at all times. *He suspects something.*

And then Sapphire made his final announcement. "Ladies and gentlemen, we have saved the very best for last."

Tyler's gaze shot up. At the back of the stage, a figure appeared in silhouette. As she came into the light, her white dress became visible, with a matching silk hood resting across the top of her head. Her brown hair was perfectly straight, and her skin was flawless. Her face radiated innocence and purity.

Tyler's heart pounded, and his eyes filled with tears, unable to rein in his emotions. *Oh, my God.*

"Emily is twenty-four . . . and a nun," Sapphire said. "She has never been touched by a man. Surely, she is our finest acquisition to date."

Tyler couldn't avoid noticing the unanimous ambiance of enthusiastic attention all around him. All eyes were fixed on Emily. Transfixed, he watched as she slowly moved along the catwalk like a human mannequin.

The numbers on the screen increased rapidly before him. Within seconds, the bids reached $100,000. Knowing how to play the game, Tyler fought back every instinct to place a bid. The way to succeed was to bid high and last. His fingers trembled on the screen, but he didn't enter a number.

Fong noticed Tyler's hands, and then he looked up to see perspiration coating his brow. The young man's rapid breathing and demeanor seemed to be more *desperate* than passionate. He'd shown no interest in any of the other offerings. Fong put it down to Tyler's own words, initially. He'd said he was looking for something different, but he was now certain there was more to it than that. Tyler Faraday was not what he seemed.

Almost casually, Fong turned his head fleetingly to Emily. He glanced back at Tyler and then back to Emily again. After quietly standing, he eased his way out onto the steps, leaving Tyler engrossed in the bidding war.

Fong hurried out to the back of the bar area, up the two flights of steps, and almost ran along the corridor. He arrived at Mae Ling's door and entered without knocking.

She looked away from her monitor screen with a start. "What—?"

"Shut up and listen," Fong cut her off in Mandarin. "We may have a serious problem."

With her hands pressed onto her desk, she stood slowly with an almost-knowing look in her eyes. "What's going on?"

"I don't think Tyler Faraday is here for recreational reasons."

Fear showed in Mae Ling's eyes. "I had a call from Landis a couple of days ago. Do you think he's with the authorities?"

"It's possible, but I doubt it. I think his interest is much more personal."

"A rescue attempt?"

"I think so."

She turned back to the screen. Emily's bids had just soared over $1 million.

She took out her cell phone and made a call. "Jin? I want to see you in my office right away."

Tyler waited with unendurable tension until the bidding stopped at $1.25 million.

"You have ten seconds to enter your bids," Sapphire said. "Going, going . . ."

With desperate speed, Tyler entered $2 million.

"Congratulations to our winning bidder."

Tyler sat back and exhaled with the relief of having won his sister's freedom.

Sapphire grinned. "That concludes *The Scramble*. Enjoy the rest of your evening. Until next time, friends." The image on the screen disappeared and the lights came on.

The auditorium was silent. The bidders stood, and Tyler noticed how their gazes were all aimed downwards. Nobody made eye contact with anyone.

Shaking, he got out of his seat and immediately felt a hand on his shoulder. He turned to see Fong smiling.

"Did you win, Mr. Faraday?"

Tyler forced a smile. "Yes, I did, it seems."

"Congratulations. If you'd like to follow me, we can arrange for your purchase to be secured. There is a procedure to ensure that you leave with your acquisition in complete safety."

"Thank you."

Fong led him to Mae Ling's office. Tyler shivered at the cruel coldness radiating from the woman before him.

And then he saw the huge behemoth standing behind the door.

"It's a pleasure to meet you, Mr. Faraday," Mae Ling said. "I am Mae Ling Cheung, the administrator of this facility."

"Well, it's a pleasure to meet you, ma'am."

She moved from behind the desk and came closer to him, her hospitable expression darkening. "I haven't got time to waste on frivolities, so I'm going to get to the point. The only question I have is—who the hell are you?"

Tyler frowned, confused. "I . . . I'm not sure I follow you."

Mae Ling took a face-down photograph from her desk. "I don't know if you are with the authorities, but the one thing I just can't get past . . ." She turned the photograph over. Tyler looked down at a close-up of Emily's face. "Is the striking resemblance."

A lump formed in his throat. *Oh, boy.*

"Jin," she said.

Tyler cried out with the pain of his left arm being twisted high behind his back.

Forty-Two

The Secret of Sapphire

"It's going down. He's in trouble!" Brandon threw the receiver onto Nikki's lap. Before she could say anything, he was out of the van.

By the time he reached the rear doors, his jacket and shirt were already off his back. He opened the doors and climbed inside, kicking off his shoes immediately. He unbuckled his jeans and threw all of his clothing to the far side behind the Turbo Swan.

He unclasped a metallic, silver chest in the corner. With desperate speed, he reached inside and took out the Kevlar pants and jacket, feeding himself into them as fast as his hands could move.

Next, he took out the boots and put them on. It took him less than a minute to secure the buckle straps along both ankles and calves

After putting on the armored gloves, he grasped the tool belt from the silver chest and secured it around his waist. Skimming it with his hands, he ensured all of his weaponry was attached to the individual compartments—two state-of-the-art machine pistols, the sonic force emitter, the laser torch, and a spider cable, among several other potentially-useful devices.

Finally, he took the helmet and brought it up to his head. As he was about to put it on, he froze with an almost-sixth sense that someone was in the van with him.

He looked to his right. Huddled behind the Turbo Swan was a sight that caused his heart to sink into despair. "Belinda?"

She stood with a guilty look on her face. "I'm sorry."

"I told you to stay with Miranda! You're pregnant. You can't be here now."

"I-I couldn't stay, Brandon. I love you. Nothing has changed since North Carolina. I'm with you to the end, remember?"

He put his helmet on, lifted the visor, and gently held her by the shoulders. "Tyler was made. I have to go, baby. Please. I'm begging you. Stay with Nikki. She's really scared."

"OK, but . . ."

"What?"

"Oh, God. Please don't die, baby."

His face expressionless, he turned away, ran to the open doors, and leaped out of the van.

***

Kevin Hobson sat in the control room of Channel 7's *Studio 6*, surrounded by technicians and TV monitors. Overseeing a late night live interview between his top anchor person, Tara Willoughby, and a particularly prominent politician, wasn't his idea of fun.

He'd continued in his function as the station's CEO, but his experience with Brandon Drake and Belinda Reese two years earlier, remained the highlight of his journalistic career. Nothing since had captured the public attention like that particular interview. Armed killers bursting into his studio had been a terrifying, but highly-publicized incident. It had thrust Channel 7 into a media league far above its original status.

His attention was distracted by the abrupt entrance of his long-standing, petite assistant, Julie Beacham. "What's going on?" he said.

"We've just had a tip from Charlie downtown. Something big is about to kick off down at the docks."

"What?"

"No specific details. Something was overheard down at police headquarters about Homeland Security, police helicopters, and the Eighty-Second Airborne Division."

Hobson stood rapidly, holding her eager look for a moment. "Homeland Security and the Eighty-Second add up to Brandon Drake. I can feel it. Get Tara and a news crew down to the docks right away."

Julie cringed. "As you can see, Tara's in the middle of a live interview."

He aggressively gestured to the politician on the monitor. "Get that goddamn, boring asshole out of here! We've got real news to cover."

"I'll use slightly different wording." She turned and exited the room.

Hobson followed her, his heart aglow with opportunistic elation.

***

Brandon reached the edge of the Hamlin factory and braced his back against the front wall. Peering around the side to his left, he saw the length of the building was clear.

After taking the sonic force emitter from his tool belt, he scurried along the side toward the rear and reached the end within moments. He leaned against the wall again and peered along the back of the building.

Two men were at the far end guarding an entrance door, both carrying machine guns. Brandon knew his armor could withstand the bullets, although the impacts would seriously knock the wind out of him. The real danger was the alerting noise the gunfire would create.

Despite the darkness, he could make out the two men were Caucasian and wearing night camos. He knew he'd have to take them out in rapid succession.

Shielding half of his body behind the wall, he reached around, aimed the sonic force emitter squarely at the face of the guard nearest to him, and took the shot. The man fell to the ground instantly.

The second guard raised his machine gun, but not quickly enough. A sonic wave bolt rendered him unconscious, and he collapsed onto his colleague.

Without a moment to spare, Brandon sprinted along the back of the building to the door. He stepped over the unconscious guards and studied the door for a second, discovering it was steel and locked from within.

Adrenaline coursed through him in the grip of self-doubt. Did he have the ability to defeat whatever awaited him inside?

He recalled the time he'd set off from the cabin to stop the attack against Carringby Industries. It was the same then as it was now. He was alone. Once again, he had to face the fact that he was afraid.

Reaching around, he gripped the laser torch on his tool belt. As he drew it out of its titanium holder, he was startled by a hand on his shoulder.

He spun around and knocked the hand away. Instinctively falling into a stance, he put his mysterious visitor in a position out of his own body range. He grasped the man by the throat and thrust him up against the wall. Only then did he see who it was. He lifted his visor and stared into the man's perturbed eyes. "Jed?"

"Yeah, take it easy. I'm trying to help," Jed Crane said.

Brandon released him and stepped back. "What are you doing here?"

"Brandon, you've got to get out of here. Wilmot and Garrett are on their way down here with the police and some of your buddies from the Eighty-Second."

"Dammit! I can't go, Jed. My brother and sister are in there, and they know what Tyler's been trying to do. If I don't go in there right now, they're gonna kill him."

Jed exhaled with a knowing look. "All right, I'll help you. Two of us are going to be more use than one. Fill me in on what we're dealing with."

Brandon knelt down and took the two machine guns from the unconscious guards. He immediately recognized them as type 05 JS nine millimeter submachine guns. *Why would American personnel be carrying Chinese-manufactured firearms?*

He hooked a gun across his shoulder and gave the other to Jed. "This should help. I've got a couple of whisper-silent machine pistols on my belt. I want to make as little noise as possible in there, but I have a feeling it's not gonna make a difference for long."

Jed hooked the machine gun across his shoulder and over his satchel. "Thanks. So, what are we up against?"

"A human trafficking outfit led by some African-American kingpin called Sapphire, who nobody has ever seen in the flesh. He only appears on a screen apparently, from different locations. That's all I know. Everybody who knows about him gets scared for their lives."

Brandon adjusted the calibrator on the pen-sized laser torch. A fine beam of orange light cut into the taut crack in the door. As he drew the laser downwards past the door lock, the odor of burning metal filled the air.

"That's an impressive piece of equipment you've got there," Crane said. "I've never seen anything like it."

"I know. All this stuff I've got on me is experimental tech. I swiped it from Mach Industries a couple of years back."

"Yeah, so I was told."

The beam cut down to the bottom and the door swung open a fraction of an inch.

Brandon lightly grasped the edge just above the point where the laser had made contact. The door creaked open.

The two men held themselves behind the door for a moment. There were no sounds coming from within.

Brandon took one of the machine pistols from his belt, braced it against his helmet, and darted around the door, aiming inside. There was nothing other than a maintenance stairwell. "It's clear. Let's go."

Jed followed him up the stairwell, both of them taking cautious steps.

Brandon caught a glimpse of what was ahead of them when he was ten steps from the top. It appeared to be an office-style corridor with several rooms on the right.

He waved Jed up when he reached the top, and slowly edged his way along. The first room was empty, save for a curious slew of Chinese regalia and paperwork.

A yard away from the second room, he could hear a rustling of activity. He gestured to Jed to be prepared. Crane held his pistol next to his ear.

They entered the small room to find three Chinese males sitting at a computer terminal. Three monitor screens appeared to show different locations within the complex.

The Chinese operatives turned in unison, alerted by the presence behind them. The momentary shock on their faces was clear as their gazes fell upon the tall, hulking, black-armored figure in the doorway. They went for their pistols concealed beneath their jackets.

With one squeeze of the trigger, Brandon sprayed them with bullets to the faint drum roll of gunfire through a silencer. The walls and floor were instantly splattered with blood.

Brandon stood silent, numb with shock. He removed his helmet and looked upon the carnage.

Jed stepped in front of him. "Hey, what's wrong?"

"I . . . I killed them. The last time was Payne."

"Then count this as four times you've done the world a favor. Those guys just tried to draw on you. You had no choice."

Jed glanced around the room. His fingers slid through a series of papers, Chinese trinkets, and insignia on the desk. There was a particular golden dragon emblem on the walls, on the paperwork, and on the lapels of the dead men on the floor. His eyebrows rose. "Oh, my God. I know what this is."

"What?"

Jed gestured to another screen in the far corner of the room with the image a black man set in freeze frame. "Is this the guy? Is this Sapphire?"

Brandon came up behind him. "I guess it has to be. Ugly son of a bitch, isn't he?"

"No, no, no. This can't be right," Crane said. "No African-American would be at the top of an organization like this."

"I don't understand."

Crane reached behind the monitor screen and followed the connection cables with his fingers. "Just as I suspected. These wires are linked to a digital enhancement computer."

"What?"

"This guy isn't being transmitted from anywhere. This isn't a live-link transmission receiver. It's a digital creative suite."

"So, what are we dealing with?"

"Tong."

"Tong?"

"Chinese mafia. Or, at least some offshoot of it. They're obviously concealing their activities from whatever Tong family they broke away from. Chances are, even their customers don't know who they really are. They're using American thugs as an outward cover, like those two clowns you zapped outside."

Brandon pointed to the screen. "So, who the hell is *he*?"

"He's nobody, Brandon. He's a computer-generated, digital glove puppet that's being used as a cover."

Brandon's mouth fell open. The answer had been staring them all in the face from the beginning. How could a man, who could put so much fear into people, be so untraceable? How could nobody have ever seen him?

The answer fell from his lips as he finally understood. "Sapphire doesn't exist."

Forty-Three

Warriors

Brandon seemed transfixed by the image of Sapphire on the monitor. The lifelike nature of it was staggering. It was clear how it had fooled so many.

"Come on," Jed said. "We've got to get out of here."

Brandon turned around, headed toward the door, and heard running feet came from the corridor.

As they reached the doorway, they found themselves blocked in by a team of Chinese goons all dressed in black security attire. The six-feet-tall, broad-shouldered leader kicked Brandon squarely in the chest, sending him flying back across the room into the Sapphire monitor.

Jed drew his pistol, but the attacker knocked it out of his hand. Jed fell under the impact of a well-placed fist to his left jaw.

Brandon got back on his feet and screamed. The leader had grasped his shoulder.

Jed looked up from the floor as Brandon cried out in agony. He remembered, from the reports of Drake's escape from Leavenworth, that he'd taken a bullet in the shoulder. Clearly, this huge attacker was exerting a Herculean grip on the wound.

But then, something happened. The pain seemed to trigger off an all-consuming rage within Drake. His eyes rapidly took on a look of unbridled hatred and became bloodshot. The scar on his forehead deepened, and Jed knew what was happening. He recalled the details of

313

Brandon's rampage during his trial at Fort Bragg. It made more sense after Brandon told him his memory had been changed, and that he used to be a psychopath known as The Scorpion. But if there was ever a time he would have wished for it to happen, it was now.

"Get your hands off me, motherfucker!" Brandon drove his elbow back into the man's solar plexus and threw him over his shoulder into the monitor screens.

Three more attackers were upon him in an instant. One grasped his throat, but he snapped the man's wrist just as quickly. As his assailant fell to the floor, writhing in pain, his right foot shot up to collide with the jaws of the other two, shattering their teeth with blinding speed.

The fourth attacker drew his gun on Brandon. Jed drew his .45 caliber and fired without hesitation. The attacker fell, holding his chest with blood oozing through his fingers.

Brandon glanced behind at Jed, momentarily distracted from the continuing threats.

Jed saw a fifth Chinese assailant pointing a gun at Brandon. "Look out!"

In the blink of an eye, Drake kicked the weapon out the man's hand.

The attacker assumed a martial arts stance, raising the blades of his hands defensively in front of his face.

Brandon reciprocated.

The assailant issued his battle cry and shot a series of kicks toward Brandon's head. However, Brandon blocked every strike and caught the man's right leg long enough to drive his elbow into his knee, inverting it irreparably. A bellow filled the room as the attacker collapsed. Brandon came toward him with a maniacal look in his eyes.

The first attacker regained his senses, pushed himself up off the shattered monitors, and drew his gun. Brandon pointed his machine pistol in his face and fired without moving his gaze from the whimpering assailant on the floor. Blood and brain matter painted the wall, but Brandon didn't give it so much as a glance.

"P-please. No shoot. No shoot," the fallen attacker pleaded in broken English.

Brandon knelt down beside him and pressed the muzzle of his gun into his shattered knee. The assailant's high pitched, banshee-like scream seemed barely human.

"Where's my brother?" Brandon growled.

"No know who you mean."

"The young, good-looking guy who came in here with Fong."

The assailant shook his head, refusing to speak.

Brandon pressed the pistol into the broken knee again, producing another ear-splitting cry.

"P-please, stop!"

"Where is he?"

"With Mae Ling."

"Who's Mae Ling?"

The man wept as his resolve gave out. "E-end of corridor . . . turn left. End corridor . . . right . . . last door."

Brandon stood and stared at his adversary for a moment. Without warning, he raised his pistol and fired until virtually nothing was left of his foe's head.

Jed watched and shivered. The man had been helpless, but Drake killed him without a second thought. His persona had changed so rapidly.

Brandon picked his helmet up from the floor, placed it back on his head, and walked out without a word.

With his pistol in hand and a machine gun and satchel across his shoulder, Crane followed him with growing unease. They might have needed The Scorpion in that moment, but he considered the possibility that the solution was just as hazardous as the problem. Brandon Drake was clearly out of control.

***

Jin kicked Tyler in the stomach, knocking him across the width of Mae Ling's office. "Who are you working for?"

Tyler gasped for breath lying on his side in a fetal position, grimacing in pain. "I–I don't know what you're talking about, man. You're making a mistake."

"Who is this Emily to you?"

"J-just some broad I bought down there."

Jin bent down and grasped him by the throat. Tyler gripped the man's wrist, but Jin was far stronger. Lifting Tyler off the ground, he pinned him up against the wall. "Wrong answer. Now, who is she to you?"

Tyler's eyes bulged and he felt his face becoming a dark shade of purple. He tried to speak but it was impossible. Jin was choking him to death.

The office door crashed in.

Jin loosened his grip. Tyler fell to his knees grasping his throat, barely able to see clearly.

The Chinese behemoth turned to the black-garbed titan and drove his fist into the helmet, but he seemed unfazed by the blow. Brandon allowed him to strike repeatedly, almost tauntingly, but the blows were having no effect.

Jin hurled himself upon Brandon, driving him back into the wall. Pinned against the plaster, unable to move his arms, he drove his helmet into Jin's nose, breaking it. Blood spattered the hoodlum's face, giving him the opportunity to break away from the loosened grip. With two free hands, he grasped Jin's head and rotated it clockwise to the sound of a hollow crack.

Jin's lifeless form fell from his grasp.

Tyler stood and approached his brother. "Boy, am I glad to see you."

Brandon turned his shielded head toward him menacingly.

Tyler swallowed hard.

***

Belinda chewed her hair anxiously. Nikki sat with her in the van and placed a supportive arm around her shoulder. "I wish there was something I could say."

Belinda opened the side door. "I've got to get out of here."

"Where are you going?"

"Nowhere. I just need some air."

Nikki followed her out, and they walked toward the end of the side street.

"This is driving me crazy," Belinda said, shaking. "They're in there, and I haven't a clue what's going on."

"I know, but there's nothing we can do. It's out of our hands."

They reached the end of the street and looked around aimlessly.

To the right, Belinda noticed headlights coming toward them in the distance. "Wait. Somebody's coming."

Nikki looked in the same direction. Another vehicle appeared behind the first. And another.

The rear cars stopped, but the first continued along the street. As it came closer, Belinda squinted. "Is . . . ?"

"What?"

"Is that a jeep?"

Nikki walked closer to it. "It's a Humvee, I think."

"Oh, God." Belinda's feet automatically stepped backward. "Come on."

Nikki followed her to the rear of the van. Belinda crouched down in the shadows, peered around the side, and saw the Humvee pass the side street.

Nikki crouched low behind her and watched through the mesh fencing. The Humvee turned onto the warehouse complex and stopped approximately one hundred yards from the front of the Hamlin factory.

The doors flew open and six men stepped out, fully armored in pale camouflage, each carrying automatic firearms.

Belinda studied the scene, and it quickly became apparent who was leading the operation. The sergeant major directed the other soldiers to disperse around the factory. Belinda recognized him even from a distance. "David?"

"What?"

"I know who that man is."

"Who?"

"His name is David Spicer. He's Brandon's friend. He helped us in North Carolina a couple of years ago."

"Well, that's got to be a good thing, surely. He's gonna be getting military help in there."

"I sure hope you're right." Belinda reached underneath her jacket and gently touched Tyler's Super Carry HD tucked into the rim of her jeans. "But we're not as helpless as you think."

***

Ten police officers set up a roadblock while attempting to keep the onlookers and TV crew at bay.

Looking particularly exasperated, Chief Tepper approached a younger officer. "Blaine, I want you to handle the reporters. I've got enough to deal with. I don't need this crap right now."

"Yes, sir." Officer Jack Blaine approached Tara Willoughby and her camera crew.

Tara pointed her microphone toward him. "Officer, what can you tell us?"

"There's no comment at this time, Ms. Willoughby, so I'm going to have to ask you to stand back."

Undeterred, she persisted. "Is there any truth to the rumors that this is a covert military operation with Homeland Security involvement?"

"Ma'am, we have no information at this time."

"Does this have anything to do with Brandon Drake?"

Blaine was momentarily silent. He was as 'in the dark' as every other officer present, but the mention of Drake's name struck a very personal chord with him. The incident of two years ago flashed before his eyes, when Drake, a man he'd been pursuing through the back streets of L.A., stopped and risked his own escape to help him. Blaine could almost feel the impact of the bullet wound again— the injury Drake had stopped to bind in order to save his life. The thought that he might now be a party to apprehending Drake was loathsome, especially if Brandon was, once again, in the process of helping innocent people. He could do no more than give an honest answer. "I sure hope not."

"Thank you, officer." Tara turned to the camera. "Are we ready?"

"Yep," the cameraman said.

She raised the microphone to her mouth again. "This is Tara Willoughby, reporting live from L.A. Harbor."

***

Brandon lifted his visor, and Tyler's concern eased for a moment.

"Are you OK?" Brandon said.

Tyler could hear the coldness in his brother's tone and the violence in his eyes was unmistakable. He instinctively knew The Scorpion persona was dominant. "I'm fine. They figured me out because I looked like Emily."

"I heard it on the receiver. Where is she?"

"The last I saw, she was being taken behind the stage with the others."

"Show me where."

Jed entered the room.

"What are you doing here?" Tyler said.

"Long story," Jed replied. "Where's this Mae Ling?"

"I don't know." Tyler gestured to Jin's corpse. "She just took off with Fong, and left me in here with *that* son of a bitch."

Brandon took the machine gun from his shoulder and motioned to the shattered door. "Show me where the stage is."

Tyler gingerly stepped past Brandon and led them out.

Brandon checked the machine gun, satisfying himself it was loaded and in order. It was a cumbersome weapon, but he wasn't about to waste valuable artillery. He decided he would eject the bullets in it first and then use the machine pistols.

Tyler led them down the stairwell into the bar area. The patrons ceased their discussions and turned to them fearfully.

Brandon and Jed made their way through the crowd with their guns trained on them. Jed's eyes showed a surge of revulsion.

Even through his dark haze, Brandon remembered he was going to become a father. The fury took hold of him again. These were sick monsters who bought children to sexually abuse and torture them. He had no control over himself any longer. He raised the machine gun and prepared to dispatch every one of them.

The sound of a stampede coming from the stairwell distracted him. Running back, he looked up to see a cadre of armed, Chinese killers coming down the steps. Without hesitation, he opened fire, and the bar area was filled with screams.

He called out to Tyler and Jed, "I'll hold them off. Get the women and children out of here. Go! Go! Go!"

Forty-Four

Big Brother

David Spicer joined his five men at the rear door of the factory and stepped around two fallen guards who seemed to be regaining consciousness. The sound of machine gun fire rang out from inside, along with a very distinctive roar.

"That's Drake. I'd know that battle cry anywhere." David turned to his men and made a very personal decision. "Gentlemen, we go in and stand with him."

The soldiers gripped their guns and ran up the steps, single file.

David quickly considered his strategy. He couldn't tell Brandon the truth of why they had come. At least not yet.

Brandon chased the attackers relentlessly through the complex. He'd driven them back to the first floor corridor and taken four of them out. At least another fifteen remained, but his onslaught was successfully keeping them at bay. He was just one man, completely outnumbered, and yet he didn't give any of them the opportunity to turn and retaliate. So much was at stake. At all costs, he had to drive them away from his brother and sister.

They turned into the last corridor toward the steps leading to the back exit.

Brandon held himself still at the sound of another hail of bullets coming from around the corner. *What the hell?*

Then he heard another stampede coming toward him. It became quieter again, as though they'd changed direction.

Readying his machine gun, he resumed his pursuit of the traffickers, having spotted the last of them hurrying through a left side door.

And then he saw David and five troopers. A dead Chinese operative was on the floor behind them, riddled with bullets. He instantly realized what the other gunfire had been. The traffickers had run into the soldiers and retreated.

David halted and frowned, raising his hand for his men to stop. "Drake?"

Brandon and David looked upon one another with mutual uncertainty.

Brandon lowered his firearm and noticed David's rank bars. He lifted his visor and saluted. "Sergeant Major. What—?"

"We're here to help," David said.

"We have to stop them, sir. They have my sister and many others. Women and children. My brother is trying to get them out of here. Those bastards are heading back down. We can't let them get to the captives."

Spicer kept his eyes on Drake and issued his order. "You heard, gentlemen. Follow Sergeant Drake and back him up."

Brandon managed a smile. "Thank you, sir."

Spicer grinned wryly. "That outfit is ridiculous, soldier."

"You can sue me later, sir." Brandon lowered the visor and headed through the side door.

He came upon the heavies as they arrived at a catwalk leading to a metallic stairwell. At the bottom was the arrival bay. Within seconds, they were midway down the steps.

Brandon glanced over the parapet and quickly calculated the architecture of the building. There had to be a door down there that would lead them back inside. Tyler, Emily, and Jed were inside.

He took the bulbous spider cable device from his belt and aimed it toward a steel rafter positioned across the middle of the bay. With the touch of a button, the cable shot out of the casing and wrapped around the beam. The metallic claw at the end of the line clasped around the wire. Gripping the cable tightly, he leaped from the catwalk and swung down to the ground.

As he landed, he saw the first trafficker heading for the door at the far end, and opened fire. The man appeared to dance to the repeated impact of bullets shooting through his body. Finally, he fell to the floor in a river of blood.

The others turned and fired at Drake. Several bullets struck the Kevlar, knocking him back behind one of the limousines. Out of the corner of his eye, he noticed Spicer and the soldiers arriving on the catwalk while he exchanged fire from behind the car. The traffickers quickly adopted the same strategy and used the cars for cover.

The troopers aimed into the bay and took out three traffickers before heading down the steps.

Tyler followed Jed across the stage to the left side behind the wings, leaving the trembling customers behind in the bar area. The sound of gunfire continued to ring out from the arrival bay above.

Jed raised his machine gun to eye level and carefully edged along the side of the stage.

Rapidly, he spun around and aimed the gun into the clearing. The women and children stood before them, barely awake.

Two American guards raised their hands in surrender.

"Get on your knees and place your hands behind your heads," Jed said.

They complied without hesitation.

Tyler came backstage into the clearing. His gaze immediately fell upon little Tiffany, the first child he'd witnessed being auctioned. Tears rolled down her cheeks. She appeared to be utterly terrified. The drugs that had been administered to her seemed to be wearing off.

He hurried over to her and knelt down, taking her hands into his own. "Hey, hey. It's OK," he said in a soft, comforting tone. "Everything's gonna be fine now, Tiffany. My name's Tyler." He gestured to Crane. "That's my friend, Jed. We're gonna get you out of here and back to your family." He looked up at the other captives and smiled confidently. "All of you. You don't know it, but we've all got a big brother upstairs, and right now he's taking care of the bullies."

Tiffany threw her arms around Tyler, and he held her tightly. A lump formed in his throat. Picking her up, he looked around at the others, studying their faces one by one.

Jed approached him. "It's all clear, Tyler. Let's take them back upstairs. Brandon and I got in through a door at the rear of the building. We can get them all outside via the stairwell."

Tyler didn't respond. He simply stood, holding the little girl, horrified.

"Hey, Tyler? What's wrong?" Jed asked.

"I-it can't be."

"What can't be?"

"I saw her come back here, dammit! I saw her."

"Who?"

"Emily. I saw her leave the stage and come back here, but she's gone."

Without hesitation, Jed trained his machine gun on the two guards. "Where is she, you bastards?"

The two men shook their heads, trembling.

"I said where the hell is she?"

Forty-Five

Warzone

The battle in the arrival bay raged. The soldiers dispatched the traffickers at the back while Brandon fired at those who were closer to the front. Within minutes, blood spattered the floor and dripped from the limousines. Brandon emptied the bullets in the machine gun, cast it down, and resumed the exchange with one of his machine pistols.

Corpses were strewn across the bay in a reflection of the horrors of war. The faces of the deceased were simply no longer—a ghastly display of gaping craters revealing the nauseating vision of crimson-soaked skull bone and brain remnants.

Brandon emerged from behind the limousine in search of the remaining traffickers.

"Drake!" David said.

Brandon looked up and saw one of the traffickers on the opposite side of the aisle with his machine gun raised. He dived out of range at the moment the trigger was squeezed. The bullets struck the fuel tank of one of the limousines, and the car exploded.

The soldiers threw themselves onto the floor, but the force of the explosion hurled Brandon across the bay. His body crashed into the front entrance doors, loosening his helmet. It rolled out of his reach as he landed.

From his position on the floor, Spicer shot the gunman, striking him squarely in the back of the head. "Drake, that's the last of them. You OK?"

Brandon shook his head in an attempt to regain his senses.

The rear entrance door latch clicked open and Emily appeared. Mae Ling held a gun to her temple.

Brandon looked up from the floor and raised himself a few inches. He tilted his head, not entirely sure if he was dreaming. She looked so much like him, he was mesmerized.

Emily looked back at him and their gazes locked. Even through the clear haze of narcotics, she muttered, "Br-brother."

Tears filled Brandon's eyes. Of all the mysteries of his past life, she was the last piece of the puzzle.

"If any one of you makes a single move, I swear I will blow her brains out!" Mae Ling said.

"No!" Brandon cried, panic-stricken.

He saw the soldiers lowering their firearms, and David's expression sank into the anguish of defeat.

Using Emily as a shield, Mae Ling moved sideways toward an iron door in the far left-hand corner of the parking area. She passed a large key she'd had palmed next to her pistol's cartridge holder into her other hand. Her gaze didn't move from the soldiers.

As she reached the door, she gripped Emily tightly with her right arm and held the gun against her breast. She glanced at the door for a split second before inserting the key into the lock.

Brandon saw the soldiers staring at her bitterly as she fumbled around twisting the key.

Mae Ling pushed the door open before bringing the pistol back to Emily's temple.

Brandon watched with a sinking feeling in his heart. Then, they disappeared through the door.

Once outside, Mae Ling kicked the door shut and locked it.

"Let her go."

She froze at the unmistakable sound of a pistol being cocked next to her ear.

"Drop the gun."

Belinda kept the .45 trained on Mae Ling, while Nikki stepped in front of her. "Give it to me!"

Bitterly, Mae Ling handed the gun over. "You."

"So, you remember me, Mae Ling."

"Of course. The one that got away."

Nikki trained Mae Ling's gun on her. "And the one who took you down. Without me, they never would have found you."

Belinda came around to face Emily and gently held her by the shoulders.

"She'll be drugged," Nikki said.

"Yeah, you're right." Belinda took Emily's face in her hands. "My God, your similarity to Brandon and Tyler is incredible. It's all right, Emily. Come with us. We're going to get you to safety."

Nikki pressed the gun to Mae Ling's chest. "Give me the door key."

"What?"

"Give. Me. The. Door. Key."

Reluctantly, Mae Ling complied.

Nikki unlocked the side door and opened it. "Get in."

Mae Ling trembled. "Look, maybe we can work something out."

"I already have. I'll let the troopers and this poor girl's brothers deal with you. Now get back in there."

Fearfully, Mae Ling re-entered the arrival bay. She heard the click of the door locking behind her and turned around slowly. The arrival bay was deserted and filled with smoke from the burning limousine. As the smoke drifted toward her, she knew she had to get out of there.

She hurried along the back wall to the door and sealed herself inside, away from the fumes. She knew she was in the safest place. The soldiers had most likely gone outside to intercept her and rescue Emily. She ran along the corridor, down the spiral staircase, and into the bar.

The cowering bidders looked upon her questioningly. None of them knew she was their anonymous host, and she had no words for them. For the first time in her life, she felt truly helpless.

Tyler and Jed led the captives out through the open back door and around the building. The women and children were delirious, and the journey was slow. Jed monitored them from the rear while Tyler led them from the front.

Tyler felt angst-ridden. He was leading every one of them to safety, except his sister.

As they came to the front of the building, he spotted Belinda and Nikki walking past the Humvee with another. "Hey!"

They turned around and his heart leaped at the sight of Emily. "Oh, dear God, you've got her," he said, and ran to them.

"H-hello," Emily said.

"Hi, Sis." Tyler sobbed, wrapping his arms around all three of them. "Oh, thank you, thank you, thank you."

Brandon, David, and the soldiers came around the building with the two stunned guards from the back door in custody.

Jed approached them. "Everything's fine, gentlemen. They're all out."

"All of them?" Brandon said.

Jed smiled proudly. "Yeah. Every last one, including Emily." He pointed to the cluster of Tyler, Belinda, Nikki, and Emily in an emotional embrace.

Brandon noticed Belinda looking across at him and ran to her. He raised his visor and she hugged him with overwhelming relief.

"You made it, baby. You made it," she said joyously.

"Yeah, babe. I did."

David appeared, clearing his throat awkwardly.

"Hi, David," Belinda said.

He smiled with a curious hint of sadness. "Hi, Belinda. It's good to see you again."

Jed held out his hand for Brandon. "Until next time, buddy."

Brandon smiled appreciatively, wondering what life held in store for his fugitive ally. "Thank you, Jed. For everything."

Crane nodded cordially and walked away while Brandon turned his attention to his family.

Jed returned to the back of the building, ran back up the rear stairwell, and back down the steps to the bar area.

Before the last turn, he heard the fearful mumblings of the bidders. What he'd seen was beyond evil.

He set the satchel down on a step mid-way down, reached inside, and took out the C4 time bomb Garrett had left under his motel bed. He'd pre-set the explosive for a four minute delay, which would give him enough time to get out.

He inserted the wire connection and the countdown began.

Running back up the stairwell, he discarded the machine gun on the floor. He quickly arrived at the rear steps and hurled himself down, three at a time.

By the time he was outside, his heart was pounding. He could hear the police sirens coming closer and knew Wilmot and Garrett would be with them.

Looking to his left, he noticed a line of ships in the harbor. The vessel farthest away was preparing to set sail. He instantly realized he'd been provided with the perfect opportunity to stow away. Having no idea where it was heading, he felt confident he'd figure out a plan when it arrived at its destination. At least he would be out of Wilmot's reach.

Summoning all his remaining energy, he sprinted toward the ship, never looking back.

Forty-Six

Swan Song

Brandon eagerly made his way toward Emily, but a hand on his shoulder halted him in his tracks.

"Brandon, I need to talk to you," David Spicer said.

"Yeah, what's going on?"

"Where'd that guy who was helping your brother go?"

"Who? You mean Jed?"

"I never got his name."

Brandon looked around. "I have no idea where he went."

"Who is he?"

"He's ex-intelligence. He saved my life a few days ago. He's certain the director of his department is corrupt, and that he arranged for the murder of the former director."

"What's this new director's name? Do you know?"

"Wilmot. He's kinda like my arch enemy."

Spicer's face became pallid. "Oh, Jesus."

"What's wrong?"

"Brandon, Wilmot is the one who had us brought here. We're under orders to bring you in."

Brandon turned sharply. The police sirens were almost upon them.

And then the helicopters appeared above.

***

Mae Ling wandered surreptitiously across the bar area keeping a distance from the bidders, determined not to identify herself. If they were to be taken in by the authorities, they would point the finger at her without hesitation. Now, they too, were the enemy.

Shrewdly, she eased her way back to the stairwell. Now that the soldiers had cleared out, she knew her only chance of escape was the back exit. And only then, on the slim chance it was unmanned.

Creeping onto the steps, she turned onto the main flight and saw the bomb before her. She had only a moment to notice the digital readout—the last thing she would ever see:

0:01

The incendiary annihilated the bar area, the stairwell, and everyone within. Fire spread through the auditorium, the force of the explosion causing a section of the arrival bay to collapse onto the lower level.

The explosion shook the earth outside. Brandon and the soldiers lost their footing momentarily in what seemed like an earthquake.

The police cars stopped in the street outside the entrance to the harbor. Wilmot, Garrett, and Chief Tepper hurried out.

David turned back to Brandon. "Did Jed do that?"

"I guess so, but don't expect me to shed a tear. David, you've got to get all personnel away from here. The fires are gonna rise up into the parking area. Those limos are filled with gasoline. It's gonna be like Napalm."

Spicer nodded sullenly. "I'm sorry there wasn't more I could do for you, buddy."

"Don't worry about me. Just get the boys away from here. And warn those cops."

"What about you? The place is surrounded."

"Everything's been taken care of. Now, go!"

David ran to Tepper, Wilmot, and Garrett. "Gentlemen. Ma'am. You have to back away. An incendiary has been detonated inside the building. With the limousines in there, there's the risk of an imminent incident."

Tepper turned to one of the younger officers behind him. "Where the hell is the fire department?"

"They're on their way, sir."

Garrett pointed to Brandon sprinting across the yard to the wire mesh fencing. "Look. Drake's getting away."

Wilmot grasped Spicer's arm. "Get after him, soldier."

Belinda and Tyler ran to David's side.

"Oh, God. What's he doing, Tyler?" Belinda said.

"I don't know, but I sure as hell hope he does."

David sank into the pits of regret and dilemma. With a heavy heart, he gathered his men and raced in pursuit of Drake.

Brandon grasped the laser torch from his belt and aimed it at the wire mesh. The beam cut through the metal with ease, creating a separation from top to bottom.

Glancing behind for the briefest moment, he saw his reluctant friend and the five soldiers gaining on him.

The walls of the fish factory blew out, and the troopers dropped to the ground. Brick, plaster, and metal jettisoned across the yard, barely missing them.

The helicopters hovered above. Brandon eased himself through the gap in the fence and ran four yards to the van.

He opened up the back, tore off his glove, and placed his fingers under the Turbo Swan's door handle. Programmed to accept his fingertips, the door rose upwards.

He climbed in, put the glove back on, reclined into the seat, and strapped himself in. With the touch of a sensor, the craft was filled with the sound of arena rock from the MP3:

It's time to break free, I'm gonna break the chains I'm livin' in . . .

The jets screeched, levitating the machine off the base of the van. He thrust the throttle forward and the Turbo Swan shot out, reaching the end of the road in the space of a heartbeat.

In a spectacular display of aerial aerobatics, he flew upwards, reaching forty feet and then came back down in a reverse loop before twisting into a straight position.

The three helicopters descended to Brandon's level. He hovered before them, an electric blue, one-of-a-kind aircraft floating static, as though initiating a face-off.

Abruptly, he shot the Turbo Swan forward between the second and third helicopters. The wind pressure automatically turned them around in Brandon's direction. In that moment, an aerial chase began.

Brandon flew around the corner and headed in the direction of the roadblock.

The helicopters ascended in order to clear the buildings on either side of them.

Brandon flew over the blockade and the TV crew. Maintaining a steady speed the helicopters could keep up with, he maneuvered the Turbo Swan through the L.A. traffic. He quickly arrived at the Golden State Freeway.

He turned the craft onto its side and flew between the cars and soared through the underpasses. The myriad lights sped past him, creating an optical illusion of neon streaks.

Exiting a tunnel, he noticed, on the monitor screen, the helicopters had fallen behind. He reduced his speed slightly, giving them the opportunity to get closer.

Within ten minutes, he'd made it halfway to San Diego, and knew it was a far enough distance for him to proceed with his plan.

He executed another inverted loop and reversed direction. Thrusting the throttle forward, he shot between the helicopters in the blink of an eye.

He reached a speed of 500 m.p.h. and returned to the location of the factory within a minute. He estimated that would give him at least ten minutes before the helicopters reached him again.

He slowed down as he flew back over the heads of the TV crew and along the street. Studying the scene before him on the monitor, he was relieved to see the women and children had been taken away from the site. He saw Belinda and Tyler were being kept back at a safe distance by the police.

David, the soldiers, Wilmot, and Garrett, were watching his approach from a position close to the Humvee. But it was only Wilmot whom Brandon wanted.

For the first time in his life, he had everything he could have wished for to live a happy life. He had Belinda, the love of his life, and their first child on the way. He had Tyler, the finest brother he could ever have hoped for. And now he had Emily, the little sister he sorely wanted to get to know and keep from harm.

He had a family and the perfect home—an untraceable cabin surrounded by snow and the beauties of nature, so far removed from the horrors of the world. Surely, it was that for which all men strived.

Only Wilmot stood in the way of it all.

Holding the Turbo Swan twenty feet in the air, he noticed Wilmot's expression change to a cunning grin. Wilmot said something to a private first class beside him. The young man's face showed refusal to whatever the request was, but Wilmot crept away toward the unmanned Humvee.

"What the hell are you doing, Wilmot?"

Spicer came to the front with a bull horn raised to his mouth. "Drake. You did good today, soldier. It was an extraordinary performance, and I'll do everything I can to ensure it's taken into account. Don't do anything to screw this up. Just bring that thing down so we can sort all of this out."

Brandon felt sorely tempted to believe David, but he had no faith in the system anymore. He knew he would be at the mercy of Wilmot, who was a murderous traitor.

And then he saw Wilmot taking a rocket launcher from the back of the Humvee. David looked back to see the director with the deadly weapon. He shouted something and ran across to Wilmot.

Brandon's heart pounded with uncertainty. He couldn't be certain what Wilmot's intention was. He could only watch as David tried to wrestle the rocket launcher away from him.

Not wanting to take any chances, he fired up the turbo. Again, the ear-shattering screech cut through the night air.

David gripped the rocket launcher and Wilmot resisted him in a potentially lethal tug of war.

"I'm not gonna use it," Wilmot said. "You can't reason with that maniac. I'm just trying to scare him."

"Put the damn thing down, Wilmot!" David forcefully pulled the rocket launcher away from the director's grasp. As he drew it toward himself, the trigger caught on Wilmot's fingers. The missile was released to the accompaniment of an oppressive force of air.

Brandon saw the missile coming toward him for a fleeting moment and then felt the impact. The shock tore through him causing him to think every bone in his body had just been crushed. The Turbo Swan's control panel became a sheet of sparks and flame. He then realized the rocket had taken out one of the two engines—the Achilles Heels of the Turbo Swan.

He caught a glimpse of Spicer, the soldiers, Wilmot, and Garrett scurrying away from the jeep and hurling themselves onto the ground.

In a frenzy, he tried to control the aircraft, but it was hopeless. The ground seemed to be shooting upwards with ferocious speed. "Shit! Wilmot, you son of a—"

The Turbo Swan crashed onto the Humvee in a cataclysmic explosion. A parachute-like plume of fiery smoke flew up over the wreckage.

Belinda and Tyler ran across to the point of impact. An agonized, horrified chorus of "No!" and "Bro!" echoed across the docks.

Fire engines sped along the street. Their sirens coldly filled the harbor as though they were the harbingers of tragedy.

Coming closer to the crash, Belinda and Tyler slowed their pace. Grief filled their hearts as their disbelieving eyes lingered, devastated, upon the sight of the blazing, smoking inferno.

Forty-Seven

The Vigil

4: 47 a.m.

The doors to the intensive care unit at Wilshire Memorial Hospital swung open. Andrew Wilmot entered aggressively to see five police officers standing in the foyer. Cynthia Garrett followed.

"Dammit!" Wilmot hissed through his teeth. "I had him. He would have landed that goddamn machine, but his goddamn buddy had to interfere."

"Take it easy," Garrett said. "It's not over yet."

"I was bluffing. I had no intention of blowing him out of the air. I just wanted to make him think I would." He stopped and rested his back against the wall.

"I know, but we don't have a prognosis yet. What do you want to do about Faraday and Reese?"

"Nothing."

"Nothing?"

"We've got too much going on right now. I'm not gonna propose *Nemesis* until everything is in order. "

A short, balding man in his early fifties brushed off his white medical coat and approached them from the far side of the corridor.

Wilmot looked up and stood straight. "Doctor Seymour."

"Hello, Director Wilmot."

"How is he?"

Belinda opened her eyes in the waiting room with a blanket draped around her. Tyler sat beside her, shivering. The events of the night had clearly taken their toll on him, and his blanket wasn't helping. Nikki sat with them in one of the adjacent chairs.

They watched the conversation between Wilmot, Garrett, and the doctor through a small window in the waiting room door. They couldn't make out what was being said.

Wilmot turned his head in their direction and gestured to them. Then he walked away with Garrett through the swinging doors. Doctor Seymour came toward the waiting room.

"Tyler." Belinda nudged him.

The doctor pushed the waiting room door open and stepped inside with a somber expression.

Anxiously, Belinda and Tyler stood.

"Mr. Faraday. Ms. Reese," Seymour said.

"How is he?" Belinda said. "Is he alive?"

"Barely."

"Can we see him?"

Seymour shook his head. "His injuries are extensive. We're just prepping him for surgery."

"How bad is it?" Tyler said. "Is he gonna make it?"

Seymour shook his head. "I'm not sure. He has massive internal injuries, multiple broken bones, and third degree burns over eighty percent of his body."

Belinda's hand came over her mouth. "Oh, my God."

"I need to see him," Tyler said.

"I'm sorry, Mr. Faraday, but that's just not possible."

"Like hell it's not. I swear, if you don't let me see my brother—"

"That's not what I meant, Mr. Faraday." Seymour placed a calming hand upon Tyler's shoulder.

"S-so, what do you mean?"

"Your brother . . ." The doctor looked at the floor, clearly reluctant to say what he had to say. "Your brother doesn't have a face for you to see anymore."

Belinda collapsed into her seat, sobbing convulsively.

"Oh, Jesus," Tyler mumbled in horror. "What about my sister and the others?"

"They're all fine. They're currently in detox. It's going to take several days, at least. They've all been subjected to repeated doses of barbiturates, cocaine, and heroin. You don't get through that overnight. We also have counselors working with them. The police are looking into the identities of the women and children in order that they can alert their families."

Tyler's expression became trance-like. "Brandon saved them. He saved *me*."

"I'm so sorry, Mr. Faraday."

Sudden rage appeared in Tyler's eyes. Throwing the blanket from him, he violently charged out of the waiting room.

"Tyler, wait," Nikki called after him, but it was too late.

Tyler waded through four police officers, almost oblivious to them. Bursting through the swing doors, he took the steps down to the next level.

He turned a corner, came to the elevators, and saw Wilmot and Garrett waiting. The doors of the middle elevator opened, and they prepared to step inside.

"Hey!" Tyler roared.

They stopped in their tracks and turned to face him.

"You did this, you son of a bitch."

"Tyler—" Wilmot said.

"Why couldn't you have just left him alone?" Tyler tore his tie and suit jacket away and cast them on the floor.

"Look, Tyler, this is ridiculous."

"You wanna talk to me about ridiculous? My brother is fighting for his life because of you. Now, take your goddamn ID or whatever out, and throw it on the floor. This is personal. Let's do this like men!" Fists clenched, his bellow echoed through the corridors. He felt his face flush, and for the first time in his life, he truly believed he could kill. His all-consuming need for vengeance overrode his caution and fear.

Before another word could be uttered, he felt his arms being gripped. Looking up, he saw two police officers restraining him.

Wilmot came forward with his right hand raised in a peaceful gesture. "It's OK, officers. This man has been through hell. Just let him be." With that, he turned, rejoined Garrett, and entered a newly arrived elevator. "We'll be back in a few hours. Go and get Mr. Faraday a coffee."

Tyler exhaled, summoning everything he had not to weep.

By noon, Tyler and Belinda had managed to remain awake as they kept their vigil in the waiting room. Nikki stayed with them throughout.

The door opened, and they looked across with a start.

Tyler rubbed his eyes, not entirely certain he wasn't seeing things. "D-Dad?"

"I got here as fast as I could," Charlton Faraday said.

Tyler stood wearily and embraced his father. "God, it's good to see you."

"What happened, Tyler?"

"What didn't?"

"How's Brandon?"

"Last we heard, they were taking him into surgery, but that was hours ago."

Belinda stood to introduce herself. "Mr. Faraday, I'm Belinda Reese. You should be very proud of your son. He helped save many women and children."

Charlton took her hand with a friendly smile. "Thank you, Belinda. I am proud of him. More than I can tell you." He turned his attention back to Tyler. "I brought someone along with me."

"Who?"

Charlton opened the door and waved his guest inside.

Tyler's eyes lit up. "Alex!"

"Hey, buddy," Alex Dalton said, and hugged him.

Charlton crept out and left them together.

"Hey, Belinda," Alex said.

"Hey, Alex."

"We're not supposed to know each other, so we just met, OK?" Alex winked at her, barely lightening the moment. He turned back to Tyler. "So, what's been happening, bud?"

"Take a seat. I don't know where to begin."

"How about at the beginning."

Tyler rubbed his eyes again, trying to remain focused. "It's a really long story. A few days ago, Brandon, Belinda, and I took off in a really cool Mercedes sprinter for Nevada."

Charlton spotted Wilmot talking to a police officer. A middle-aged man in a suit came through the swing doors and approached Charlton.

Faraday pointed Wilmot out to the man. "That's him."

"All right. Let's find out what his intentions are, and we'll take it from there."

The two men approached Wilmot as he concluded his discussion with the officer.

"Mr. Faraday," Wilmot said with a cordial tone.

"I'm gonna cut to the chase, Wilmot. If you plan on pressing charges against my son, you've got one hell of a battle on your hands."

"Is that so? Do you think you can buy off the law to get your boy off of an aiding and abetting rap?"

Charlton felt his retaliatory spirit rising and grinned. "Well, let's see here. He failed to alert the authorities to his brother's whereabouts. In the process, he helped in the rescue of their sister and a number of others, women and children, from a human trafficking outfit. Is that accurate?"

"Pretty much."

"Then you go ahead and press those damn charges, and I'll push the story through every major TV station and newspaper in the land. When the riots start kickin' off, you'd better hope you can run pretty damn fast. I'll also have a dream team of lawyers on the case that'll keep your department tied up in litigation for the next thirty years." Charlton gestured to his companion in the suit. "This is Kent Ulrich. He's just one of 'em."

Wilmot smiled condescendingly. "Mr. Faraday, you are overreacting."

"Am I?"

"Yes. I can certainly see where Tyler gets it from."

"What are you talking about?"

"I have no intention of pressing charges against Tyler, or Ms. Reese. SDT is intelligence, not law enforcement. In fact, I'm doing everything I can to dissuade the police and the FBI from going after them."

Faraday and Ulrich frowned.

With cavalier arrogance, Wilmot continued. "You see, I've just returned from police headquarters. Only two of the personnel from this slavery ring were taken into custody, and that's because almost all of the others were blown to four points of the compass. These two didn't know much, but what they did know was very interesting."

Charlton glanced at Ulrich, and then back to Wilmot. "Interesting in what way?"

"Well, they weren't even aware who they were really working for, but they gave us two names. Mae Ling Cheung and Han Fong."

"So?"

"We ran checks on both of these people. It seems they used to be with one of the Tongs. According to the two who were taken in, Han Fong left the building around five minutes before the army arrived. He wasn't there when it exploded, which means he's still out there."

"What has any of this got to do with my son?"

"That all depends on how friendly this Fong is with the Tong families, and how vengeful they might be if he has their favor."

Charlton's expression darkened and he felt his blood pressure spiking.

Coyly, Wilmot said, "As far as we're concerned, sir, your son had nothing to do with this. We don't want him taking the stand. The US government has better things to spend the tax payer dollars on than securing Tyler in the Witness Protection Program. I suggest you consult your lawyers about that." Grinning smugly, he walked away and disappeared into the ward, leaving Charlton with profound concern.

"We didn't even see what happened," Tyler said. "We saw the Turbo Swan hovering and there was this really loud bang. Then it just fell onto the Humvee and exploded."

Alex looked away, speechless. It was the most remarkable story he'd ever heard.

The door opened again. Alex, Tyler, Belinda, and Nikki looked up to see Miranda and Tamara in the doorway.

"We came as soon as we heard," Miranda said. "How's Brandon?"

"We still don't know," Belinda replied.

Alex stood awkwardly. "Hi, Mir."

"Hi Alex. I wasn't expecting to see you."

"Yeah, well I . . ." Feeling uncomfortable, he made his way toward the door. "I need some air. I'll be back shortly."

"Would you like some company?" Miranda said.

He glanced back at her and hesitated for a moment, still processing his friend's incredible tale. Now he had to face the appearance of his former lover. Finally, he conceded. "Yeah, why not."

Enthusiastically, Miranda followed him out.

"I'm going to see what I can find out about Brandon," Tyler said, and stood.

Oozing with trepidation, Belinda joined him.

Alone together in the waiting room, Nikki moved over to Tamara and hugged her.

"I've wanted it to be over for so long," Nikki said, choked. "But not like this. Oh, God, not like this."

"Have you spoken to your parents?"

"Not yet."

"Maybe you should."

"Y-yeah. You're right."

Nikki took out her cell phone, pausing to recall the number. As it came back to her, she tapped in the digits with trembling fingers. A female voice came through the earpiece. Nikki attempted to compose herself, but her tone quivered uncontrollably. "M-Mom?"

Tyler and Belinda headed toward the operating room. Both were exhausted, but they sorely needed information about Brandon. *Anything.* Perhaps one of the surgeons would give them some indication of Brandon's status.

The operating room door opened and Doctor Seymour stepped out. He removed his surgical mask and looked up.

Tyler and Belinda slowed their pace and studied his expression, looking for even a glimmer of hope.

With a pained visage, Seymour simply shook his head.

Tyler broke down with a sadness the likes of which he'd never known.

Belinda's eyes didn't move from the doctor. Her face assumed a blank, emotionless expression, as though she was unable to feel anything at all within her own protective vacuum.

Forty-Eight

Requiem

"Approximately forty miles behind me, in an isolated cabin, a private requiem is taking place for the man who single-handedly divided the nation—Brandon Drake," Tara Willoughby said into a microphone before a Channel 7 camera crew. "High within these snow-covered mountains surrounding Aspen, Colorado, Drake's family and closest friends are remembering the life of a man who perished in an explosion, while confronting members of his own former division a week ago. This reporter was a witness to the incident.

"Channel 7 has a remarkable history with Drake, from his exposé of the staged terrorist attacks instigated by the late Senator Garrison Treadwell, and Channel 7 studios falling under attack by the senator's operatives, to his last stand in Los Angeles. With the arrest of Commissioner Jason Landis for his alleged involvement in human trafficking, there is no doubt that Drake's story is destined to become one of the most captivating chapters in the annals of American history."

***

In somber reflection, Belinda, Tyler, Emily, Charlton Faraday, Nikki Hawke, and David Spicer stood in the cabin's living room awaiting Brandon's imminent burial. Insulated coats covered their black suits and dresses. Their dark snow boots made for the most unorthodox funerary attire, necessary though it was. Mumbled chatter among them enabled the avoidance of agonizing silence as they waited.

Tyler approached Emily. She seemed vacant and was keeping herself distant from the rest of the group. The doctors had decided it was in her best interests to attend the funeral, although her counseling and rehabilitation required considerably more time. "Hey," he said. "I thought you might like some company. Are you all right?"

She turned to him sadly. "I–I'm not sure."

"You're doing fine. If there's anything you need, just tell me, OK?"

She nodded sorrowfully. "I'd like to know about him."

"Brandon?"

"Yes. I only saw him once."

"You saw him? When?"

"It's difficult to explain. I felt as though I was out of my body, like in a nightmare. The woman was holding me, but it didn't seem real. That's when I saw him. He looked at me. I saw his eyes. I instinctively knew he was my brother. He made me feel so safe, but then he was gone. I never saw him again."

Tyler hugged her gently. "I had no idea, Emily. But you were right to feel safe with him. There was nobody better to be with if you found yourself in a jam."

Tears came to her eyes. "I see him in my dreams. Every night it happens. If only I could have known him. He died because he saved me."

"He loved you, Emily. I love you, and we're gonna take care of you."

"And that's a promise," Charlton said from behind them. "Take as much time as you need, Emily. When you're ready, we'll help you to start a new life, if you'll let us."

She stepped forward and hugged the older man. "Thank you so much, Mr. Faraday. You are both so very kind."

David Spicer moved over to Belinda. She'd been comforted by Nikki, but he felt he should at least try to say something to console her.

"Hi, David," she said.

He noticed her tone was weak and quiet. "Hi. I'm so sorry for your loss. Is there anything I can do?"

"No, David. I really appreciate you just being here. I know it's what he would've wanted. He thought highly of you. I can't tell you how much you're helping by doing the eulogy. I don't think I could have coped with that."

"Oh, believe me, it's a privilege."

"I couldn't even kiss him goodbye," she said. "Apparently, he was burned beyond recognition."

"So I was told, but I didn't want to bring it up. It was a horrific crash." David looked around the cabin, eager to change the subject. "So, this is the place he got himself sent down to keep secret?"

"Yes. He was happiest when he was here. We both were. We only had trouble when we left. Its secrecy is meaningless now that he's gone. Burying him here is the only way I can still be close to him in our special place."

"I can understand that. I also think it's interesting that you've chosen to give him a secular burial."

"Yeah, well, I'm not religious, and Brandon never gave me any reason to think he was. I want to celebrate his life the way I knew him. With honesty. I ask only that you do the same. Speak about the real Brandon, David. Not a bullshit fantasy. Can you do that?"

He swallowed hard at the request, but nodded in concurrence.

A man in his early forties entered the cabin. His fulsome brown hair and wholesome features complemented the compassion in his eyes.

"Hello, Mr. Bixby," Belinda said to their Humanist celebrant.

"If everyone would like to follow me, please," Bixby said in a gentle tone.

Belinda began to hyperventilate. "Oh, God. This is really happening. He's gone. Brandon is really gone.*"*

David placed his arm around her shoulders. "It's all right. Just take your time."

Slowly, they all followed Bixby out of the cabin and round to the clearing at the back.

The mourners stood before an ornate white casket, which Tyler had financed, positioned above a six-foot-deep grave.

Belinda knew there was no other place to lay her lover to rest. It was perfect. Snow covered the ground, and the aspen trees provided an ideal, picturesque vision of peace.

Bixby began his commentary on Brandon's life. Most of what he said was what Belinda and Tyler had told him, including Brandon's battle with alcohol. He made reference to what he'd personally witnessed when

Brandon's privately-made video recording was broadcast, two years earlier. He commented on how sincere, passionate, and honorable Brandon had appeared to him. The way in which he'd taken on three gunmen, live on national television, hadn't failed to captivate all who'd seen it.

Bixby summed up the emotion Brandon stirred in all people, even in those who opposed him. Drawing reference to him being adopted into comic book culture, he referred to him as a 'marvel'.

As Belinda listened, it all came back to her. From the moment she first met Brandon as the mysterious stranger on the Carringby rooftop, to the love they came to know in the cabin, and the extraordinary rescues he'd performed. Every act and escapade had left her with the subconscious belief that he was invincible. Such was the nature of her sense of shock.

Tyler recalled the first time he'd ever laid eyes on his brother in the Fort Bragg courtroom, and the dazzling combat skills he'd displayed against the MPs. He'd known at the time that Brandon was seriously damaging his chances, but he remembered how impressive the fighting moves had been. It had instilled his heart with awe.

His first actual meeting with his brother at Fort Leavenworth flashed before him. He'd discovered such a contrast to the warrior in the courtroom. Brandon's emotional state revealed a man of deep sensitivity and profound vulnerability. Brandon had wept copiously at the realization he had a brother, like he'd been given an anchor to a true, tangible identity. In that moment, Tyler wanted nothing more in life than to help him find happiness again.

Tears rolled down his cheeks with a combination of unbearable sadness and rage at such a cruel injustice.

Nikki placed her arm around his shoulders. He turned to embrace her. Their relationship was developing quickly, and he couldn't deny his need for her.

Emily absorbed Bixby's words. They filled her with a yearning to know everything about Brandon. She continued to struggle with the knowledge that she would never actually meet him. His face, as he looked at her in the factory, persistently haunted her mind.

"And now ladies and gentlemen," Bixby said, "a very special guest has come here to help complete the story of the man whose life we have come to celebrate today. Sergeant Major David Spicer of the Eighty-Second Airborne Division."

David stepped forward and positioned himself beside the casket while Bixby joined the mourners.

David was hesitant for a moment, but quickly gathered his thoughts. "I served with Brandon for six years on many tours of duty in Iraq and Afghanistan. On the field, he was the finest combat soldier any of us had ever known. He was the best with weapons, hand-to-hand combat, and he had the engineering skills of a genius. We never lost a battle when he was on our team. But it came at a price."

He looked up and saw Belinda watching him. The slight nod she gave permitted him to continue with a clear conscience. "I was asked to give a true and honest account

357

of Brandon. What I have to say may not be easy for some of you to hear."

Belinda nodded again.

"Nobody ever liked Brandon," he said. "He made it impossible for anybody to like him. He was one of the coldest men I had ever met. Nobody ever got close to Brandon Drake. We didn't think it was possible for him to love anyone, and we even had a nickname for him. We called him The Scorpion, because that's what he was.

"On our last mission together, he saved my life and almost died in the process. But he didn't pull me out of the way of a grenade out of a sense of duty or camaraderie."

The mourners hung on David's every word, the air dense with anticipation.

"He saved my life because I owed him money from a poker game."

David noticed Belinda's sad smile as she touched her abdomen. It was as though his words were completing a very real picture of the one who had left his one true legacy with her.

He continued. "And then, two years ago, I had the shock of my life. I met a man who looked just like Brandon Drake, but who was nothing like him. This man was kind, selfless, and immeasurably courageous in the way he stood alone. He had a sense of honor that the Brandon Drake I knew couldn't have even contemplated. This was someone I was proud to be associated with. He was committed to justice and compassion. The Brandon Drake I knew was no longer, and regardless of how he got that way, he was the epitome of—" David became choked with emotion and paused to collect himself. "The *All American* hero," he said finally, invoking the motto of the Eighty-Second Airborne Division. "He died taking on every kind of bully you could imagine." David placed his hand on the casket affectionately. "Rest easy, soldier." With that, he returned to the mourners.

They were alerted by a rustling in the trees. Belinda tilted her head, and her eyes widened in disbelief as *he* came into sight.

She made her way forward slowly, and David gripped her arm protectively. "Belinda, don't."

She looked behind at him and smiled. "It's OK, David. I know him."

Reluctantly, he let go of her, and she continued to move along through the snow.

More memories came back to her. *How does he always know?*

He had been there for Brandon when he needed him the most, to help him through his period of loneliness. Brandon had loved him, cared for him, and he only left after Brandon had found Belinda—after he knew that Brandon was no longer alone.

The huge, brown bear finally stopped at Belinda's feet and lay flat on its stomach. It had the saddest eyes she had ever seen.

"Hi, Snooky." She knelt down in the snow and petted his brow. "You know, don't you? He's gone. How do you always know?"

She finally broke down. Her tears fell upon the bear's fur, and he looked up at her with an impossibly empathetic stare.

She wrapped her arms around his neck and he allowed her to hold him until her grief was spent. She glanced behind her to see the mourners watching, open-jawed.

She eventually let go of Snooky. He raised his head to the heavens with a roar so powerful it reverberated throughout the mountains—a mournful wail of anguish that was beyond human understanding.

Belinda listened to the remnants of the cry. For the briefest moment, she was certain she could hear Brandon's voice, almost as an echo on the wind. She just couldn't make out what he was trying to tell her.

Epilogue

Wilmot and Garrett briskly stepped out of an elevator into the lower levels of a sprawling, neon-lit complex.

"You were right, Cynthia," Wilmot said.

"Right about what?"

"Treadwell had another cabin, and Drake was holed up in it all along."

"Deductive reasoning."

"We actually did it," he said with victorious pride. "It couldn't have worked out better."

"I still have concerns about Kane Slamer."

"Slamer's formidable."

"He's a maniac."

"So are you. Warriors have to be. There's no other way."

Garrett lightly held his wrist to halt him. "What about Crane?"

Wilmot's joviality faded for a moment. "We'll get him."

He pushed open a white door marked *Testlab 9* and Garrett followed him in. The pristine lab offered an array of monitor screens, medical apparatus, and shelves filled with a myriad of drugs.

"Cynthia," he said. "Welcome to the future of *Operation: Nemesis.*"

Doctors Matthew Seymour and Frederick DeSouza greeted them in white coats.

"Good morning, gentlemen." Wilmot shook Seymour's hand. "I can't tell you how much we appreciate your help with this project, sir. I understand how difficult it was for you in Los Angeles, but we couldn't have done it without you. The department will certainly make it worth your while, and your cover will be protected."

"Thank you, Director Wilmot," Seymour said. "It was painful to say the least. But this *is* in the interests of national security."

Wilmot offered his hand to DeSouza. "It's good to have you on board, sir."

"Director."

"So, how's the patient today?"

"We're keeping him in an induced coma, but he's fine," Seymour said. "A few cuts, bruises, and fractured bones. Nothing serious. His recovery period will be approximately four to six weeks. Come and take a look."

Seymour and DeSouza led Wilmot and Garrett into an adjoining cell-like facility with a hospital bed in the corner.

Brandon Drake's unconscious form lay motionless under the sheet, his face severely bruised, his eyes swollen, and his arms and legs in casts.

Wilmot grinned. "Perfect. The world thinks he's dead, the cadaver of a homeless vagrant is in his grave, and we've got another weapon who's now, officially, off the grid."

"I'm seeing it, but it's difficult to believe," Garrett said. "We were both there, Andrew. We saw the crash. I still can't imagine how he survived."

"He knew what he was doing when he took all of that equipment from Mach Industries," Wilmot said. "The Turbo Swan was constructed from a concussion-resistant alloy, which absorbed most of the shock when it crashed. The helmet he was wearing had a similar composition, and his armor was made from an advanced, heat-resistant form of Kevlar. Without those advantages, he would have been incinerated."

Wilmot's expression darkened as he turned to DeSouza. "When do you think he'll be ready for the new revision?"

"Now would be as good a time as any, while he's still unconscious. But as I told you before, introducing another persona to his consciousness could result in permanent catatonia."

"And I always pay attention in class, doctor, which is why I'm not going to ask you to do that."

DeSouza looked at him with bemusement. "Then, would you mind telling me what it is that you want me to do?"

"Treadwell made a grave mistake, and I want you to undo it. Eradicate Drake's current persona and his memories of the last four years. Everything we need to replace them with is already in there."

"You mean, you want me to—"

"That's right, doctor." Wilmot paused momentarily before affirming the order. "Bring back The Scorpion."

To be concluded in

Run!

Hold On! Season 3

Run!

Hold On! Season 3

Excerpt

Drake took in the extraordinary scenery surrounding him—hundreds of meager homes piled upon one another. Rising up into the hills in such vast quantities, the properties formed a giant, sprawling cluster. It was the most elaborate example of poverty he had ever imagined, so far removed from the thriving, bustling city. Unique to Rio, the favelas were a sight one would find nowhere else.

Slamer took out a palm-sized satellite navigation device, and Drake looked over his shoulder, noticing a flashing red dot in the middle of the map screen.

"We're here," Slamer said. "Crane's apartment is on the other side of this shithole." He tapped the brickwork that made up part of the rear of a dilapidated structure.

Drake looked up and saw a flat roof approximately thirty feet above them.

Slamer took a twelve inch cylindrical tube from his belt. A targeting sight was fixed to the exterior. "You ever used one of these?"

Drake took an identical device from his own belt and looked at it curiously. "Nope."

"It's an upgraded spider cable launcher. Apparently the originals had the cable inside a ball-like container. Pretty clumsy, if you ask me."

"I've never seen one."

"Well, let's get up there." Slamer aligned the targeting sight with a railing close to the edge of the roof and depressed a button on the casing. A high-tensile steel cable shot out and a metallic claw clasped the rail.

Drake aimed and fired his cable. The claw gripped the railing almost a yard apart from Slamer's.

They put their helmets on and secured them. The visors covered their eyes. After hooking their gun-carrier straps over their shoulders, they pulled out hand grips from either sides of the cable launcher tubes and held them tightly. Depressing the quick-release switches at the ends of the grips, motors within the devices reeled the cable in, drawing Drake and Slamer up to the railing.

As Drake held on to the handgrips, a feeling came over him. There was something familiar about the sensation of being pulled up from the ground, but it wasn't exactly a memory. It was a feeling akin to déjà vu, although it seemed as though he shouldn't be pulled *upward*. It should have been a *horizontal* glide.

They arrived at the top, climbed over the railing, and detached the cable claws. Drake shook his head trying to assimilate the strange sensation that had come over him.

Slamer ran across the roof to the other side, took out a set of small, advanced, electron binoculars, and brought them up to his eyes. "Got it . . . Oh, fuck."

Drake hurried over to him. "What's wrong?"

"Take a look for yourself."

Drake took the binoculars. "Which apartment is this guy supposed to be in?"

"Third level. Fifth from the left, with the entrance steps at the front."

Drake immediately saw the problem. Crane's was the only apartment in the line where the drapes were closed. If they couldn't see their target, they weren't going to be able to take him out. "Shit."

Slamer removed his helmet, took out his sat-scrambler cell phone, and selected his contact. "Wilmot? Slamer. We're going to have to go directly into the apartment. The son of a bitch has the drapes closed . . . Right, I'll tell him." The call ended.

"Tell me what?" Drake said.

"Switch on your helmet camera and radio. He's gonna be monitoring the operation. We're taking it from the rear."

Wilmot stood with Garrett in the Mojave base's situation room facing a wall filled with monitor screens. Several technicians attended the control panel.

A young male technician approached the director and handed him a head set and mike.

Two of the screens suddenly showed images of the favela. The movements were shaky and difficult to decipher. Drake and Slamer were apparently leaping down onto the balconies of the homes beneath. Occasionally, the screens became blank flashes of white as the two operatives tore through numerous clotheslines of sheets and threadbare towels. Sweeping shots of screaming women appeared for fleeting seconds. The residents were clearly startled by the two aggressively-contemptuous, armored soldiers wading through their homes.

Drake and Slamer arrived at the bottom, and the jerky movements indicated they were running across the street. Perturbed looks on the faces of the pedestrians were cause for concern.

Wilmot gripped the mike. "Boys, you don't have much time. You're creating a scene, and there's a risk of alerting Crane."

Slamer's breathless response came through Wilmot's head set. "You think we don't know that?"

Wilmot rubbed his eyes with anxious tension. "Don't screw this up, Slamer."

The screens became clearer. Drake was ahead of Slamer as they ran along an alley. They turned right and came up behind Crane's complex. A few steps later, they stopped at a rear metallic door.

"This is the one," Drake said. "It's locked."

"Blow it!" Wilmot ordered.

Drake took a small, C4 charge device from his belt, placed it against the door, and it adhered magnetically. After setting it to five seconds, he and Slamer rapidly moved away a few feet, shielding their faces.

The door blew open. Smoke shrouded the immediate area, accompanied by the unmistakable scent of pitch and burning metal. They drew their automatic rifles, discarded the leather carrying cases on the ground, and ran inside.

Taking three steps at a time, they scaled the stairwell, oblivious to the screams and protestations of the first floor occupants.

They arrived on the second floor. A middle-aged, slightly overweight male, wearing a filthy off-white singlet and what appeared to be pajama pants, stood before them angrily. Without hesitation, Drake drove the butt of his rifle into the man's face, shattering his nose and knocking him to the ground.

Within moments, they were on the third floor. Crane's floor.

Drake heard sounds of commotion coming from below. He looked down three flights of stairs and saw a team of police officers entering through the open rear door.

"No, no, no!" Wilmot bellowed through their headsets. "I covered this and ordered them not to interfere. This is a top secret operation. What the hell are those assholes thinking?

"What do you want us to do?" Drake said.

"It's on their heads. Blow out the stairwell."

Drake took a grenade from his belt, pulled the pin out, and dropped it down the stairwell. The first floor steps shattered. The detonation sent two officers flying out through the open door. Two others careened into the walls with bone-shattering force before falling, lifelessly, to the ground.

Flames rose through the remains of the stairwell, filling the complex with smoke.

Slamer turned around, his rifle poised, ready to dispatch any who might try to interfere.

Drake came to Crane's apartment door and kicked it in, surprised by how easily it came open. It wasn't even locked.

With his rifle raised, he cautiously stepped inside, rapidly aiming his weapon in every direction. It was a basic room with no wallpaper, paintings, or plants. There were only bare stone walls, but nobody was in sight. The smoke impaired his visibility, but it was clear enough to see nobody was there.

He moved around and kicked open the kitchen door. Huddled in the corner was a twenty-something, Latina female, weeping and visibly terrified.

"Where's Jed Crane?" Drake demanded.

"I-I no know," she said in broken English.

"I said where the fuck is he?"

"No know. P-please don't kill me."

Suddenly, an excruciating, stabbing pain shot through his head. It felt as though his skull was being crushed. The rifle fell from his hands and he dropped to his knees, screaming.

The smoke and the woman's words merged into voices from elsewhere:

P-please don't kill me.

I'm not going to kill you.

"Oh, God!" he cried, and tore his helmet off. He grasped his head, unable to bear the pain, and collapsed into a fetal position.

Wilmot and Garrett looked at one another, mystified. They'd seen enough to know Crane wasn't in the apartment. Who the woman might have been was irrelevant. A neighbor? A prostitute? Crane's roommate? It didn't matter. Whatever was happening to Drake had negated the operation.

"Slamer, abort the mission," Wilmot said. "Something's happened to Drake. I'm having you picked up out front. Get him the hell out of there!"

About the Author

Peter Darley (P.D. to his friends) is a British novelist, whose professional history is in showbusiness. He is a graduate of the Birmingham School of Speech and Dramatic Art, and he studied television drama at the Royal Academy of Dramatic Art (RADA). His television credits include guest-starring roles is UK productions such as BBC's *Crime Limited, Stanley's Dragon* for ITV, *The Bill*, Sky One's *Dream Team*, and numerous TV commercials. He also worked as a model, presenter, and voice-over artiste for ten years, and has been an agent for several variety acts.

His lifelong admiration of heroes, and love of roller-coaster-style thrills have been a huge influence on his writings.

He is a keen athlete and body builder, a professional close-up magician, and lives with his wife in rural England.